REIGN *of* SHADOWS

REIGN

of

SHADOWS

SOPHIE JORDAN

An Imprint of HarperCollinsPublishers

HarperTeen is an imprint of HarperCollins Publishers.

Reign of Shadows
Copyright © 2016 by Sharie Kohler
All rights reserved. Printed in the United States of America.
No part of this book may be used or reproduced in any manner whatsoever
without written permission except in the case of brief quotations embodied
in critical articles and reviews. For information address HarperCollins
Children's Books, a division of HarperCollins Publishers, 195 Broadway,
New York, NY 10007.
www.epicreads.com

Library of Congress Control Number: 2015939000
ISBN 978-0-06-237765-4

Typography by Brad Mead
16 17 18 19 20 PC/LSCH 10 9 8 7 6 5 4 3 2 1
❖

First paperback edition, 2017

For Jared, because when I imagine a world
like this I want you by my side . . .

YEAR SEVENTEEN
of the
BLACK ECLIPSE

ONE

Luna

THE ECLIPSE SPANNED all my life. It invaded everything. A deep, seeping blackness that poured into every crack and fissure like pooling blood. The darkness was especially dense outside my tower, sliding like ink to where I stood on the lighted balcony, listening to the hum of hungry insects and animals. And them.

Sighing, I rested both elbows on the balcony railing. Coals popped and crumbled in the stove behind me, emitting a cozy warmth that contrasted sharply with the damp cold nipping at my nose and cheeks. Heat and comfort lapped at my back while darkness stretched before me. And yet I wanted Outside with an anxious energy that buzzed along my nerves.

Longing pumped through me as thick as the chronic night. A small animal scurried in the forest far below my window. I dipped my chin in that direction and cocked my head, tracking it as though I could see through the gloom and treetops, as though the creature were visible at the base of the stone tower.

The animal snuffled at the outside wall, probably trying to decipher the obstacle in its path that wasn't part of the natural world. A tower didn't belong in these woods. No hint of civilization did. After a few moments nosing around, the animal returned to the woods. I followed its movements through the underbrush, envying its freedom.

From high in my perch, I listened. My hearing had long adapted to the darkness. From the quick thump of paws, I guessed it was a rabbit. They were bountiful in these woods. They bred quickly and were fast enough to escape the dwellers. Most of the time.

A distant sound emerged. I lifted my face to the sky as the droning chirps swelled from the east, building to a crescendo. I wasn't the only one who heard them. The rabbit tore through the undergrowth.

My fingers clenched the stone railing, knuckles aching, heart beating hard in my chest.

Hurry, hurry.

I dropped my chin again, urgency burning in my veins as I willed the rabbit to move faster, to live. Which was ridiculous. We ate plenty of rabbits, but somehow I identified myself with this one.

The army of bats drew closer in a great sweeping cloud, their giant, leathery wings slapping on the air. Bats were once pocket sized. Since the eclipse they had grown, now averaging four feet tall. No longer did they consume insects. They hunted bigger prey.

Go, go, go.

They buzzed all around the tower with high-pitched yips that made my skin jump.

"Luna, come," Perla called. "The last thing we need is one of them getting inside."

I couldn't move. Riveted, I stood in place, listening for my rabbit.

The bats spotted it and lunged for it as one giant beast. Leaves rustled and branches cracked as they dove through the treetops. Their song grew frenzied, excited as they closed in.

The rabbit screamed shrilly as its body was ripped apart, flesh and bones snapping like parchment and quill. I flung my hands over my ears against the terrible sound.

Perla was suddenly there, tugging me inside and shutting the door, drawing me into the warm glow of lantern light. She gathered me into her soft, yielding arms until I stopped shaking. I could still hear the bats. The rabbit's shriek echoed inside my head, taunting me even though it was long dead.

"There, now." She patted my back as though I were still the little girl she used to read to at night. "You're safe."

I sagged against her, accepting her comfort even though it troubled me that she thought I needed it. Because none of this

changed anything. I still wanted out there. I still had to learn to
make that world my own.

I'd spent my entire life within these walls. I wouldn't spend
the rest of it in here, too. I couldn't.

According to Sivo, life was supposed to be a balance of light and
dark. Each time we cleaned our weapons after a hunt it was this
bit of truth he shared with me.

Before, the moon reigned for only half the day. The sun
occupied the sky for the other half, burning brightly enough to
scorch your skin if you stayed outdoors too long. It was incredible
to imagine such a thing, as illusory as the fairy tales that Perla
told me as a girl.

I only knew this existence—the black eclipse and thick walls
that kept us safe from an army of dark dwellers. I only knew Sivo
and Perla and isolation. This life consisted of sporadic runs into
the great maw of night with Sivo at my side trying to teach me
survival in the shadow of our tower.

A slaughtered rabbit was a casualty of the war being waged.
I would not be such a casualty. I knew this because I knew the
dark. I knew the taste of it in my mouth. The feel of it on my
skin. It clung. Smothered. It carried death in its fold.

The dark should terrify me, but it did not. It never had.

The rabbit wasn't me. It was prey, and I would never be that.

Perla stepped back and lowered her arms from me. "Come
now. These linens won't fold themselves."

I glanced back at the closed balcony doors. "It's quiet again."

My ears strained for the sound of bats, but they'd moved on, their cries lost in the distance. There was nothing beyond the normal noise of the forest now. The throb of blood-swollen insects on the air and the cawing of carrion birds. An occasional tree monkey scampered through branches.

The whisper of fabric told me that Perla had started folding.

"It won't last," Perla replied in her usual perfunctory manner. "Never does." She snapped a linen on the air.

I turned from the balcony and faced her. "How long before I can go out there? On my own?" I went out often enough, but only ever with Sivo. "I have to know how . . . I have to be able to live out there."

It was a familiar argument. Sivo used it every time he took me with him. There was logic in it even she could not refute. But what I was asking for now—to go alone—had never been permitted. And yet I had to try. How was I ever going to learn to cope in this world if Sivo did everything for me?

"You don't live out there. You live in here. And I don't care how good you think you are at handling yourself," Perla said. "You're not stepping one foot outside these walls alone."

"Let me go on a quick run for berries. It's his birthday," I wheedled. "Let me do this for him."

"No," she replied, swift and emphatic.

Sighing, I sank down on the bed, the brocade coverlet stiff under me. I plucked at a loose thread. The coverlet was old, belonging to the first occupant of the tower—a purported witch who wrought havoc on this forest long before we came here. Long before the eclipse. We had her to thank for the tower. Apparently she enjoyed luring travelers to her door and then making a soup out of them. It was the stuff of fairy tales, but I knew anything was possible. This life, the way the world was now, had taught me that.

Sivo and my father had explored the layout of the kingdom long ago. They knew every inch of it, including the Black Woods. The two of them discovered the tower in those years, before I was born, before the eclipse. Now only dark dwellers roamed the thick bramble of vines and towering trees. The world belonged to them.

The nearest village was over a week's walk, if it still stood. We didn't know anymore. We didn't know how many people were left at all. Our world was the tower and the surrounding forest.

Sivo had selected our tower for its remoteness and because the Black Woods were rumored to be cursed. The witch's fearful reputation lasted long after her death, keeping man, woman, and child from traveling into this forest. A fortuitous circumstance for people like us who didn't want to be found.

"If you're going to sit there, make yourself useful," Perla prodded.

I plucked a linen from the basket, snapped it once on the air, and began folding. The linens smelled of the outdoors. We hung the wash to dry on a stretch of line on the balcony of Perla's room. I carefully added the folded towel to the stack, inching closer to the woman who had raised me as a mother would. Without her

I would have died alongside my mother the night of my birth, but that fact didn't stop resentment from bubbling up inside my chest.

"Perla, please." I touched her arm. "Sivo—"

"Sivo will understand, and we've prepared his favorite flatbread for the occasion. He will be satisfied with that."

With a groan, I dropped back on the bed.

Satisfied. There was that word again. Being satisfied with our lives was enough for her. She didn't understand the need for more. *My* need for more. She thought I should be content with what I had. Sanctuary. A roof over my head and food in my belly. It was more than so many people had.

"Do you want to end up like that rabbit out there?" she asked.

"Bats don't attack humans," I reminded her.

"I'm not talking about the bats and you well know that."

I did know that. She was talking about dark dwellers.

Sitting up, I crossed my arms over my chest and tried another tactic. "Sivo thinks you should let me start going out alone."

I could hear the faint grinding of her jaw. The habit had worsened lately, and I suppose I was to blame.

Sivo's heavy footsteps thudded outside my room, halting at the threshold. He brought with him the loamy aroma of the woods. "I'm back," he announced unnecessarily.

"Are those boots dirty?" Perla demanded, adjusting her weight onto her back foot and cocking out her hip.

"What, these?" He scuffed his boots, lifting first one and then the other, examining beneath them.

"Yes . . . those things on your feet," she snapped. "You know I spent all day yesterday mopping."

"No. No mud," he assured her.

Perla grunted, clearly unconvinced. I fought a smile, accustomed to their bickering.

"I don't know why you insist on dumping refuse when it's dark," she grumbled.

Perla didn't approve of unnecessary risks, and as far as she was concerned Sivo took far too many of those.

"Midlight doesn't last long enough to do all the things that need to be done in a day." He didn't sound annoyed as he uttered this. A remarkable fact considering he uttered it almost daily. Midlight lasted no more than an hour, but it was the only time a semblance of light emerged to push out the night. "Besides, root truffles don't bloom in midlight."

Perla gasped with delight. I smelled their pungent aroma as soon as Sivo pulled some from his pocket and held them out for her to see.

"Make a fine dinner," he murmured. "Especially if you cook them with some of those potatoes the way you do."

She cleared her throat and tried to sound gruff as she said, "Put them in the kitchen. We'll have them on the morrow for your birthday. Still not worth the risk." She had to add that last bit.

"I look forward to it." Sivo's voice rang out cheerfully. In the grimmest hour, he was forever optimistic. "Well, I'm off to bed. See you girls in the morning."

"Good night, Sivo," I called. Normally he would hug me, but he hastened away. Probably to remove his boots and clean up any trail of mud he'd left.

Alone in my chamber with Perla again, I moistened my lips. "I could have helped Sivo pick more." Silence. "Four hands can gather more than two. . . ."

"I've said all I'm going to say on the matter." She lifted a stack of towels and moved to the armoire. Her joints popped as she bent to store the linens inside. She slammed the doors shut with decided force. "Don't bring it up again tomorrow and ruin Sivo's day. Can you promise me that?"

I exhaled, nodding. "I won't bring it up tomorrow."

She snorted, not missing that I promised for only tomorrow. Stopping before me, she cupped my cheek with her work-roughened palm. "I've only ever wanted you safe. Protected."

I squeezed her hand and appealed one more time. "What will keeping me locked up inside this tower ever accomplish?"

"You'll live." Frustration rang in her voice.

"Not forever," I argued. "We all die, Perla."

"Some sooner than others." Her voice hardened. "Your parents met their deaths too early. I won't have the same fate befall you. You're the queen of Relhok."

The words never ceased to startle me. I didn't feel like a queen. "A queen stuck in a tower. What good is that to the people of Relhok? How is that a better fate?"

"What good will you be dead?" she countered. "Someday the eclipse will end and the dwellers will go away—"

She stopped at my choked snort. No one knew when it would end. If it ever would. The pressure of her hand stopped me from commenting further.

"Someday it will all end," she repeated. "And then you'll be free of this tower. Until then, you'll stay inside and be safe."

Her hand dropped from my face. Her steady tread moved away, and she lifted the remaining stack of linens from the bed. I felt her gaze linger on me. "That is your fate."

She departed the room then, the soft leather soles of her shoes whispering over the stone floor.

Alone in my chamber, I opened the balcony doors again and stepped back outside. My chest burned with an uncomfortable tightness and my face flushed hotly as my conversation with Perla tracked through my mind. Suddenly I couldn't draw enough air into my starving lungs.

Frustration wasn't a new sensation, but tonight was the first night I felt anger bubble up inside me. I clasped the cold stone railing until the blood ceased to flow through my fingers and my knuckles ached. Perla couldn't determine my fate. Only I could. If I decided to do something, even she couldn't stop me.

"This tower isn't my fate." The words flew out over the deep mist, a pledge to myself.

TWO

Luna

SEVERAL HOURS AFTER Perla and Sivo retired for the night, I crept through the darkness down the winding stairs leading to the bottom of the tower. The rabbit's scream echoed faintly in my ears as I made my way, a reminder of what awaited me on the Outside. I didn't push the memory away. I clung to it, letting it keep me vigilant.

I had accompanied Sivo enough times that I didn't need to feel my way in the dark as I descended. I didn't need to skim my hands along the dank walls, where moss and bracken grew between the cracks. I knew where to place my feet. I knew the precise moment to duck at the low threshold. I knew where to squat in the circular room, where to clasp the latch that led into the antechamber and to another door—this one on the ground floor.

Closing the door to the antechamber behind me, I disrobed in the cold, inhaling the moist, moldy air. My fingers trembled slightly as I unlaced the ties at the front of my bodice and stripped off my gown, my uneven breath a whisper in the chill. Everything had to go, right down to the ribbons in my artfully plaited hair and the slippers on my feet. Perla insisted on the ribbons as though we were still at court, where things like coiffed hair held meaning. Instead of here, where there was only the passing of days. Existing and not living. Fresh resolution swept through me.

I hung my garments on the peg near the door, my bare skin puckering to gooseflesh. I donned the appropriate attire, always left in this room that smelled of bracken and earth. It was a precaution. Dwellers possessed an excellent sense of smell and we didn't want the aromas of the tower—baked bread, crushed mint and leaves, and beeswax candle—that clung to our everyday clothes attracting them. My hands found my outdoor wear easily. I reached past Sivo's bigger garments hanging on the peg next to mine. Thanks to Perla, mine were less worn than his, the doeskin jacket not as soft as Sivo's. Tonight they would see some use.

My palms skimmed over the supple leather of my snug trousers. The fabric was ripe and well seasoned. Sivo had seen to that, rubbing and dragging the clothes through leaves and dirt until they smelled as pungent as loamy earth.

I plucked a satchel from where it hung on another peg and

then picked my weapons from an array on the shelf. A knife for my boot. A sword and scabbard at my waist.

A distant, almost imperceptible sound pulled me up. Angling my head, I listened, picking out the noise. It wasn't from within the tower. Sivo wasn't awake. This sound floated from Outside. I heard it almost every day from my perch on the balcony. One of them was moving about. Perhaps more.

I stepped closer and touched a palm to the solid stone wall. Several inches thick, it was sturdy and reliable. It kept us in and them out. And yet Perla still worried. Always she worried.

I listened longer. I was good at listening. Waiting. Knowing when to move. Sivo said it was my gift. The thick, cloying dark made picking out sounds easier. Sounds and smells lingered, never seeming to dissipate.

After a few moments, I decided it was only one creature dragging its feet over leaves. Its tread was a steady staccato of shuffling thuds. I could count them one after another. A beat hovered between each footfall with no other overlapping of footsteps.

The dweller breathed in that way they did with deep saws of wet, fizzing breath passing through the feelers squirming at its mouth.

I waited for it to pass and move deeper into the forest. Satisfied that it was too far now to hear me when I emerged, I unbolted the door in the floor. There was only one visible entrance to the tower. The most obvious way in and out. We rarely used it in case anyone was ever watching the tower and waiting to see someone emerge. Another one of Sivo's precautions.

Clutching the metal hoop in my fingers, I swung the door open, grateful for the silence of the well-oiled hinges. I descended into the tunnel, mindful of the slippery moss as I secured the door over my head, making certain it was shut firmly.

Lowering my hands, I turned, grinding the heels of my soft-soled boots into the slick stone floor. I hastened through the tunnel beneath the tower, slowing as I neared the end. Lifting my hands, I sought the dangling latch for the secret door above. Seizing it, I climbed up the few footholds in the rock wall, and waited in the dripping dark, listening for any nearby sound.

After several moments of silence, I unbolted and pushed open the door, sliding out into the night. I eased the hidden door, flush with the forest floor, shut and covered it back up with leaves and dirt.

Rising, I inhaled a freeing breath. Life buzzed all around me. No tower walls hemmed me in. A murder of crows squawked, tearing through the air with wildly flapping wings. Frogs croaked. A monkey scampered in a tree above, jumping from limb to limb, clicking its tongue down at me. Blood-swollen insects buzzed and chirped. One of them whizzed past me, its wiry legs brushing my shoulder. Perla thought they carried disease, but they never bit us. They were so fat and well fed from feeding off the dwellers. We were paltry temptations.

The wind rustled through branches and leaves, lifting the tiny hairs that framed my face. There was no time to savor it though. I needed to be back before Sivo and Perla woke.

My feet moved swiftly toward the stream where the berries grew. Even if I hadn't made the walk several times with Sivo by my side, my nose and ears could guide me through the press of perpetual blackness. I had learned how to use the wind currents, how to listen and feel the airflow change and alter given the location of objects. The world had its own voice and I listened to it.

I heard the swift burble of the stream before I smelled the crisp water. I risked moving a little faster, knowing that the sound of running water helped mask any sound I inadvertently made.

I stepped from the tree line up to the stream and squatted along the pebbly ground and drank greedily. Icy water dribbled down my chin and throat. I swiped at it with my hand as I sank back on my heels, listening as a fish splashed close to the surface.

Aside from the rain catch we rigged atop the tower, the only water we had was what Sivo carried back in buckets. It was a laborious and dangerous process.

Rising, I dried my hands on my jacket and moved to the boonberry bushes. I flipped open the flap to my satchel and began plucking berries, stuffing a few into my mouth as I worked, letting the dark, tart flavor burst on my tongue. My bag was almost full when I heard the anguished shout. I felt it like a vibration through me.

I ceased to chew. That very human scream was close. My mind raced, mentally mapping the area, seeing so vividly what I couldn't see in darkness. The stream. The tower. The direction in which the shout originated.

With a sinking sensation, I realized the reason for the shout.

It was one of several traps Sivo left out to catch game. Sometimes he caught a dweller and finished it off. One less to plague the land.

I flinched as another agonized shout stretched long over the air. A person was out there and in trouble because of us. My stomach muscles convulsed. I didn't even know this faceless individual, but I wanted to grab him, shake him, slam a hand over his mouth, and command him to silence. He couldn't have lived this long and not known the importance of silence. Sivo's voice whispered through me, ordering me to turn my back and come home.

Listening to that imaginary voice, I dropped the flap on my satchel and turned for the tower, my footfalls just short of a run over the spongy ground.

And then I heard the first dweller.

It was a signal cry, beckoning forth more of its brethren. Long and keening, sharp and discordant as no human could make. The eerie call ground through me like nails on glass. My heart seized and then kicked into a full sprint. Where there was one dweller—

An answering call followed, then two more in fast succession. I counted rapidly in my head. Four dwellers.

Inhaling, I searched for the sound of them, trying to determine how close they were. Weaving through clawing vines and trees, I listened, tasting the air for copper. The blood of the dead always drenched dwellers. They were coming. The air was already thicker with a layer of loam and copper over the forest's usual odor of rotting vegetation.

I pulled my sword free as I ran, flexing my sweating palm around the aged leather hilt. The wind thinned, the current shifting, blocked by a large object ahead. The tower.

I recognized the slope of the ground beneath my feet as I neared home. I was going to make it. Elation bubbled up inside my chest. The cold hand of fear began to loosen and slip free.

Then another cry came. Longer, plaintive and hungry. Ice shot down my spine. That made five.

I was almost home, but for the person caught in the trap, fear was just beginning.

I stopped a few feet from the hidden door. My chest heaved from my run, blood surging hotly through my veins. Sivo's and Perla's voices whispered in my head, urging me to uncover the secret door and dive inside the tunnel so that I survived.

I shook my head. There had to be more to life than hiding and counting the days until your last breath. There had to be more than looking away when someone lost his life. There had to be . . . more.

Adjusting my grip on the hilt of my sword, I turned from the tower and plunged back into the woods.

THREE

Fowler

I FLUNG THE iron trap to the ground with a curse. Bits of Madoc's flesh stuck in its angry, bloodstained teeth. Dagne whimpered and jerked to the side even though the trap was in no danger of hitting her. She reached out and lightly touched her brother's arm.

Her huge eyes settled on me. "You can fix it, yes?"

A huff of disbelief escaped me as I squinted down at Madoc's ruined leg. I couldn't see much, and not just because of the dark. Blood covered his shin, soaking the shredded fabric of his trouser leg. He would have been better off if the trap had snapped his neck.

"You can carry him, right?" She nodded, as though expecting that I would agree.

Absolutely. I could carry a thirteen-year-old boy and fight off dwellers simultaneously.

I looked up as though I could find a way out of this in the tight canopy of vines and branches overhead. A glimpse of moon winked down between leaves, mocking me.

Dropping my gaze, I focused on the bedraggled boy and girl at my feet. Fat, blood-engorged insects swarmed around them in the feeble moonlight. Garbed in grimy clothes, faces streaked with dirt, they reeked of fear and rot, blending perfectly with their surroundings.

"It's going to be fine, Madoc. We have Fowler. He'll take care of you." She patted her brother's shoulder and lifted her gaze to me again. "Right?" She was bobbing her head again, willing me to promise her lies. "Fowler?"

She was tenacious like an old hunting dog I once had. The hound would fetch the pheasant, but getting him to drop the bird from his teeth was another matter entirely. Eventually my father killed him, having no patience for such willfulness. He would have had no patience for Dagne or her brother. The fact that I did would have disgusted him.

I dragged my hands through my hair, fingers curling in strands that had grown long in the last year. I tugged hard as though ripping them from my scalp would give some relief. A gust of breath expelled from me. Against my better judgment, I'd let the siblings tag along with me and now I'd pay for it. It wouldn't have been so bad if they possessed an ounce of stealth. My mouth twisted into a grimace. They were dead weight pulling me down with them.

I could have slipped away. I'd considered it. But I stuck it out, telling myself that it was just until the next village. I'd leave them there. Perhaps it was that I didn't want to be like my father, that I was determined not to be, that kept me from abandoning them.

I glanced around, peering into the dark, gauging if any of the shadows were more than shadows. If the shapes sifting around me in the inky air moved with purpose. If we were already being hunted. I stared hard, straining my eyes in a world gone cold with relentless night.

"Fowler, do you—"

"Quiet," I rasped, looking behind me into the yawning stretch of night, straining to hear beyond the sounds of buzzing insects and a far-off scream of a tree monkey.

I sniffed, detecting the smoke of peat fire somewhere nearby. I thought I had noticed it earlier and dismissed it. Where there's fire, there were usually people, and people didn't live in these woods.

It was several hours until midlight—that gloomy haze of hour when the barest amount of light filtered out from where the sun hid behind the moon. The only time during the day when the earth was free from dark dwellers. But even then there was tension, a fine edge of panic so sharp it could cut glass. A choking urgency to outrace time and hurry before the murky light vanished and they returned.

Dagne started weeping—a small, piteous sound like a mewling kitten fighting for its last breath. She wrapped her thin arms around her brother's chest and struggled to haul him to his feet. He cried out and I flinched at the sound that seemed to echo around us. "Are you going to help me?"

I held up a hand for her to be quiet, cocking my head to the side and listening to a forest that had fallen suddenly too quiet.

"We should never have come this way," Dagne complained. "I told you this forest is cursed."

I had heard the tales as a boy, but didn't care, assuming the Black Woods would be less populated. And where there were less people there were less of them. "I don't recall inviting you to join me."

"Just go before they come. Leave me," Madoc whispered.

I let out a breath. It was tempting. He'd screamed when the trap snapped on his leg, and again when I pried the steel teeth from his ankle. A swarm of dwellers was probably en route to us. Even if we did escape, what were the odds that we would do so unscathed? It only took one bite for infection to set in. One drop of toxin would make you so sick that even if you didn't die, you couldn't function. Couldn't run.

We all froze at the first cry. Now there was no doubt. They were coming.

Other dwellers chimed in. The eerie cries bounced off one another from every direction. It wasn't the first time I heard them, but the sounds they made were no less terrifying. Monkeys went wild in the trees, jumping and rattling vines and branches, safe in their perches, but no less agitated.

A strangled sob spilled from Dagne. She clutched her brother closer. "I'm not leaving you!"

In a sudden surge of energy, Madoc shoved his sister at me and I caught her. The effort made him lose his balance and he fell back to the ground. "Take her! I can't go on."

Dagne was fragile in my arms, as easy to snap as dried kindling. She was only sixteen, but she felt smaller. She reminded me of Bethan with her slight stature and eyes big like a wounded animal's. I couldn't protect her. I couldn't be responsible for another life.

I wouldn't be.

I glanced down again at Madoc's crushed leg. He was right. He wasn't going anywhere.

"Fowler." He bit out my name. "Take her and go. I—I'll delay them."

Delay them. He meant they would be too busy slaughtering him to come after us. Dagne choked out a little cry, understanding his meaning, too. I nodded once and tightened my grip on her arm, tugging on her to follow me. She struggled, pleading, and I knew, despite my nod, this wasn't going to work. Not with her. Not with me. Not together.

A twig snapped.

I released Dagne and shoved her behind me. Yanking an arrow from the quiver at my back, I swung my bow into position. Blood pumped fast and hard in my veins. I drew my string and lined up my arrow in one fluid move, pulling back until my curled fingertips brushed my cheek. As effortless as breathing.

Body braced, I rotated on the balls of my feet, my gaze scanning the area. The moon's glow relieved the black pall of night to a deep plum. I marked the darker motionless shapes of trees and shrubs easily, searching for the slightest movement.

My nostrils flared. The usual odors were there. The ripe, loamy odor of the outdoors infused everything. But an underlying whiff of something else mingled there, too, ribboning through the familiar. The source was faintly mint, a little peppery, like the black tea grown in the hills of Relhok. It wasn't a dweller but something else. Someone else.

The new arrival stepped cautiously forward from the thick press of trees and low-hanging branches, moving slowly.

I peered through the gloom at his face. Not a him. A her. A girl.

Her eyes gleamed darkly in a pale, dirt-free face. The clean face gave me pause, instantly telling me she had a shelter nearby. A safe place.

I lowered my bow a notch. Her arrival meant a chance for Madoc and his sister. I opened my mouth, but before words formed, an arrow whistled past my ear on a trajectory straight for the stranger.

The girl jerked to the side at the last possible moment, swiftly dodging the arrow. It vanished into the darkness. I whirled around, grabbing Dagne's bow from her bone-thin fingers.

She sputtered, "I need that—"

"You kill what needs killing."

Dagne's eyes widened. "I thought she was a dweller!"

"Quickly. This way." At the girl's voice, I turned. She stood in front of me, oddly composed. She motioned to Madoc on the ground. "Can you carry him?"

"Who are you?"

"Luna," she answered, as though her name were explanation enough.

She angled her face, head cocking sideways. Listening the way animals did. "They're coming," she announced in a voice as smooth as water-polished stones. "Too many to fight."

Almost on cue, the familiar cry split the night. It sent off a cacophony of responses.

"We don't have much time." She uttered this with such confidence, such knowing.

"Figure that out all by yourself, did you?" I slung my bow around my shoulder and leaned down. Wrapping an arm around Madoc's waist, I hauled him to his feet. He draped an arm around my shoulders, lips compressed so that only a small groan escaped.

"Keep up," she said in that sleek-as-glass voice.

"You heard her. Keep up," I ordered Dagne.

I propped up Madoc as we walked, his feet dragging over the ground. I grimaced at the rustle of leaves and crack of twigs in our wake.

The girl moved fast, cutting through the dark foliage.

I could hardly track her. And then I couldn't. She was gone like a flame snuffed out. One moment there. Gone the next.

I stopped and blinked, peering around with quick turns of my head.

The dwellers were on top of us, their musky scent everywhere. I couldn't use my bow while holding up Madoc, so I pulled the blade from my side with my free hand.

"Where did she go?" Dagne clasped my arm, shaking it, edging into hysterics.

My sword wobbled in front of me. "Let go," I ordered, but it was too late.

A creature materialized in the night, its body near my height. No hair sprouted anywhere on the gray, dimpled body. Even though its flesh resembled molding clay, I knew its body was dense, composed of sinewy tissue not nearly as yielding as the tender flesh of a human. They were still vulnerable enough to a well-aimed arrow and a precise, strategically thrust blade, however. One simply had to get close enough.

Its mouth gaped wide, long feelers rising out of its face to taste the air and detect the presence of prey. The eyes were small, dark orbs that saw very little—if anything. But they hunted us just fine without sight, relying on their hearing and those feelers that vibrated like a nest of snakes, seeking us.

Dagne screamed.

The dweller lifted its chin, jerking its head to the side at the sound.

I dropped Madoc as the thing came at us, walking a direct line, its hairless head listing to the side as it assessed our movements.

Still in a panic, Dagne wouldn't release her grip on my sword arm. Cursing, I snatched the sword from my right hand with my left. The delay cost me. The dweller was on me before I could bring up my blade.

The stocky body slammed into me, solid as rock, and we went down. My sword flew from my hand. Wet, rotting breath panted in my face, a rancid gust on my cheek. The mouth yawned wide, revealing sharp, serrated teeth trying for a bite as its thin feelers shook and stretched for my face like hungry serpents, ready to release their toxin.

I shoved one hand at its thick throat, forcing distance between us. It lunged for my face. I dodged its mouth, turning my head and watching a drip of toxin narrowly miss my nose. I spotted my lost sword, just out of my reach.

Giving up on it, I located the dagger strapped at my thigh and yanked it free. With a grunt, I brought it up and sawed at the throat, pressing deep into thick, corded skin. The small eyes turned glassy, reminding me of an onyx-beaded necklace my mother had always worn.

Blood soaked me, pouring from the deepening slash in its neck. The creature fell limp on top of me.

Grunting, I flung off its weight and scrambled for my bow.

Dagne cried out. A thump behind me had me spinning, bow at the ready, arrow trained straight ahead and pointing directly into Luna's face.

She held a dagger, blood dripping from the blade. A dead dweller sprawled at her feet between us.

I lowered the bow a fraction. "You came back."

Her eyes glinted in the dark. "I told you to follow."

I huffed. "I can't move as fast as you when I'm carrying someone else."

She turned her back on me and started moving ahead again. "More are coming. From the east. Hurry."

I glanced to my left as if I could see them through the night. Almost in response to her words another keening cry stretched on the air, soon answered by another, then another.

Already her slight figure was hard to detect in the swallowing dark. Bending, I hauled Madoc up again. He was weaker than moments ago, a heavier burden.

With a sniffled whimper, Dagne fell in close behind me as I hastened after the girl. Ignoring my exhaustion, I kept moving, pushing ahead, one foot after the other.

FOUR

Luna

I STRETCHED MY arms beneath the trapdoor, my fingers securing and locking it in place, sealing us in. I could still hear the dwellers Outside—their tromping feet and uneven breaths. Their odor chased me down into the tunnel, sour in my nostrils and bitter copper in my mouth.

"This way." I turned briskly, leading them through the narrow space, jumping a little when I heard Sivo call out my name ahead of us.

"Who's that?" the boy at my back demanded.

I shook my head and squared my shoulders. I'd been practicing different explanations in my head, but didn't think I would have to use them until after we went upstairs and I woke Sivo and Perla.

Sivo thundered toward me. His large, square hands closed on my arms, fingers flexing as though assuring himself that I was whole and uninjured.

"What were you thinking going out on your own?"

"I wanted it to be a surprise." I glanced down to the satchel at my hip as though he could see within to the contents. "For your birthday."

"You daft, soft-hearted girl." He shook me slightly as his voice cracked. "Getting yourself killed would have made for one memorable birthday."

"That didn't happen though, did it?" I asked gently, patting his hand. "I'm right here. I'm fine."

Sivo's sharp intake of breath told me he'd spotted them in the gloom behind me.

"What have you done?" Sivo bit out, his voice strained tight—it wasn't how he usually talked to me and for a moment something twisted inside me.

I stepped to the side, revealing the trio behind me.

Sivo's hand clamped on my wrist and tugged me back as though I needed protection from this ragtag group that I had saved.

Then I remembered how quickly the archer dispatched the dweller. He wasn't totally helpless. He could likely fend for himself if he wasn't looking after the other two. The other two . . . I couldn't imagine they would remain alive much longer. Not with one of them injured.

"Is there a problem?" The boy's boots stepped closer, scraping over the stone floor. Fowler. That was what the weeping girl had called him.

He couldn't be much older than me. He moved with an agility that surpassed Sivo's. An air of competence resonated in the deep pitch of his voice and in the sure way he moved. He didn't waste precious moments, life-and-death moments, debating what to do. He just acted.

"Sivo, I had to." I motioned to Madoc. "He stepped in one of the traps."

The tremble in my voice must have given me away. Guilt, maybe? It wasn't our fault. We needed the traps for our survival. No one ever came into the Black Woods. No one was supposed to.

"The traps? Are they yours?" Fowler demanded.

I uttered nothing.

Sivo admitted, "We set the traps. We have to eat."

"Yes, well, your trap caught Madoc here. Nearly got us all killed."

"If it wasn't for me, you'd all still be out there. Dead," I added in case he missed my point. "You're welcome for bringing you here."

His focus snapped back on me. I felt his gaze slide over me like a palpable touch. "If it wasn't for your trap," he countered, "we wouldn't even need your hospitality. We'd be safely on our way."

I snorted. I couldn't help myself. "Indeed? You think you would be safe? For how long?" I nodded toward his companions.

"These two traveling with you are as quiet as stampeding horses."

"How quiet would you be with your leg shattered to bits?" the girl complained.

"Enough," Sivo declared, his voice settling over the group with authority. "We'll take you up—see what we can do for that leg. Your weapons stay here though."

Fowler adjusted his bow on his shoulder, the arrows rubbing against each other. His distrust flowed sharply in the space of the tunnel. He was the one who kept them alive. This I knew. He was primal. His weapons were as much a part of him as his own limbs. He didn't move to set his weapons down and Sivo's body tightened beside me. The point was nonnegotiable.

I rested a hand on Sivo's arm and addressed Fowler. "If I wanted you dead, I would have just left you out there," I murmured. "I never would have brought you here. You present as much risk to us as we to you." More, I silently added. Sivo tensed beneath my fingers. He didn't like me being this honest.

"Fowler?" the girl said softly. "Please." Clearly they followed his lead, but she wanted inside.

After several moments, his deep voice replied, "Fine."

I smiled slightly, amused that he thought there was ever any other possibility. Out there, death waited. In here, with us, they had a chance.

He stripped off his weapons. Once they were unarmed, Sivo turned, leading the way through the tunnel, his great shape cutting a path ahead of us. I hurried after him, lightly touching his sleeve, the sounds of weapons falling on the stone floor echoing behind me.

"Sivo?"

"Yes," he grumbled back at me.

"Happy birthday."

I was the first to reach the second floor and find Perla waiting. The fire in the hearth popped and crackled but it was nothing compared to the angry energy radiating off her. The warmer air sighed over my chilled skin. We gathered in this space daily. It was where we ate and where Perla knitted before the fire after meals. Where Sivo and I cleaned weapons and practiced knife throwing. The minutiae of our lives unfolded in this room. For Perla, it was her universe. To an extent, mine, too.

A hollowness spread through my chest, pushing everything else out. It was a familiar sensation that plagued me whenever I thought about my future here. Perla and Sivo wouldn't be around forever. What would it be like when they were gone? They were the only people I had ever known. I talked to no one else. Touched no one. Heard no one.

Until now.

The air stirred as Perla paced before the hearth. When I cleared the threshold, she turned on me, snatching me up and embracing me with her soft, yielding body. Not that hugging let her forget her annoyance with me. She pulled back and gave me a small shake.

"You know the thoughts I've been suffering since waking up

to find your bed empty? It's bad enough when you venture out with Sivo . . . but to go alone when—"

"We have guests," I interrupted, stopping her short.

Loosening her grip on my arms, she assessed the newcomers as they cleared the threshold behind Sivo. I could hear her thoughts spinning. Her breathing altered, too; grew raspy and agitated. She wanted them gone.

"You're dripping blood all over my rug," she finally muttered. "This way. You can use Luna's room. She can bed with me." Her joints creaked as she led them to my chamber.

I held back. Sivo hovered at my side. "You shouldn't have brought them here, Luna." His voice came out gravelly, tired—not like his usual self—and I felt a little guilty for being responsible for that.

"Did you expect me to leave them?"

"We cannot let them think we are vulnerable. They cannot know who you are—"

"They don't know." I understood his meaning. "There's no reason for them to ever know."

He released a rattling sigh. His breaths were like that a lot lately. Phlegmy and wet like he suffered from a perpetual ague. I didn't want to think about what it might mean.

"That boy's leg is going to take time to heal. It may never be right."

"Whatever his leg is at the end of all this, it's better than him being dead. Which is what he'd be if I left them out there. They'd all be dead." Maybe not Fowler. He had been on the verge of running and leaving them. When I first stepped into their midst, I'd felt that. I'd known.

"What I'm saying . . ." His voice gentled into the tone he used when he talked me down from a tantrum. I hadn't heard that voice since I was a child. I realized then just how defensive I felt. As though these strangers belonged to me, as though they were mine to keep. Stray pets that I found and intended to have with me forever. ". . . is that they can only stay a little while."

And what was so wrong with them staying indefinitely?

Thankfully, I held back the question, knowing it was counter to everything I had ever been taught about surviving this world. *Let no one in. Keep our existence secret.*

The three of them were the most interesting thing to happen to me in the entirety of my life. A sad testament, but there it was. Even though I knew next to nothing about them, I didn't want to see them go.

"That older boy. The leader . . ."

"Fowler?"

He hesitated. Heat crept over my cheeks at the quickness of my reply. "There's a look to his eyes. He's dangerous." I resisted pointing out that perhaps this was a good thing. Being a little dangerous in this world was a requirement. "As long as they're here, you're not to be alone with him. With any of them. Understand?"

I nodded. Sivo didn't say any more, but he didn't have to. The truth was there, a cloud hovering over us. If we were to keep our secrets, then they couldn't stay.

And yet the thought left me hollow. I'd never been given a taste of anything else. I'd certainly never confronted a boy who smelled of ferocity and life and vitality. A boy with a deep, rumbling voice that made everything in me tighten in a way that I couldn't comprehend. It was new. Different. It was feeling.

Guttural cries drew our attention toward my chamber, where Perla had started to work on Madoc's leg. My mattress groaned and squeaked from his thrashing. Perla's brisk, efficient voice shushed the boy and then instructed his sister and Fowler to hold him down.

I winced as Madoc's moan stretched over the air. The terrible cries twisted into shrill pleas. "No, no, no, no . . . stop, please, no . . ."

This was even worse than the death cries I occasionally heard from my perch in the tower. This was the sound someone made who wanted to die. I shivered, the noise worming its way beneath my skin. I pressed a hand to my twisting stomach and inched closer to the hearth, lowering my face and soaking in the warmth.

Sivo claimed that because I had grown up under the mantle of dark, my senses of hearing, touch, taste, and smell were keen. He claimed it was an advantage in this world without light. Right now, with my throat closing up at the noises coming from my chamber, I wished myself free of the advantage.

"Go back down and change," he instructed. "I'll ready breakfast."

Glad for the escape, I descended the winding stairs, leaving

Madoc's sobs and the crunch and grind of bone as Perla reset the leg.

I entered the anteroom and quickly undressed, shivering in the cold air of the tower's bowels. My heart still beat swiftly, body humming with exhilaration. The events of the morning left me in a strange daze. Almost like I had woken from an especially vivid dream and didn't know quite where I was anymore. But of course, I was where I always was. Only now, at long last, things were different.

I tied up the laces at the front of my gown with deft fingers and smoothed a hand over the soft fabric, once again the girl Perla preferred me to be. The queen of Relhok.

The title meant nothing anymore except to Perla and Sivo. Even to me, it rang dully. A royal assumed dead. Lost and forgotten. Trapped in a tower within a cursed forest, surrounded by monsters. It was the kind of fairy tale villagers entertained their children with on long winter nights when the world was good and right.

I returned to the second floor, my silk ribbons with their fraying ends clutched in my fist. The room was empty, the pop and crumble of a log in the fire even more pronounced in the vacant space.

Sivo's deep voice rumbled from my bedchamber and I knew he was in there with the others. I thought about joining them, but the ribbons in my hand reminded me of my fallen hair. Self-consciousness seized me. For some reason my appearance mattered.

Deciding to tidy myself in Perla's chamber, I moved across the stone floor and pushed open the door to her room. As I stepped inside, a swift intake of breath greeted me. The sound, combined with a warm, musky, undeniably male smell, was freshly familiar.

Too late, I realized the room wasn't empty.

FIVE

Fowler

"EVER HEARD OF knocking?" I faced the girl, annoyed at the intrusion. In truth, annoyed at everything. I shouldn't have been here with any of these people. I should have been far away, my only distraction avoiding dwellers.

Propping my hands on my hips, I gave Luna an eyeful, waiting for her shock, her embarrassment, but it didn't come. She stared straight at me, still that oddly composed girl from the forest unaffected by arrows flying at her head or approaching monsters.

Or by me standing naked in front of her.

"I didn't realize you were in here," she explained.

I didn't bother to reach for my clothes. I angled my head,

waiting for her to move, to avert her eyes, to turn. Expected behavior. She did none of those things. She didn't even blink.

"Your mother—"

"Perla is not my mother."

"Your friend then." I lowered my hands to my sides. Awareness prickled over my skin at the proximity of this girl to me when I wasn't dressed. "She complained that I reeked of blood and the outdoors. She told me to change in here."

Luna angled her head in that curious manner of hers. "Perla doesn't like the Outside. Not even the smell of it. Reminds her of them."

My bare feet moved across the cold stone as I approached her, waiting for her to bolt. I swept my gaze over her, inches from her now. Still, she gave no reaction. Unlike me. My breath grew shallow. I was reacting but she didn't seem to notice.

I studied her. She was too clean and her attire far too fine. The gold thread woven into the bodice transfixed me. It was a long time since I had seen a female wearing so fine a dress. Most people wore threadbare garments, worn and patched.

Shaking my head, I looked at her face again, from the smooth and shining hair to her bottomless dark eyes. Now, in the lamplight, I could detect tiny flecks of amber in the deep brown depths that I hadn't noticed outside.

Her lips parted slightly with unspoken words. I was close enough that I could count the smattering of freckles on her nose. They weren't sun-kissed freckles. There was no chance for that. Not in this life.

She stared back at me, her stare fixing dead center on my chest. An alarm went off in my head, warning me that something wasn't right. Something wasn't as it should be.

"You . . ." My voice faded as I struggled with an idea that couldn't be possible.

"What?" She lifted her chin, her expression mild, unaffected, her eyes now looking directly at me.

Through me.

My heart hammered in my ears as I slowly lifted a hand between us. Not touching, but simply putting it out there with all the stealth of a hunting predator. "You should have knocked."

"Why?"

"Why?" I echoed like I was testing the word, tasting it. This close, her body radiated a warmth that settled into the pores of my exposed skin. "Are you really so bold you don't . . ." My voice constricted into that strangled hoarseness again. I looked down at myself and then back up to her face again. Still no reaction on her part. She folded her hands in front of her, the fingers laced. She wasn't this bold. No. She was something else.

I took her hand. She started at the sensation of my callused fingers on her softer skin. My pulse jumped and skittered at the base of my throat, but I ignored it, placing her chilled hand, palm flat, against my bare chest. Her fingers spread wide, each one a burning imprint.

She made a choked, mewling sound.

"Because"—my voice scratched out of me—"I'm naked."

Fire scored her cheeks. It was the blush I expected when she first walked into the room.

Now she knew.

But she hadn't known before.

She gasped, tugging her hand. I held it against me for a moment before letting go. She pulled away as though stung. I stepped toward her, this time waving a hand before her face.

"Stop that," she snapped, sensing the air stirring in front of her. Only sensing though. Not seeing. She swatted at my hand, stopping when her back hit the door.

"You—" My voice broke off and I dropped my arm.

She shook her head fiercely. Her eyes gleamed, panic moving over her features. She reached for the door latch at her hip, ready to flee.

But it was too late. I knew. And I said it.

"You can't see."

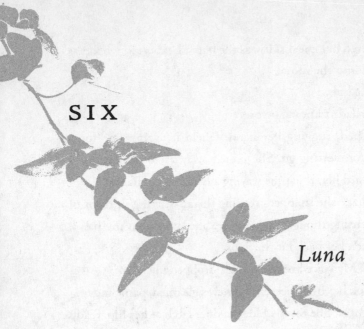

SIX

Luna

THE EXACT MOMENT of the eclipse, as darkness descended on the land, I entered the world. No one was paying much attention to my arrival in that moment except, of course, my mother, and the servants attending her. Even my father didn't know, already off fighting the mad crowds banging for entry at the gates, unaware that there was nothing he could do to stop the dark tide from rolling in.

But beyond that night, beyond my birth, the people ushering me into this world did not know that I lacked sight. There would have been no way for them to know then. Especially not with the distraction of thousands of dark dwellers breaking through the ground and swarming like ants over the land. Such a distraction made it easy to ignore the birth of a princess.

Perla, the wet nurse standing by at my birth, fled with me before I, too, was slaughtered. Sivo, one of my father's royal guards, found us in a corridor. A mercenary in his earlier years, a warrior at heart, he reacted quickly, leading Perla from the castle. Together, they escaped through the melee of the capital and made it across the country to the secluded tower Sivo had discovered with my father all those years ago.

My father had turned the tower into his private retreat, stocking it with supplies, enjoying its isolation and that no one knew of its existence. According to Sivo, he didn't believe in cursed woods in the same way that he had not believed in the legends of monsters living beneath the ground, waiting for darkness so that they could emerge. Those tales had been part of childhood. Adults knew better than to believe in such fantasies. My father would bring my mother to the tower occasionally to enjoy the solitude and life away from court. It was hard to fathom wanting solitude. I had more of it than I could stand.

I was almost two years old before Sivo and Perla realized my condition. I was already walking, running, and talking. I behaved as a normal toddler in the confines of our tower, if not too active for Perla's tastes. She would laugh and say that I needed a leash—a fact that almost came to pass when she caught me scaling the wall tapestry in my bedchamber. I was almost to the domed ceiling. She was overwhelmed in those days. With my lack of caution, life was just as dangerous within the tower as it was out of it.

I behaved as though I possessed sight, recklessly barreling full speed ahead. They only discovered the truth because Perla asked me to pick out the blue ribbon for my hair one morning and I handed her the green. I didn't understand blue. Upon further investigation, she realized I didn't understand the difference between porridge and stew until I tasted them. I couldn't understand because I couldn't see.

And apparently I couldn't identify when a boy stood before me naked either. Strangely enough, this was both a relief and a disappointment.

I bit my lip, my teeth sinking in and clinging deep to the sensitive flesh until I tasted the copper tang of blood. Fowler was naked in front of me. I released my lip and inhaled a raw breath that expanded my lungs.

I lifted my chin as though I wasn't completely unnerved. My lack of vision had never felt like a handicap before. Not as it did in this moment.

He was naked.

I inhaled his scent and it was stronger, proof that not a stitch of clothing covered his body. The salt and musk of his skin hit me sharper than before—and something else. Another scent that was indecipherable to me. I felt it as much as I smelled it. It was raw and deep and visceral. My skin almost ached from the presence of it, pulling tight and breaking out into gooseflesh. My stomach knotted like a thousand butterflies were rioting inside me.

"What d-did you say?" I demanded as though I hadn't heard. As though "you can't see" wasn't running over and over in my mind.

"You heard me," he replied evenly, his voice without inflection.

"Of course I can see." I channeled all my feelings, outrage, shock, fear—other unidentifiable things—into a reaction that I hoped translated into bemusement. Not panic. "Of course I can see."

He took his time responding. "You're lying."

I shook my head.

He continued, "Your face burns red right now, but not before. Not when you first walked in here."

"You're wrong," I insisted.

"No. Not about this I'm not."

I turned then, managing a shrug.

"Why don't you admit it? You think I'll see it as a weakness? Is that it?"

That was exactly what Perla and Sivo thought, but everything in me rebelled at this.

"I'm not weak." My voice shook out of me, a tremor on the air that seemed to belie my words.

He stepped closer. The air grew thicker and I felt the subtle ripple in its flow as he shook his head. "I know you're not weak."

I inhaled. My chest felt too tight. He was close enough for me to touch and the memory of his skin, smooth and hard under my fingers, roped with sinew like one of the rangy wolves that hunted the woods, plagued me. Touching, feeling another human, someone who wasn't Sivo and Perla, who wasn't family, was as strange to me as the idea of sunlight that lasted half the day every day.

His voice hit me like sparks popping and flying from a fire. "I won't hurt you," he murmured, like he was coaxing a wild animal closer—in this case, me. He was the stranger here. The interloper. It was he who should tiptoe around me.

"I'll leave tomorrow, and what you are . . . blind or not." He uttered "not" with heavy skepticism. "It won't matter."

"Then why do you care what I am?" I demanded, trying not to reveal how much he had just shaken me. He was leaving tomorrow.

Leaving us to care for the boy and girl, I presumed. Dusting his hands clean and abandoning them both to us. I wasn't sure if I was bothered more for Madoc and Dagne or simply because he was removing himself from my sphere. He'd filled what had been empty only to remove his presence just as suddenly.

Except I would remember he had been here. In the tomb of my tower, in dark silence, I would remember his voice, his smell, and the way he handled himself on the Outside. His vital energy. His animal intensity. He was what it meant to be alive.

He made the urge to experience life outside these walls pound deeper inside me—stronger than before. I pressed my fingers to my pulse thrumming wildly at my neck.

"Call it curiosity," he replied.

"You'll just leave Madoc and Dagne? Abandon them—"

"They're not my responsibility."

"They were with you. You were together. How can you be that . . . selfish?"

The air stretched thin, and I felt his stare on my face, harder than before. "This world demands it. Only the selfish survive."

"I don't believe that—"

"What do you know of the world? How often do you even step outside these walls? The way Sivo reacted when you returned with me, I don't imagine very often. You're blind. You can't know."

I hissed a stinging breath. Not only was he selfish, but he was cruel and narrow-minded and he saw too much of the truth. "I left these walls long enough to save your life. Fortunate for you, I was not struck with a surge of selfishness then."

"I didn't ask it of you."

"No, but you took my help, didn't you?" I swung back around. "My mistake. I wish I hadn't bothered." I paused with my hand on the latch. Swallowing, my voice came out thankfully stronger. "Next time I won't."

A lie on both counts.

If the same circumstances presented themselves, I would react the same way. I knew that much about me.

"Don't worry. There won't be a next time."

Turning, I stepped from the room, closing the door with a dull thud behind me.

* * *

It was a long day.

Perla emerged a few times from my bedchamber for fresh linens and water. I lifted my head in her direction at the first sound of her tread, as though she might reveal something in manner or speech about Fowler. Had he mentioned to her that he knew I was sightless? Had he said anything about me at all?

Perla frequently accused me of being quick to provoke. She always pointed to my bloodlines. Apparently, my father had been hot tempered. I punched the dough I was kneading and flipped it over.

Fowler had emerged fully clothed shortly after I left him. His scent had been less potent, and I knew I would never make the mistake of failing to recognize him unclothed again. He'd walked a hard line for my chamber. I didn't even feel his gaze upon me. He would be leaving tomorrow. Unless he changed his mind and intended to leave this very day. I didn't know and, of course, I couldn't inquire. That would call too much attention to the fact that he affected me.

"How's the boy?" I asked Perla as I set the dough in a bowl and draped a linen over it.

Her response was a grunt. Madoc still lived, and she was frustrated that I had made him our problem, that I brought him here and threatened our sanctuary.

I didn't press for more. Perla was in no mood for it. The air felt strained and tenuous enough, brittle like the ancient parchment of the few books we possessed.

I held silent as Perla gathered what she needed. Sivo hummed lightly from the chair where he sat. She banged through the cupboards, searching for something.

"What are you looking for?" I asked tentatively.

"The large bowl with the chip in it."

I automatically reached for it behind the basket of root truffles Sivo had gathered yesterday.

She grunted again as I handed it to her, her chapped fingers brushing mine. This grunt translated to: "thank you but I'm still angry with you."

She returned to the chamber, her tread heavier than usual.

"She's not happy with me," I murmured.

Sivo stopped humming. "What makes you think that?"

He was teasing. I smiled and shook my head. "Oh, just a feeling."

"She's scared. She loves you more than herself. We both do. We worry about what will happen to you when we are . . ."

My smile slipped as his words faded, but the rest was there. I heard it even if unspoken.

I thought of Fowler's words. *Only the selfish survive this world.*

They rang ominously, an echo that I couldn't banish. If that were true, then Sivo and Perla had long outlived their life expectancies. That should disprove his statement and not make me feel like their demise was an impending fate chasing them like a bloodhound. It shouldn't make me feel like my own time was slipping through my fingers like water through a sieve. My throat tightened at the notion. It wasn't so much that I could die. Everyone died. I wasn't afraid of death.

It's that I would die with so little to show for my life. A long stretch of days spent trapped in a tower.

I was afraid that was all I would ever have.

SEVEN

Luna

THAT EVENING I ventured into my bedchamber. Slinked really, pressing flat against the wall, hugging a fresh pitcher of water to my chest—my excuse for entering the room.

Madoc was awake, thrashing and pleading for relief in a voice that cracked. I could smell the earthy bite of sweat beading his skin. The copper of his blood tainted the room.

Dagne sniffed softly from beside the bed and adjusted her weight in the chair. "What's your name again?"

"Luna."

We were both quiet for a long while until her chair creaked again and she said, "You're lucky to have this place. I don't think

I've ever been anywhere so clean and warm. So safe. I didn't know places like this exist."

A sudden laugh had my head whipping around.

"No place is safe." Fowler sat in the corner. He had been there all along. His body was utterly still in a chair near the balcony. I'd occupied that seat for countless hours with the balcony doors open to the outside world, listening to the winds and drone of insects and the distant sounds of dark dwellers. Occasionally, I could hear the death of some poor animal as it fell victim to their ravenous appetites. We weren't the only things they fed upon.

The seat cushion bore a permanent indentation from my weight, and now he filled it, altering its shape so that the next time I sat in it I would only think of him and remember the boy—man—who wore his selfishness like a badge of honor.

My awareness of him burned a path through me. I brushed a stray strand of hair back from my cheek and tried to pretend I didn't feel his stare. And yet, like an animal aware of something else in its orbit, I knew he was there, watching me, thinking about our last encounter and the truth of my existence. A girl without sight in a world where we lived as prey.

I could feel him thinking about me, the knowledge whispering in the space between us like a ghost's breath. Sivo and Perla would panic when they learned this vulnerability had been exposed. And then they would only worry that he might discover the rest. That he would figure out who I was.

But he would be leaving tomorrow.

A desperate breath welled up inside me as though I was on

the verge of losing something, a chance . . . an opportunity for something new and strange and exciting. A short time ago I stood alone in a room with him. The air churning from cold to hot, thin to thick, in a way I had never felt before.

He rose and left the room without a word.

I exhaled, feeling like I was balancing on a knife's edge, anxious with the knowledge that he was going to leave and that would be the end of all this. A return to monotony.

I turned my attention back to Dagne. "Your friend—" I stopped short of saying leader, but the moment the word "friend" escaped I knew that didn't fit either. "He's good out there."

"He doesn't want us with him." She said this as though it was a simple truth. "And he won't wait for Madoc to recover."

"I'm sure that's not true." I winced at the lie. By his own admission, it was the truth, but a part of me believed, hoped, that he wouldn't be so merciless as to walk out on them. Would he abandon them so carelessly? As though they were nothing to him?

She laughed harshly. "Oh, it's the truth. You have been living in this tower a long time, haven't you? You can rely on no one."

Heat broke out over my face for revealing my naïveté.

"Life is unkind. That Fowler even stopped for us at all, that he didn't kill us or hurt us . . ." She paused. "Well, that's as generous as you can expect anyone to be."

I didn't want to believe that. There had to be more. People had to be . . . better. I couldn't let her destroy my hope for more. "Where are you from?"

"It doesn't matter. Every place is the same. Except for here.

It's nice here. Your hair . . . it's so shiny and clean. Those ribbons are pretty."

Reaching up, I removed a ribbon, threading it free from my hair. I offered it to her. It was a small thing to do, but it would bring her pleasure. I was certain of that.

The ribbon slipped from my grasp, and I knew she took it. "Th-thank you."

I nodded.

She sighed. "We left our village years ago. My father, Madoc, and I. We've been moving ever since. Even after Papa . . ." Her voice faded.

He wasn't with them now. That was explanation enough.

Her voice softened and I heard the whisper of her fingertips through her brother's hair. "Sometimes we found a place that seemed safe. An abandoned cottage. A cave. Once we found an old mill. We stayed there a couple months. Others came; they took it from us. They took—they took everything—" Her voice broke a little and it was minutes before she said anything else. I didn't know what to say. I could only imagine with a shudder what *everything* was to her. "I'm glad Papa wasn't around anymore when that happened. This tower is a small slice of heaven."

She wanted to stay here. It was obvious. But would Perla let her? Would Sivo? Their goal was to keep me alive and protect my identity. They would see keeping her and Madoc as being at odds with that goal.

"Perhaps Fowler will wait," I suggested, even knowing in my gut that he wouldn't.

She released a laugh that twisted into a sob. "No. But don't worry. I don't expect you to let us stay here. I don't expect anything from anyone. We keep going, right? That's the only thing to do."

I nodded. Keep going. Except for me. I had to stay put.

Her words, Madoc thrashing on the bed, the coppery tang of his blood—all of it was too much, too ripe in my nose. Dagne's tears flowed unchecked down her cheeks, flavoring the air with salt.

With a murmured good-bye, I moved to the doorway and passed through it, anxious to get away.

I occupied myself in the kitchen, preparing a tray for Sivo to bring to Madoc and Dagne. Perla returned to the room. She would see to the needs of our visitors—and likely make certain that they didn't get any ideas about staying any longer than necessary.

After I made the tray, I took up the knitting—a task I loathed, but I needed to keep my hands busy. My fingers moved deftly with needle and thread through the supple leather, darning the hole in Sivo's jacket. I tried not to concentrate on the sounds floating from my bedchamber, but my ears were too keen to shut off. At one point Fowler emerged from the other chamber to rejoin Dagne and Madoc without a word to me.

Finished with the jacket, I folded it across the basket and started preparing dinner. Perla had already cut up some vegetables, so I finished what was left, cutting them on the wood table and tossing the modest amount into a pot.

Vegetables were few and far between. We'd rigged a garden

on top of the tower. Sivo worked on it constantly, trying to encourage what he could to grow with only the paltry sunlight offered during midlight. I often joined him. It was outdoors, after all, and it won out over inside chores.

I liked standing near the edge with my shoulders back, my fingers dusted with soil. I would lift my face to the wind and inhale the loamy musk of the Outside as Sivo worked, stabbing at the ground, cursing his undernourished greens, radishes, and beets. Occasionally peas would flourish, and that was a good day when we would actually have pea soup. Perla would make it with bits of rabbit meat and Sivo swore it was nearly as tasty as when his mother had made it with ham.

I'd never tasted ham. Boars had not lasted long after the eclipse. They didn't move fast enough to avoid the dwellers.

Sivo sat at the table, the smooth swishing sound of him sharpening knives a familiar rhythm as I placed the lid back on the pot over the hearth and then moved to slice the loaf of bread baked yesterday.

The creak in the floor signaled Perla's approach. I knew her tread well, the length of time that stretched between each steady step. Sighing, she set down the basket full of soiled bedding and rags she used to tend to Madoc. She moved to the washstand. The gentle splashing of water filled the room. After she finished, Sivo collected the basin and dumped it out the window, returning within moments.

"Dinner ready?" she asked, patting her hands and arms dry with the towel.

I nodded. "Almost."

Sivo resumed sharpening his blades. "How is he?"

"If his fever breaks, he'll live. He's young. Strong. Whether or not he will walk again is another matter." She moved beside me. I felt her gaze on my face. "What were you thinking?"

I sighed. "I was thinking they would die if I didn't help."

And I was thinking I was tired of being alone. That I would go stark mad staying all my days inside stone walls with never once encountering another soul.

I didn't say that, of course. It would make me seem ungrateful. It would make it seem like Perla and Sivo weren't enough—that they hadn't done enough for me.

When the high chancellor slew my father and my mother after she had just given birth to me, Perla snatched me from the nursery and fled. Cullan had clearly been waiting for an opportunity to seize power, and he found it the night of the eclipse, in the outbreak of chaos and wave of blood and death.

I shouldn't have lived. If not for Perla and Sivo, Cullan would have ended me, too.

I held my tongue, determined not to say anything that made this life they had miraculously carved for us seem too little.

"And why should whether these strangers die concern us?" Perla grumbled. "It's enough to keep just ourselves alive."

I felt Fowler's arrival even before I heard him step from my bedchamber. I lifted my head, wondering if he had heard Perla's comment. And if he cared one way or another.

His tread vibrated along the floor with a stealth that even Sivo couldn't manage.

"He's asleep," he announced.

"Fallen unconscious more likely," Perla responded. "Pain will do that to you. Knock the fight right out of you."

After a long pause, he replied, "If that's what pain does, it's a wonder any of us still live."

I stopped sawing on the bread and lifted my head in his direction. We all fell quiet at these words, and I knew that Sivo and Perla were staring at this stranger, wondering at him. Afraid of him.

And there was me, overcome and eaten alive with curiosity, the back of my neck prickling with awareness. I wanted to know about him. Where did he come from? Where had he been? Where was he going?

He was too new to be anything other than fascinating.

Heat scalded my cheeks and I lowered my head lest anyone see how he affected me. I concentrated on arranging the thick slices of bread into a basket.

"It smells good," Fowler offered, easing the awkward stretch of silence.

"Help yourself if you're hungry," I offered.

"Of course he's hungry," Sivo proclaimed. "A strapping fellow like him needs his nourishment if he's to make it on the Outside." A nongentle reminder that he was to go. Sivo wasn't much for subtlety. He might as well shove Fowler's belongings at him and show him the door.

I set the last slice of bread in the basket and dusted loose crumbs off my fingers, and heard myself saying, despite what he'd already told me, "Well, I'm sure he won't depart until Madoc is on his feet—"

"I'll leave on the morrow. At midlight."

He hadn't changed his mind. Had I expected him to? That somewhere over the course of a day, with warm bread in his belly and walls safely surrounding him, he might have changed his mind?

I turned my head in his direction, still inclined to persuade him. "But your friends—"

"They're not my friends." His voice dropped hard and absolute. "We traveled together. Briefly. I have to keep going."

His deep, rumbling voice wrapped around me, squeezing like a fist. He had to keep going. Alone. That's what he meant. He wanted no one. Like one of the slippery fish that I managed to seize for a fleeting moment in the stream before it escaped through my fingers. Gone.

There was no keeping him here. He would be leaving. "Why? Why would you want to go out there? It's safe in here." Strange, I mused, that I would be using the same argument Perla used against me every day. Perla, who preferred to die in this tower. This thought scudded through me with a wilting shiver. Dying in the tower. Living the entirety of my days within its walls. My presence, my life, unmarked. Unremembered. Unimportant. As though it never happened at all.

"Luna, don't be rude. The young man has a right to come and go as he pleases. We can't force him to remain." In Perla's voice, buried beneath the muted tenor, was the message for me to simply let him go. Release him and good riddance.

"There's a place. The Isle of Allu." Even as he said this to me, there was a thread of something in his voice. Surprise, perhaps, that he felt compelled to justify his actions. "It's reported to be free of dwellers—"

"Oh, and the sun shines there, too, I am certain," I snapped. "What a lovely fairy tale."

And yet even the remote possibility of it intrigued me. Which only infuriated me because I would never know if such a place actually existed. He could leave. He could go in search of this fantasy island. Whether it existed or not, he would never return to tell me.

I turned, my movements sloppy in my frustration. I grasped the lid off the pot, forgetting to grab the mitt to protect my hand. I cried out and dropped the lid.

Air rushed around me as Sivo jolted from his chair. Perla's heavier gait came forward, too, but there was another movement. Someone who moved faster, his stride fluid as water running free between my fingers.

"What have you done there?" His voice was a deep rasp, curling warmly like peat smoke. Warm fingers circled the bones of my wrist, turning my palm over.

"It's nothing," I grumbled, sensing Perla and Sivo hovering close, watching. Whatever they were thinking, they made no move to stop Fowler from touching me or curtail his attention on my hand.

"It's a burn. What were you thinking? Cooking and handling yourself near a fire."

I sucked in a breath and held it for a moment, my chest full with outrage over his presumption. "Who are you to chastise me—"

"Someone with eyes to see that you shouldn't—"

Tears stung the backs of my otherwise useless eyes. I felt them there, but thankfully they did not fall. I did not have to endure the humiliation of weeping in front of this boy who saw fit to judge what I should or should not do.

I reacted without thought. My hand snatched the knife that I used to cut the bread. My fingers circled the hilt unerringly, fitting it perfectly within my grip. It hissed as I swung it, stopping the serrated blade before his throat.

"I can see just fine without seeing. Fine enough to cook. To cut anything. Don't doubt that I can handle myself. Wasn't it me who brought you here and saved you?"

The utter stillness of the room told me neither Perla nor Sivo moved. They watched—whether for fear that I would indeed cut his throat or fear that he would turn the tables on me and retaliate, I wasn't sure, but I liked to think that Sivo was proud. He had trained me well.

Of course they could simply be shocked that Fowler knew of my blindness.

I heard the rustle of fabric as Fowler lifted his arm. The point of the blade gave way under the slightest pressure—but only because I permitted it. If I wanted him dead, he would be.

"Whether my death was so certain or not, point made. I'll not mistake you for helpless again," he murmured.

I stepped back, lowering my arm, but kept the knife in my grip. For now, I felt better holding it. I took a calming breath. It didn't matter what he thought of me. He was leaving.

With that reminder, I ignored the pulsing burn on my hand and dished up dinner, setting the bowls in front of each of us. Steam wafted up to my face.

"Where are you from?" Sivo asked as I was in the process of lifting my spoon to my mouth. I hesitated slightly before bringing the warm broth the rest of the way to my lips.

"I was born in Relhok City. I gather from your accents that you're from there as well."

Perla tensed. "We left before the eclipse," she lied, distancing us from the truth of what had happened inside the royal quarters, from the slaughter of my mother and her attendants.

"Fortunate for you. After the eclipse everything . . ." His voice faded, words unnecessary.

We didn't need to be told how bad things were in the capital during the eclipse. Sivo and Perla remembered and they'd shared those details with me. Knowledge was power, and a girl without sight needed as much power as she could seize.

"Did you ever see the high chancellor?" Sivo tensed beside me as he posed the question, his spoon clinking inside his bowl.

"You mean the king?"

His spoon clattered into the bowl. "He's no king of mine. Assassinating the old king and declaring yourself king doesn't make you the one true king." Emotion bled into Sivo's guttural voice. I patted his hand under the table, cautioning him not to reveal so much emotion. Why should a family such as ours, isolated and eking out a meager survival in a cursed forest, care who ruled over Relhok?

"I left the city over a year ago, but last I heard he was working on an alliance with Lagonia. Those were the rumors at least."

"Lagonia?" Sivo scoffed at the reference to Relhok's neighbor. "They're enemies of Relhok. They block all routes to the sea."

"Nothing like a mutual foe to turn enemies to allies."

"What mutual foe?" Perla asked.

"Dark dwellers," I whispered, understanding. They were everyone's enemy. The rivalry between Relhok and Lagonia paled beside the threat of the dark dwellers. I felt Fowler's attention on me then, his stare crawling over me. He had heard my whisper.

"Yes," he replied. "The king will do anything to secure a trade route. The country is starving and we need the sea for fishing and trade to other countries."

Sivo rose then, taking his bowl with him. He stomped from the room. I knew he couldn't stomach to hear the high chancellor discussed in such a manner—as a king that might be doing something good for Relhok. As far as he was concerned, the high chancellor deserved a sword at his throat for what he did to my parents. I was inclined to agree, except I didn't see what could be done about it now. We were here, far away from any chance of evening the score.

"Did I say something wrong?" Fowler asked in a voice that reflected nothing.

"He's not an admirer of your king," Perla sneered.

"He's not my king," Fowler replied in that even voice. "He's mad. Everyone knows that, but he rules with an iron fist and the people of Relhok are still alive because of him. That's enough for most."

"But not you. You left," I said.

"It's enough for most," he repeated.

Silence stretched and I wondered at his words and what was enough for him. Allu?

Perla rose and dished up more soup. "I'll bring a bowl for the girl and check on the boy." She hesitated before moving off. I knew she wondered at the wisdom of leaving us alone together. She didn't want me to grow attached to him. It was probably the memory of me holding that knife to his throat that satisfied her.

I listened to Perla's departing tread before shaking my head and returning to the task of cleaning up the dishes, trying my best to ignore him.

"Afraid to be left alone with me? I have my clothes on this time."

"Should your naked form frighten me? I can't see you, remember? So I needn't be repulsed."

He laughed at that, and I stopped, quite undone by the low, smoky sound. It rippled over my skin like the stroke of fine ribbon. His laughter stopped abruptly, almost as though it startled him as much as me. When he spoke again, his voice held no hint of that laughter. "Rest easy, I've not sent many females running away screaming before."

From what I'd felt of him, he was well formed, but I couldn't resist needling him. He was too confident and I wanted nothing more than to knock him from his perch.

"Oh. You're in the frequent habit of prancing about naked, are you?"

"Not frequent, no."

But I wasn't the first. I waited to see if he would elaborate on that, tucking a stray strand of hair behind my ear with suddenly fidgety hands. I wanted to hear more about him. I wanted him to talk about his life. I wanted to know about where he came from, what he'd seen, the people, including the girls who had or had not seen him naked.

I gulped a breath, pressing the back of one hand to my flushed cheek.

I wanted more of the strange flutterings inside me when his deep voice addressed me as though we weren't strangers. I liked that familiarity. I wanted more of it. I shook my head, harder this time. I needed to remember he would be leaving tomorrow, and I did not intend to be left reeling in the sudden quiet of his absence.

His voice broke through the unquiet of my mind. "Why are you so angry?"

"I'm not."

"You are. Is it because I figured out you're blind?"

If it were only that. I hefted the tub of dirty water.

He rose, his chair scraping back on the stone. The air stirred as he stretched a hand toward me. "Let me help—"

I stepped back quickly. "I can do this. I've been doing it for years." And I'd be doing it after he left.

Turning, I walked across the room, presenting him with my back, unwilling to reveal to him the confusing tumult of emotions twisting inside me.

Fear. Want. An ache for something more that went bone deep. I wanted. I needed. I had felt a fraction of this yearning when I sat beside my window, hugging my knees to my chest as I breathed in the outside world, thinking that maybe someday I would find a life beyond the tower. Only a fraction though. Because before him my need was amorphous. It had no distraction. No face. Unlike now. With a grunt, I hauled the wooden bucket up to the stone edge of the window. These feelings had become more intense, more pressing since he arrived here, and when he left, he would not be taking them with him. The feelings would stay long after he departed. They would be with me always.

EIGHT

Fowler

I PUSHED THROUGH the other prisoners to stare out between the bars, gripping the cold steel until my knuckles went white. None dared stop me. Perhaps they read something of the desperation in my face—or they were too weak, too broken from years of imprisonment to care.

The outer gate closed shut with a vibrating clang, and I spotted her in the fading purple of night. She passed over the drawbridge for the first time in her life. A deep throb pumped through my chest as I realized it would be the last time.

I had envisioned her crossing it with me. That had been the

plan. Eventually. We'd talked of it countless times. But now it was too late.

Today she would die.

Sitting in the back of the rattling cart, her knees tucked close to her chest, she looked so small. So defenseless. Her head turned, scanning the battlements, and I knew the truth deep in my bones. She searched for me and I wasn't there. Did she think I betrayed her? That was salt in the wound.

Torches flickered, illuminating the numerous faces, all pale smudges with coal-dark eyes looking down at her. Her mother was there among the spectators. Her little brother, too. As stoic and silent as everyone else. As helpless as I was to save her.

I wasn't there. I was stuck in here, failing her.

The wagon rolled to a stop and the guards hopped down. They reached up and helped her descend. With cold efficiency, they led her to the waiting pole. Even across the distance, I could see the rusty stains of blood soaked into the wood. The deep gashes and rips embedded in thick oak. Those details told the story of what was to come.

I flexed my hands around the bars, palms slick with sweat.

She didn't resist as they backed her to the pole. The solid length hit her square along the spine. I wanted her to fight, to run, even though if she broke free there was nowhere to go. An intense gray fog hugged low to the ground. The flat expanse of land that surrounded the walls of the keep was long eradicated of trees. In the far distance, the land gave way to shrubs and then trees so thick and dense it was impossible to determine what lurked within. She peered in that direction, gazing into the fleeting glow of midlight.

With every passing moment my throat felt like it was tightening from an invisible noose. The dark would soon return to swallow everything.

The guards made quick work of the rope, pinning her to the pole tightly, tying off the ends into knots she could never hope to loosen. They stepped back and returned to the wagon.

The creak of wheels and the jingle of harnesses filled the air as they circled back around, the horses' hooves kicking up earth. The drawbridge lowered with a rattle of chains, hitting the ground with a thud I felt vibrate through my bones. The wagon hastened into the shelter of the keep, rattling over the wooden drawbridge.

The gate descended with a clang, closing behind them. Everything inside me wilted as the drawbridge cranked back up and slid home with a jarring clank, shutting her out. Snuffing out that tiny flame of hope inside me.

Silence fell, an eerie quiet after all the noise. She looked around, her head the only thing mobile. The immense, stone-walled keep gazed back at her solemnly. I shivered, feeling the cold in the cell.

Watching her, I knew how she felt. I knew the loneliness. The king's voice rang out, shattering the silence.

My gaze found his robed shape standing atop the battlements. Hatred welled up inside me at the sight of his face. "May this humble token serve as a testament to our deference, to our limitless respect and awe. . . ."

The rest of his words faded into a droning buzz. I knew them by heart—had heard them all my life.

She scanned the firelit faces, searching for one, her lips moving, mouthing what I knew was my name in a soundless plea. It was there, wordlessly humming between us. She clung to the feeble hope that I would come. That I would stop all this from happening.

That I would keep my promise.

I shook the bars with impotent fury.

The king finished and silence fell again. The gray deepened to purply black and the fog melted, giving way for night again. I scanned the distant tree line. Dark shadows swelled from the thicket, their black, growing claws stretching across the barren land toward her.

My chest hurt. Each breath an agony. She held herself so still. Her gaze trained on the faces watching her. Family. People she'd known all her life. No one to help her.

I'm here. I'm with you. I willed the words to her as though she could hear them.

She couldn't believe that I didn't care. She had to know. I had not abandoned her.

At the first inhuman cry, her body came alive, struggling against the ropes. Just as I'd seen countless others do. I had always marveled at that, wondered why they bothered fighting when it was so clear they couldn't escape. Now I knew. The will to live was a powerful thing.

I screamed her name, shouting it between the bars until my voice grew hoarse.

They were coming and still she fought, choking on terror. Even though she knew there was no going back inside the keep, she battled for life. The keening cries increased in volume and overlapped. She struggled, her hair flying wildly.

Finally their horrible cries stopped. And so did she. She stilled.

I watched, my throat raw, my eyes wide and aching as I searched the darkness, fear bubbling like acid inside me. I knew what it meant when they quieted.

My heart thudded a deep, rushing beat in my ears. I sagged against the wall, utterly broken, my hands numb on the bars as my eyes strained against the relentless dark—darting, seeking, searching for their shapes in the impenetrable black where they hovered.

They were there. A single whisper escaped me.

"Bethan."

The only answer I heard was her scream.

I woke with a ragged gasp, hands gripping the sheets like they were the bars of the prison cell from all those years ago.

It was the same dream. Except it had been a while since I last suffered it.

I inhaled, steadying my heart rate and forcing the images away. Lacing hands behind my head, I stared into the dark. It had been a long time since I felt a bed beneath me. I had spent many a night staring into the dark, sleeping in far less comfortable accommodations, storing up my strength.

I should have been enjoying a dreamless sleep. This was the most secure I'd been in a long time. I should have been taking advantage of that. Instead I was trapped in the old nightmare. I scrubbed a hand over my face as if I could rid myself of all thoughts of Bethan and that day.

After a few moments I succeeded in rerouting my thoughts. They strayed in the most obvious direction. A pair of bottomless dark eyes that saw nothing and yet saw everything floated across my mind. Luna.

It was almost as though her lack of sight made her stronger. Someone like her should be dead, but she wasn't. She was thriving. Maybe a world of dark was best suited for the blind. I expelled a heavy breath.

She'd made me laugh.

I didn't know the last time I had laughed. For a moment my chest had loosened. I felt lighter until I remembered that laughter didn't belong in this world.

A knock at the door brought me upright. "Yes?"

The door creaked open. Perla stuck her head in my room, wisps of steel-gray hair floating around her. "It's the boy."

I slipped from the bed, pausing to slide my feet into my boots, knowing nowhere was ever safe—including this idyllic tower. I needed to be ready to run at a moment's notice.

I followed Perla into the bedchamber. Madoc whimpered in the middle of the bed, his face flushed and sweaty. Dagne sat on the edge, wiping his brow with a cloth.

Sivo stood in the corner, looking bleary-eyed. Luna was beside him, her arms crossed in front of her defensively as though she was trying to shield herself from me.

"What's happening?" I asked.

Perla nodded to the boy on the bed. "His fever has spiked. I fear it won't break. We're losing him."

Dagne choked on a sob, burying her face against where his arm rested limply on the bed, her fair hair a pale banner of gold against the bedding.

I searched Perla's face, wondering why she was telling me this. If he was dying, there was nothing I could do about it.

"That's too bad," I heard myself saying.

If they were expecting sympathy, they weren't going to get it. People died every day. This world was more about dying than living. The goal was that it just not be me lying fever-ridden in a bed—or becoming food for dwellers. Some days even that goal felt insignificant. Fighting for survival had become reflex and not something I even considered anymore.

"You sound real shaken over that," Luna's voice chimed in. My gaze shot to her. For a girl without sight, she pulled off the scathing glare rather well.

"Are you sorry for him then?" I challenged. "You just met him."

"I am sorry for him, yes. Any loss of life is something to grieve."

Dagne lifted her face, her cheeks wet from tears. "Would you stop it? He's not dead yet. Stop talking about him like he is."

"I'm sorry." Luna shook her head, looking truly morose.

I snorted. Such a soft heart. She cared too much over one boy dying. Didn't she know yet? People you loved, the ones you cared about the most, they all died eventually. No one was spared. When you lost them, everything you had, all of your heart, was lost, too. It crippled you. Left you an empty shell, functioning on instinct alone.

"You're horrible," she whispered, so softly that I perhaps wasn't supposed to hear her.

My mouth kicked up at one corner. "You haven't any idea what I think or feel. You live in your private sanctum. You don't know what the world out there is truly like."

Even if I wanted to care about someone again, there was nothing left in the shell of me. My heart might beat, but that part of me was gone.

Luna's gaze rested in my general direction. "I've been out there—"

"Have you ever been a stone's throw from this tower?" At her silence, I knew she had not. "When things get messy you dive back into your hole, right? You're fortunate. You haven't had a taste of what it's really like."

Color splashed her cheeks. "So if I did . . . I'd be as heartless as you?"

"Yes." He paused on a breath. "If wise. Because the heartless survive."

She inhaled a deep, rattling breath. I tried not to notice. Not this. Not anything about her. Still, my gaze assessed. As slim as she was, she had curves.

My gaze flicked to Sivo, noting the rigid set to his big shoulders. My assessment was not overlooked. Protective fury hummed from him. I understood the silent threat. He'd kill to protect her. I nodded once to him, letting him know he wouldn't have to worry about me.

"You say that as though proud," she accused. "How can you think that's right? That being *heartless* is right?"

"Nothing about anything is right anymore."

She shook her head. My words hung between us as I committed her to memory. Luna was all emotion, her face like a glimmer of daybreak amid perpetual night. She gazed at me, her eyes somehow fixed on me, her expression full of reproach.

Silence hung in the room, the faint sniffling from Dagne the only sound.

Sivo closed a hand over her shoulder and squeezed gently. She offered him a weak smile.

"There's a chance for the boy yet," Perla offered with a heavy breath. "Nisan weed."

"Nisan weed?" I frowned, vaguely familiar with the herb. When I was a boy, my nurse had taken me with her to hunt for herbs at midlight. Nisan weed had been a prize find. I could still see her holding the little flower up to the feeble light, stroking its petals as though it were the greatest jewel. "Large red and yellow flowers with the dark centers?"

"Yes." Perla nodded. "It works quickly, which is what he needs with a fever raging such as this."

"I saw it on the way here," I replied before I could consider what admitting such a thing signified.

"You did?" Sivo asked. "Not near here. I've picked it clean over the years."

"Perhaps farther than you're accustomed to traveling. It was about an hour's walk from here."

"You must go and bring it back," Dagne pleaded, her fingers desperately clenching her brother's limp hand.

I shook my head and faced Sivo. "I'm leaving at midlight—"

"Please!" Dagne cried, her face deepening to an even brighter red as new tears poured down her cheeks. "Do this one thing before you go."

"You know the way?" Sivo pressed me.

"I can create a map directing you to where I spotted—"

"You said it's an hour's walk. Midlight won't last that long. You could find the herb faster. You know directly where to go."

I sighed, unable to argue with the truth of that. He would waste precious time searching.

I looked around the room. A sick boy. An old woman. A scared, weeping Dagne. And Luna, a blind girl even if she was the most capable of them all. I choked out a dry, humorless laugh. If they lost Sivo, how well would they fare? And for how much longer?

Luna pressed her lips into a tight, mutinous line. "What's so amusing? Our request for help? Or that we're even attempting to save his life?"

She didn't know me. Not at all. I could say yes.

Her chin lifted a notch. It was uncanny, as though she read my thoughts and was challenging me to go against my avowal to leave this place . . . my determination to live a selfish existence.

"I'll go."

NINE

Fowler

I SLIPPED OUT a little before midlight, knowing that the task would take more than a full hour. I'd rather be making my way in the dark at the beginning of this errand than at the end.

I studied the sky and then glanced around, feeling that familiar restless energy. The air always felt this way moments before midlight—when all manner of life, animal and man, was ready to burst free, and roam freely in the brief window of time that dwellers went to ground.

A snap sounded behind me.

I whirled, lifting my bow. I waited, staring into the gloom, my gaze darting over the terrain of trees and brush.

I held myself still, ears straining.

No other sound came. I didn't hear the sloughing, wet breath of a dweller. No dragging steps. Not even the rotting, loamy odor that signaled they were close.

A shape materialized, only slightly less dark than the ink of night. I pulled my arrow taut, the pull of string a sweet, faintly audible creak near my ear.

"Don't shoot."

A shock wave rippled through me. "Luna?"

She stopped before me. She was garbed in trousers again.

"What are you doing here?" I demanded, my voice a low hiss.

"Coming with you." She actually smiled.

"No. You're not."

She propped a hand on her hip. "It looks like I already am."

I lowered my bow and pointed beyond her. Shaking my head, I realized the motion was lost on her. I dropped my hand. "Go back."

"No," she answered evenly. "We've already covered this much ground, and it's almost midlight. Why send me back now?"

"Why are you even here? I said I would fetch the nisan—"

"Because we need to know where it grows. After you leave, we may have need of it again."

"And you couldn't have pointed that bit of logic out sooner? So Sivo could have joined me and not you?"

At this, her smile broadened. "I could have."

"You said nothing deliberately."

She shrugged a thin shoulder. "I need to know these things

for myself, too. I can't rely on Sivo for everything."

I cursed. She blinked as though my colorful speech was something new, and I supposed it was. Her guardians had spent all these years sheltering her.

I sighed and dragged a hand through my hair, scanning the horizon. She was right though. They wouldn't be around forever. What would become of her?

I ignored the voice inside that reminded me this wasn't my problem and snapped, "Fine."

She smiled again, her lips curving wide to reveal bone-white teeth. "Stop smiling so much," I grumbled, turning away.

She followed close behind me, moving noiselessly. "You walk like you're part of the night." The words escaped me like an accusation. It didn't make sense to me. How could a sightless girl be so proficient at maneuvering this terrain?

"I am part of it," she replied. "Aren't you?"

"I'm not a part of anything." Not anymore. I started to think about those days when I was, but stopped myself from going there. I wasn't that boy anymore. I couldn't be him ever again.

"Will you be a part of Allu?"

My reply was immediate. "I have to be."

"But what if you're not? What if it's not like you think?"

I held silent at the question, letting it drape over the night, sinking into the dark abyss through which we waded.

"How do you even know that place is real?" she pressed.

"Allu exists. It's on every map. It's always been there."

"Yes, I'm aware. I've studied my geography and history. But

how do you know it's free of dwellers?"

I hesitated before saying, "It's all I've ever heard. Everything I've ever been told. That gives some weight to the stories."

"Have you met anyone who's ever actually been there? And returned to tell of it?"

"Who would ever wish to come back once they reached Allu? Why would they risk themselves?" It was ironic hearing myself use Bethan's logic. She had been chipping away at my resolve near the end. I had started making plans for us to leave. A bitter irony now that it was too late for her.

"Hm." There was a wealth of meaning in that single sound. She doubted. Just as I once had. "Childhood is full of fairy tales. I had my share, too. What makes yours real?"

"I knew someone," I snapped. "She believed. She convinced me." And yet her faith hadn't been enough.

"Where is this girl? Why isn't she with you?" Turning, I faced her. She stopped and tilted her chin, waiting for my answer.

"She's gone." A flying beetle the size of my fist zipped over my shoulder, heading in her direction. She pulled her head to the side, dodging it as if it were nothing, as if she had seen it coming.

Her throat worked as she searched for words. "You mean dead."

"Dwellers took her." Which was as good as dead. Anyone dragged underground never came back. The details of that day weren't something I ever shared.

"I—I'm sorr—"

"If you apologize for every person I ever lost, we'd be here all day." I swung back around. "Let's keep moving."

"What was her name?" she whispered at my back.

I expelled a breath and looked skyward. "What does it matter now?"

"Her name?"

I closed my eyes. It had been two years now, and the sound of her voice was a dim memory. She had been full of laughter. Even with monsters at the gate she could find happiness.

I didn't know what I was holding on for anymore. It was pure instinct that kept me moving. My lungs knew how to expand with each breath, and somehow I had mastered the art of not dying. Survival was an easy thing to accomplish when there was nothing left to live for.

"Bethan," I bit out, experiencing a sharp release of pressure inside my chest at uttering it aloud.

"Bethan." She rolled the name on her tongue as though she were testing it out.

"Satisfied? Now make haste," I snapped, although she wasn't moving all that slow.

As midlight arrived, the tension ebbed from me. Or perhaps it was because she had ceased nagging me with her uncomfortable questions.

Secure in the soft glow of light, I increased my pace, caring less for the noise of my tread. I tried not to look over my shoulder. She had fallen back a bit and was struggling to keep up. I forced myself not to wait for her. The old impulse to be kind and courteous instilled in me by my nurse was still there.

She wasn't my responsibility. She had forced herself on me, and I was stuck with her. I should just keep walking. Follow the plan and keep moving east. She'd keep up with me. Or not. I had no doubt she could figure her way back to the tower. She had an uncanny sense of direction.

I turned to monitor her regularly. My compulsion to check on her was a weak thing inside me. It dawned on me that she couldn't see if I looked back. The knowledge that she wouldn't know that she had roused some kind of protective instinct freed me to glance back whenever I felt the urge.

Looking back frequently, I studied the way her head was always turning, her nostrils flaring as though she were some animal exploring her surroundings.

Her slim, pale hands looked like small doves, skimming trees and brush, memorizing with touch. She looked peaceful. The dark wisps of hair surrounding her face fluttered in the breeze as those unseeing eyes moved and flitted. As though she could see.

At one point, she stopped and looked directly at me, her dark eyes deep and penetrating, a bottomless well that seemed to hold so much. Impossible, I knew. She couldn't see me. She couldn't know I watched her, but then she spoke.

"I'm not going to stumble into a hole or run into a tree if that's worrying you."

I blinked, unnerved. Facing forward, I said nothing and increased my pace.

"I've never been this far from the tower," she called after me, her voice breathless as she attempted to catch up to me. "The trees feel a little slighter here and the air less pungent."

I didn't reply. Not that my silence seemed to matter. She continued talking, chatting like a magpie.

"Sivo always worries about straying too far from the tower." She sighed as if someone worrying about her safety too much was her greatest grief.

She reminded me of Bethan in that moment, blissfully unaware of all the dangers in the world. Blissfully unaware that I was her greatest threat.

I kept going, lightly touching a fallen log and vaulting over it, biting back the reply that Sivo should worry. She should.

I didn't call back a warning, but Luna somehow knew it was there. She lifted one leg over the log, then the next, carrying on indifferently.

I adjusted my quiver of arrows hanging on my shoulder and faced forward again. Sivo worrying was probably what kept them alive so long.

The tower was safe, virtually undiscoverable within the thick press of trees, far from any road or path. If I were a different manner of person, I could try to steal the life they'd carved for themselves. It wouldn't be too difficult. A cut to Sivo's throat while he slept. Perla presented no threat. The only other real threat was Luna. I'd seen her at work.

She reminded me of a flower that used to bloom in Relhok. The scarlet buds once dotted the hills outside Relhok City. They were wrapped up in my earliest recollections, tangled amid memories of sunshine on my skin. The flower had faded from existence a few years after the eclipse, like so many things since then.

From the moment I could walk, my nurse had taught me to avoid them when we went outdoors. I would lie in the tall grasses surrounding the castle, directly beside one such flower, and study the red petals. So beautiful and delicate in their seeming harmlessness. I would hover a fingertip over a petal, tempted to touch for myself, to delve into the deeper darkness nestled at the root of those petals. One day I did.

It was only the slightest brush of my finger, but the burn had been swift like a wasp's sting. My hand swelled and my nurse had clucked at me, shooting me fearful glances as she applied a salve to the injury. It was not that she thought the sting would kill me . . . but that I would kill me—a boy who had to touch and see for himself what danger felt like.

Luna was like that flower: innocent on the outside, but dangerous to anyone who got too close. Even me.

She kept up, following me as we ascended a steep crest. When we reached the top it would plateau to the exact place I had spotted the nisan weed. Was that only yesterday? It felt like a good deal more time had passed since I first met this girl.

"You're taking a long, dangerous journey based on rumors." Her words circled me like an insistent gnat. She didn't know when to quit. "What if you cross the continent and find it's not even there—"

"It's there." My steps hit the ground harder. "You talk too much."

"You're angry," she announced, her tread quickening to match my pace.

"No." My tone and brevity didn't seem to affect her.

Usually a scowl worked. Or a look. It was something in my eyes. When I left Relhok City, Govin, the bowman who trained me and the only person left I felt compelled to say farewell to, had told me that my eyes were dead.

I'd seen a lot of dead eyes over the years. It was impossible to understand unless you witnessed it happening—the moment life departed and slid away like a wisp of smoke. The light in one's eyes, a light you didn't even realize was there, faded to nothing.

She'd never have to witness that. Scowls and dead-eyed stares were useless on her.

She pressed on, blithely unaware. Or indifferent. "What if it's not as you say though? What if dwellers are there?"

I stopped and faced her. "Then it won't be any different from any other place, will it?"

"Except you will have gone so far. . . . What about your home—"

"I'm trying to forget where it is I come from."

We topped the crest. Sprawling bushes rose up before us. I stopped before the thick hedge of nisan.

"We're here."

Luna reached out a hand to touch the wild bramble.

"Careful," I warned. "There are thorns." I squatted, flipping open my satchel. She followed me down, her hand reaching out and gently touching the flowers. A soft smile lifted her lips. I couldn't remember the last time I thought about any girl's smile. Blinking, I looked away. I started to pull at the herb, stuffing it in my bag.

"Wait, stop. Don't pull up the root." She removed a dagger from the sheath at her waist and carefully began to snip bits of the plant's flowers. "We want it to regrow."

"Optimistic, aren't you? That it will ever regrow with so little sunlight? It looks as though it's barely hanging on as it is."

"And yet it's here. Seventeen years after the eclipse." She worked intently, her forehead creasing as she carefully snipped at the nisan and tucked it into her satchel. "The eclipse can't last forever."

"It can't?"

She turned to face me. "There was light before. There will be again."

"That's what the Oracle has been saying for years and it hasn't come to pass."

"It will though. She's right."

The Oracle was not right. Everyone could play tribute at her altar, but not me. She was a puppet for the king. As bad as he was.

She continued, "Maybe we won't be lucky enough for it to happen in our lifetime, but it will happen again someday. This happened before. I'm certain you heard the folk tales."

"Yes. So."

"Well, it happened before and it ended before. We merely need to hold on until then."

"You're a fool to put faith in anything except what's before you." Rising to my feet, I snapped, "Come. We need to head back."

We moved swiftly, conscious of passing time.

I scanned the area. Just because it was midlight didn't mean it was safe to relax. This was the one time of day when people could move without fear of dwellers. Everyone came out of hiding, including the good and the bad, and there were more of the bad. Desperate times brought out the worst in people. Opportunists and scavengers abounded. The good were too trusting. They had perished first, many lost in those early years of the eclipse.

As we hastened back to the tower, I peered where the branches hung the thickest. Rumors of a curse in the Black Woods didn't keep everyone out. It hadn't kept me out.

We were making good time when suddenly I realized it felt too quiet.

I glanced at Luna and saw that she had paused.

Her head was bowed, and she had a look of concentration on her face.

"Luna? What is—"

She held up a hand, hushing me with the barest shake of her head.

I waited, my pulse throbbing in my neck in the suddenly weighted air. My hand drifted up, went for an arrow in the quiver behind my shoulder.

"There," she murmured. "Do you hear that?"

I shook my head as if she could see me. "No. It's quiet—"

"Under the quiet." She turned her face in the direction we came from. The tower. "It's there—"

I listened longer, and then shook my head again. "I don't—"

"No! Sivo, Perla . . ." A stricken look passed over her face. She sprang into a sprint.

"Wait!" I took off after her, cursing as she flew down the steep incline we had climbed. She was remarkably quick, taking the same path that brought us to the nisan weed—almost as if her feet had somehow recorded the route and now pulled it out from memory.

I was fast, but I had to push my legs just to stay behind her.

"Luna," I growled, acutely conscious of the fact that the forest was deathly still. It was the type of silence that happened when dwellers emerged. A quick glance up showed a sliver of sun peeking out around the moon. It couldn't be them. We had more time.

Luna raced ahead. I finally caught up with her before the ground sloped down toward the tower. I closed the distance between us, stretching my fingers for her shoulder, catching hold of her. I dragged her down, stopping her from running full speed into whatever lay ahead. Together we toppled to the ground, rolling.

I splayed my body over her, using my larger size to pin her down. She struggled. She was giving me little choice except to let her go and walk into whatever danger waited over that hill.

I should let her go. She wanted to go. I should get to my feet, hand her the bag of nisan weed, and leave her to it. If she wanted to race headlong into danger, then so be it.

I would have done this yesterday, but today . . . somehow I couldn't. Today, with this girl pinned under me, my hardness aligned to her softness, I wasn't going anywhere.

TEN

Fowler

"LET ME GO," Luna said, trying to buck me off. "You don't understand. The tower has been discovered."

I tightened my grip on her shoulders. "Then shouldn't we proceed with caution? If someone found your home, we should—"

I was rewarded with a swift kick of her boot directly to my shin. I grunted. She might be small, but she packed some force. That's all it took. She wiggled out from under me. I pushed to my feet after her.

She was almost to the hilltop when I caught her. She released a startled cry, and I covered her mouth with my hand, cutting off the noise.

Dragging her down, I draped my body over her squirming one. I peeked over the hill above her head. The familiar tower loomed tall in the murky air—surrounded by an entire company of soldiers, a hundred strong garbed in the blue and black colors of Relhok. I knew the colors well. I scanned the faces. It had been two years since I last mingled with the Relhok cavalry, but I had grown up with some of those boys.

I pressed my mouth near her ear. "At least a hundred men surround the tower."

She stilled, tensing beneath me.

Convinced she wouldn't flee or make any sudden sound, I adjusted my weight so that I was no longer atop her. She angled her head in that way of hers, listening.

"They're on horseback," she whispered, her voice a raspy breath.

I looked at her, surprised. The horses were quiet. Not the slightest neigh. They'd been bred for stealth. The soldiers covered ground silently, moving almost like ghosts over the land, creating as little noise as possible so they didn't alert nearby dwellers. They rode hard only during midlight. That must be how Luna heard them originally.

"What do they want?" she asked, as if I would know. I was her only connection to the outside world. A girl who's spent a lifetime stuck in a tower wouldn't have any idea what these soldiers wanted. "How did they find us?" she added, the faintest trace of accusation in her voice.

Did she think I led them here? If soldiers from Relhok were

after me, they probably would have found me long before now.

Several soldiers had dismounted, including the company commander. His dark blue cavalry tunic swayed around his knees as he moved, the kingdom of Relhok's coat of arms emblazoned on the center of his chest. The sight of it was an ugly reminder of all I left behind.

A dweller I could outrun or dispatch. My memories of Relhok were harder to shake.

The commander turned so that I had a better view of his face. I inhaled, recognizing him. Henley. He was only a few years older than me. He'd risen through the ranks quickly, but then, he had a vicious nature. Viciousness was rewarded. Especially under Cullan's reign.

"Are they here because of you?" The words escaped her in a puff of breath.

"No."

"Then what brought them here?"

"I don't know. I can't imagine why a force this size is so far east, but they're not after me." At least I didn't think so.

"You know something though," she whispered.

"I don't know what they want," I muttered, annoyed that she could read me so well without even seeing me. What was it that gave me away?

"You're tense," she whispered as though I had asked the question out loud.

I shook my head. "There's an army below us. That might have something to do with how tense I am."

I turned my attention back to the scene below. The tower door stood open. We had only ever used the secret door that led to the tunnel beneath the tower. I didn't even realize there was another door. Sivo stood in the threshold, facing the commander.

I marveled that he had opened the door to greet the soldiers, but then there was little choice. A group this size . . . if they wanted inside the tower, they would eventually find a way. Better for Sivo to open the door and behave as though he had nothing to hide. He eyed them neutrally. Gone were the days of armor and chain mail. The clink of steel on the air was a song dwellers responded to like a bell ringing them to supper.

"Sivo's outside," she announced softly, a tremor in her voice as she started to lift up.

I pushed her back down with a hand on her shoulder.

"I have to go. Let me go," she choked out hoarsely.

"To do what? Let Sivo handle this."

She nodded slowly, clearly uncertain, but I wasn't letting her charge down that hill. Dark flyaway strands of hair surrounded her face. She looked even paler than usual with worry and concern. Something pricked at my chest, loosening memories buried there of when I had cared that much for someone else.

I watched as Sivo and the commander spoke.

"What's he doing?" The fear in her voice pulled at me.

"He's talking to them. It looks . . ." I was about to say "friendly," but she would know that for a lie.

Sivo talked, his lips moving quickly, his movements anxious. Henley seemed impatient. He glanced to the sky and the waning midlight. I followed his gaze, assessing that sliver of sun. The ground beneath us would wake soon.

That shard of sun peeping out around the moon robbed Henley of the last of his patience. He flicked his fingers to several of the soldiers and they moved swiftly at the unspoken command, shoving past Sivo and disappearing inside the tower.

Luna's shoulders surged up slightly, lifting her head higher. Her voice took on a panicked edge. "What's happening now? Is Sivo—"

"They haven't harmed him." Yet.

I tugged her back down again. She strained against my touch. "Why are they here? No one has ever bothered us before."

"A company that large, coming into these woods—" Woods that even a hired soldier wouldn't want to brave. "They're looking for something."

I arrived at the realization the moment the words passed my lips. They were seeking someone. Hunting. The king wouldn't risk losing a force of cavalrymen this size without cause.

"They can't be here," she insisted in a small voice.

Again, the thought entered my mind: they are here for me. Then I dismissed it. Perhaps once the king would have sent men after me, but he had greater concerns now. A kingdom to oversee and an alliance with Lagonia to secure.

She tensed the instant Perla stepped from the tower. Maybe it was the soft curse that left my lips or something more innate. Maybe she felt a connection between herself and her surrogate mother and sensed she had emerged from the tower. I tightened my grip on her, predicting her surge of movement.

"It's Perla! Let me go—"

I covered her mouth and flattened her to the ground again, heedless of my roughness. If they found us, any treatment Luna suffered at their hands would be far worse. The king's men weren't known for their gentleness with commoners. Especially with the fairer sex.

"I can't let you go." I told myself it wasn't just to protect her, but to protect me. If they discovered her, they discovered me. "Understand?"

A quick peek over the hill again had me ducking down. A soldier was headed up the hill, his expression drawn tight. He'd heard us. I dragged her down, rushing us into a thick shrub of prickly bramble that surrounded an old gnarled oak tree.

"What are you—"

"Quiet," I growled into her ear. "A soldier."

I forced us into the stabbing vines, ignoring the gouging thorns tearing at every exposed inch of skin. She sucked in a pained breath. I pushed her deeper into the hedge, girding myself against a thick thorn carving a hole in my neck. Blood trickled down my throat beneath my collar, but I uttered no sound.

I folded my body around her, shielding her as much as I could. We felt as one, no part of us not connected. She trembled, but thankfully held silent. Her breath fanned hotly against my neck in violent little puffs, and then her fingers were there, finding my cut, lightly pressing at the wound as though she could slow the flow of blood.

I stared, unblinking, through a gap in the viny gorse, watching as the soldier crested the hill and took guarded steps down it, his sword drawn and ready. He studied our tracks on the ground.

I felt her heart pounding against her ribs and directly into me. Or maybe it was my heart. Curled against each other like two locked pieces of a puzzle, I could not tell where I ended and she began. There was just this. Us. One shared heart. And, if things continued to deteriorate, our joint death.

The soldier turned in our direction. I loosened a dagger from my boot. He neared our hiding spot, his steps easing cautiously closer. I could no longer see his face, just the scuffed cavalry boots encasing his calves so close now I could see the film of dirt coating them. I adjusted my grip on my dagger, preparing to jump out and thrust it in his heart. From there my only plan was to run—to take Luna and run.

Something exploded from the tree behind us, arcing through the air and landing on the soldier in a spitting, hissing ball of fury. He fought off the tree monkey that lunged at him, crying out as its sharp nails scored his face. Flinging the creature to the ground, he stabbed the reddish brown ball of fur repeatedly with his sword. He didn't stop there either. His bloodied face twisted wrathfully as he stomped on it, his curses flying.

"Sangar!" a soldier called from the top of the hill.

"Coming." With a final kick for the pulverized carcass, he turned away.

I watched him stomp away before looking down at Luna. I winced at the sight of her. She was a mess of oozing scratches, the wet crimson an obscenity on her skin.

"He's gone." I barely spoke the words. They were more like a breath against the side of her face.

She nodded.

Awareness swelled inside of me as I eyed her. Felt her curled under me. It had been a long time since I held anyone. Since I felt a girl's body wrapped up in mine. She felt so small and soft—so very breakable.

A jarring reminder that everyone broke under the cruelty of this world.

I pulled back and was rewarded with a fresh thorn to the base of my neck.

"What's happening now?" she whispered.

"Let's find out." We extricated ourselves from the gorse, earning new scratches for our trouble, and crawled side by side back up the hill.

I inched high enough to glimpse down at the tower. "Sivo is talking to them. They've forced Perla outside," I whispered. "Dagne and Madoc, too. Two soldiers are supporting Madoc."

A shiver rippled through her, and she bit her lip before saying, "Perla hates the Outside." Her voice sounded small—almost childlike in its helplessness. "She must be terrified."

I watched the scene unfold. The commander pointed at Dagne. Sivo shook his head and waved his hands in the air as though he was trying to pacify Henley. He wasn't going to succeed. I had a flash of memory then, a fractured image of when I was a boy and happened on Henley in the royal kennels, torturing one of the dogs with a riding crop.

I blinked, chasing the image away, and focused on the present reality.

Madoc was clearly still in the grips of fever. His head lolled on his shoulders. He could hardly keep his gaze fastened on the group of soldiers. Dagne, on the other hand, looked wholly aware and alert. She stuck close to Perla as if that made her less visible to the eyes of all the men in the company.

Henley finally had enough. He shook his head as if finished listening to Sivo. He snapped something at his men and one of them stepped forward, grabbing hold of Dagne and pulling her away from Perla. She looked around wildly, crying out when Henley pulled the sword from the scabbard at his waist in one smooth move. She struggled, but the soldier held fast, pushing her forward. The freed blade sang on the wind as it cut through air and swiped down. Blood sprayed, spattering Henley in the face. It happened so quickly, the man's actions mild and effortless as though he were scratching an itch and not snuffing out a life. As though he was not slicing into a young girl.

Luna jerked against me as though the sharp edge of steel was cutting into her—leaving me no doubt she was aware of the violence taking place below.

Dagne dropped to the ground, limp and lifeless. Perla tried to grab her. Madoc cried out. He struggled against the soldiers holding him. It was a weak attempt that didn't last long. Drained, he bowed his head low and hung between them, shoulders shaking with sobs.

Air hissed out of my lips. She had done nothing to provoke them. It was an execution. Plain and simple.

"Is it—"

"Dagne," I supplied.

Luna choked back a sob, her fingers digging into my arm. "Why?" A shudder passed through her. "Why did they kill her?"

A cold familiar numbness stole over me. "I don't know."

There was no reason to kill the girl, but Henley had. He'd struck her down like she was some disease to be cut out and removed with swift excision.

Henley pulled a handkerchief out from beneath his tunic and cleaned his face, his movements almost elegant as he wiped away Dagne's blood. As though it were no more than grime from a day's travel.

Luna's voice escaped a fraction too loud: "What of Sivo and Perla? Are they unharmed?"

One of the soldiers at the edge of the group shifted in his saddle and turned to face the hill where we crouched.

I dropped flat, shoving Luna several feet down the rise with me. "At the moment, they're fine," I growled, "but we won't be if you don't lower your voice."

She didn't care. She strained against me, fighting to get up. She was ready to launch herself down the hill.

I seized her shoulders and turned her, pinning her to the spot. "Stop trying to get yourself killed. They killed Dagne. They won't hesitate to slaughter us, too. Now wait here and I'll see what's happening."

I crawled back up and looked down the hill again. Henley pointed a finger in Madoc's face, questioning him. Madoc gazed at his slain sister, a crumpled and broken life on the ground. His sobs tore through the wood, loud and ugly. As if midlight wasn't fast fading and this wasn't the time for silent breaths and swallowed words.

I glanced around at the encroaching darkness. Madoc's sounds weren't going unheard. The dwellers might not be aboveground yet, but they were waiting below, listening.

The soldiers exchanged uneasy glances. They knew the hour was fading fast and all the noise did not bode well. One dweller, even ten, they could easily dispatch, but Madoc was likely rousing dozens of drones.

I couldn't hear Henley's words from this distance. Sivo nodded once at whatever was said, his features drawn and pale, lips compressed in a flat line. When the commander finished, he turned and mounted his horse, circling his hand once in the air for the men to move out.

"They're leaving," I announced, watching the horses retreat in practiced stealth.

Before they disappeared entirely from the glen, the commander pulled his mount around to address Sivo. He surveyed the tower as well, his gaze stretching over its walls and then back down again. He was evaluating it. It would make an excellent outpost. He or others from the capital would be back. Or others from the king would. Everything had changed. Luna and her family were no longer safe here.

I looked down at Luna, my hand closing around hers. "Come. They're gone."

"Midlight is over," she announced dully, almost as an afterthought.

I lifted my face up to the darkness. "So it is."

We walked swiftly to the tower. I was still aware of her trembling beside me.

A movement to the right caught my notice, and I turned, watching as a dweller clawed itself free from the dirt, gray, talon-like fingers churning soil. Its square-like head broke the ground's surface, the receptors on its face shaking loose dirt as it tasted air.

I hurried our pace. We'd be inside before the creature could reach us.

Perla supported Madoc, guiding him to walk. Sivo lifted Dagne's body in his arms. He looked up as we approached, his shoulders slumping in obvious relief. For the first time I saw him as he perhaps was: a tired, old man. "Luna"—he breathed her name—"you're safe."

Perla squeezed her hands together in prayer. "Heavens be praised."

More dwellers stirred the ground behind us. I stepped forward and took over supporting Madoc. "Let's move inside."

Perla glanced around, her eyes rounding in terror. "Yes, of course." She ushered Luna into the tower. I followed with Madoc.

Sivo brought up the rear. He lowered Dagne's lifeless body to the ground with a grunt and then bolted the tower door behind us. "Wouldn't be right," he muttered. "Leaving her out there for the dwellers. I'll bury her tomorrow."

I didn't bother pointing out that the dwellers would find her either way—buried in the ground or left above. Inhaling, I smelled the faint odor of the soldiers who had invaded this space. Leather, horse, and sweat. Those had been the smells of my childhood. At one time comforting, but now they only reminded me of pain.

Sivo's gaze connected with mine, grim and brimming with emotion. Perla's, Luna's, and Madoc's steps shuffled away, fading as they made their way up the stairs.

"They killed Dagne. They simply struck her down."

I nodded. It was senseless. But I knew that violence in these men did not have to make sense, especially when it came from the likes of Henley.

"They found us," he declared, looking a little dazed. "More will come."

I inhaled a deep breath, knowing this to be true, and knowing I shouldn't care. I wasn't supposed to care. What happened to these people . . .

It changed nothing. I was leaving, and they would have to continue to survive on their own.

ELEVEN

Luna

PERLA DISAPPEARED INTO my bedchamber with Madoc. I took the bag of nisan root to the work table and began tearing the petals and dropping them into a pot of water. I was still shaking, but I had to keep moving. If I stopped I would think about what happened. I'd think about those soldiers. I'd hear that sing of blade on the air and Dagne's scream.

If I did that, I would start to cry and I wouldn't be able to stop. I should have given her more ribbons. A sob welled up in my throat. I should have done that. I should have done more.

"Luna!" I realized Sivo had been saying my name.

I nodded jerkily. "Yes. I'm fine." I continued tearing the nisan into bits. Satisfied that I had enough, I moved the pot to the hearth, brushing past Fowler and hooking it into place so that it could reach a proper boil. I returned to the table and began weaving the herbs onto twine for drying.

"Can you stop for a moment?" Sivo asked.

I shook my head. "We need to get this into Madoc." Considering what had just happened, his will to fight the fever plaguing him was likely low.

"Well, you've set the pot to boil now. The rest can wait." Sivo's heavy steps advanced on me anyway. He pulled me away from the table and into his arms. I resisted, but his arms wrapped around me. For the first time, I noticed that his biceps and forearms weren't like before. When I was younger they reminded me of tree trunks, so solid and strong. Now they were half that size. Somehow over the years they had diminished. I hated this. I hated the evidence of his age and growing frailty.

I relaxed against Sivo, conscious of Fowler in the room. I could feel his eyes on me. I imagined he thought this display of emotion weak. He wouldn't succumb like this. He was too hardened.

Madoc's sobs floated from my bedchamber and I stiffened in Sivo's arms.

"Never thought I'd be happy to have you disobey me," he said against my hair, his bearded cheek rustling the strands. He meant me sneaking out of the tower. I tried to smile, but the curve of my lips felt brittle and pained.

I inhaled, smelling the molding stone. This place had

hemmed me in all my life, but for once, I was glad for its walls.

Not that it had saved Dagne.

I pulled back from Sivo's embrace. Fowler stood near the hearth, holding his hands out to the fire. I could smell the salt on his warming skin. I suppose he was accustomed to death.

I sucked in a deep breath, something new occurring to me.

If Fowler hadn't come, then I would have been here when those soldiers came. It could have been me instead of Dagne.

Also perhaps he wasn't as selfish as he claimed. He had led me to the nisan weed, and he had pulled me back on that hilltop when I wanted to charge into that group of men.

"It's all right, love." Sivo's large hand patted my back. "We will be fine."

It was with that assurance that I knew we would not be fine. The tower was no longer hidden. We were no longer hidden.

Our world had changed.

I sat near the fire, my hands folded tightly in my lap. It was the only way to keep them from shaking—or hide the fact that they shook at all. I focused on stilling all of me, listening as Madoc's cries turned to muffled sobs and then nothing at all.

Perla emerged from the room. "He's asleep. I put a sleeping draft in with the nisan tea."

I envied him the oblivion of sleep. I thought of Dagne below, broken and lifeless near the door we never used.

Except today we had opened the door.

Perla moved beside my chair, and the earthy musk of herbs

and baked bread enveloped me. She rested her thick, chapped palm on my shoulder.

I reached up to pat her hand.

"They'll be back," Sivo announced.

"You can't know that," Perla objected, a sharp, defensive ring to her voice.

"They've found the tower now. They'll tell others. Either they'll be back or someone else will. And that commander . . . he recognized me."

"What?" Perla demanded. "Did he say—"

"He couldn't place where. He must have been a very young boy when I worked in the palace, but mine isn't the easiest face to forget." He was referring to his heavy beard. He'd always had it. According to Perla it was ginger bright. "He'll remember. Eventually."

And when he did, he would tell the king that he had seen one of the dead king's guards. He would send soldiers back based on that alone. I could feel it all unraveling. The safe little world we had built was falling apart, stone by stone. The secret of me, my identity—it was one breath from being exposed.

Perla moved her hand from my shoulder and crossed the wood floor, sinking into a chair at the table with a rattling sigh.

Sivo continued, "They'll do what they did to Dagne to each of us—"

"Don't say that!" Emotion shook Perla's voice.

A hushed silence fell over the room, the pop and crackle of the fire the only sound. Fowler said nothing. I wondered if he even cared. Sivo was skirting the truth of our identity, saying more about us than he ever had before in Fowler's presence. He must feel confident that Fowler would not guess. Or perhaps he simply trusted him now.

I moistened my lips, searching for an answer—a way out of this. A solution didn't present itself and I had to face the truth. There might not be one.

We lived in this tower and now those soldiers knew of its existence. They would report what they had found and when the king realized who Sivo was, they would be back.

"Luna can't stay here." Sivo's announcement was softly worded but no less grim.

Perla didn't react at first. No one did. Then she finally snorted. The sound was part laugh, part grunt, but entirely dismissive. She did not take Sivo's words seriously. "You're being ridiculous. You want us to leave? I can't leave this place. I would not survive a day. And Luna? You want her to go out there? How long will she survive? She cannot see, Sivo! No. Our chances are much better here."

"I've trained her well. She goes." Sivo's voice was firm and unyielding. "And I said nothing of us going."

My heart pounded in my suddenly too-tight chest. Words hung on my lips, but I could think of nothing to say. To leave the sanctuary of the tower and exist on the Outside was equal parts terrifying and thrilling. To leave Sivo and Perla, however? No. I could never do that.

I turned my face in the direction of Fowler. He'd made so

REIGN OF SHADOWS

little sound up to this point that I could almost believe he left the room, if not for the sensation of his eyes on me.

"You want her to go out there without us?" Perla's tone left no doubt how absurd she thought that plan was.

"You said it yourself, Perla. You won't survive."

"No! Absolutely not! She stays—"

"They'll come back. And when they do, when they discover her, they will kill her. You know that, Perla." I'd never heard Sivo speak to her in such a way—so hard and final. Usually, he let her have her way, but not in this.

"You know what they can do," he continued, his words heavy with the implication, with the reminder of who they were. Who *I* was.

Perla sucked in a raw breath, and I knew she was remembering, too. They were the king's men—and he had killed my parents. He was supposed to believe I perished that night, too. If he suspected otherwise . . .

They had killed Dagne. They would kill me, too. Of that, I had no doubt.

"Perhaps," Perla allowed, stubbornness lacing her voice. "But I'm not letting her go out there by herself—"

"She won't be alone," Sivo countered.

I suddenly found my voice. "What do you mean?" Did Sivo intend to go with me? He couldn't leave Perla here. She wouldn't be able to fend for herself without his help.

"She goes with him," he said evenly, calmly. As though it were the obvious solution. *Him.* I didn't need to see to know he

109

was talking about Fowler. I even felt them looking at Fowler now. "He'll take her with him to the Isle of Allu."

"We don't even know him," Perla insisted.

"Perla, I'm not leaving you here. If soldiers return to the tower, then we'll make a stand together. We've lived a long life. It's our responsibility to give Luna the best chance to live hers. Don't you see? This boy coming here was meant to be."

Perla was weeping now. "You and your signs. And how do we know he won't harm her?"

I turned in Fowler's direction, waiting for him to say something, to tell them all this back-and-forth was for nothing because he wasn't taking me anywhere. He wouldn't do something so noble. He had his own quest and it didn't involve me.

"I know he won't abandon her." Sivo's deep burr rumbled on the air. "He lives by a code. Don't you, boy?"

Fowler still said nothing, and I wanted to retort that Fowler's code was all about self-preservation, not altruism.

"Don't you?" Sivo repeated. "You'll see she comes to no harm. And you'll see she gets to Allu. Won't you?"

I waited for his denial. Once he dissuaded Sivo of the notion that he was some manner of hero bent on saving girls, we could come up with another plan that did not involve me leaving Sivo and Perla and heading off on a quest for some fantastical place that probably did not even exist.

Finally, he spoke. Only, the words were not what I was expecting.

"You have my word."

TWELVE

Fowler

I HAD NO idea where the words came from within me. I recognized my voice. I knew I uttered the words, but they weren't mine. They couldn't belong to me.

Listening to Sivo and Perla arguing, with Luna saying so very little and looking as stunned as I felt at Sivo's suggestion that she depart with me—his logic had begun to sink in.

Those soldiers would come back, and next time, she would be here. It couldn't be assumed they wouldn't harm her. Not after seeing what had happened to Dagne. They had an affinity for killing.

And yet doubts assailed me. I had committed to taking

a blind girl with me to Allu. Aside from the fact that no one around me ever lived for long, it was madness, no matter how adept she was at handling herself. I didn't want to take a girl *with* sight, much less one without.

The thought crossed my mind long after Perla took Luna to pack for the journey—I could slip away without a word. While they slept, I could simply leave. Skulk away like a thief in the night. A bitter taste coated my mouth at the cowardly image.

I lifted my mug to my lips, taking a long swig of the hot tea that Sivo had prepared after Perla and Luna left the room.

Sivo's voice wove over the room. "You know I can only let her go because I trust you."

In a flash of clarity I realized that's why I agreed. My throat tightened and I drank again, trying to loosen my windpipe. This man looked at me as though I was an honorable person. Someone to be trusted. It had been a long time since anyone looked at me that way. I didn't like it. I didn't want it.

I sent him a glance and then looked away, his stare too penetrating.

"There's something in you," he said.

I shifted uncomfortably, feeling the old man's gaze. I didn't know what he could see in me except failure. That's all I was, something broken.

I took another drink, calling myself every kind of fool. Luna was not my second chance.

I faced him. "I thought you were letting her go because you don't have any other choice."

He gazed at me long and hard. Luna's and Perla's voices carried from the bedchamber. He turned in the direction of that room, and I studied his profile as he listened to them. Orange firelight flickered over his face, doing little to soften the craggy features.

He dipped his chin and closed his eyes for a long moment, as though he were absorbing the sound, taking it inside himself and imprinting it into memory. "There is that, too," he acknowledged.

I leaned forward, draping my arms loosely on my knees. "Staying here . . . you will die."

It had to be said. There was no "if" about it. No doubt. The tower was no longer a secret. Luna wasn't the only one in danger. Once the soldiers reported to the king and he decided what to do—they would return. And Sivo, Perla, and Madoc wouldn't be spared. At best, they would be turned out. At worst, they'd be dealt with in the same manner as Dagne.

"I know."

"Then why stay?" My voice took on an edge.

"Because Perla can't survive out there. And there's the boy now, too. He's not fit to travel." Sivo ran a hand down the length of his beard, fingers delving into the pepper-dusted ginger strands. "You've given me your word. You're strong. You know how to survive on the Outside. Luna's smart. She might lack sight but she makes up for it in other areas. She might even be of help to you."

"I can believe that."

"She's special, Fowler." It was the first time he said my name. His gaze captured mine and held.

I nodded, flexing my hands around my mug.

"No," he bit out, leaning forward in his chair. "You think you understand me, that it's the love of a father talking, but I mean it. She's different. A day may come . . ." His voice faded and I could tell he warred with himself about whether he wanted to say something more.

Shaking his head, he dropped back in his chair, turning his attention to the nest of flames in the hearth. He looked almost mesmerized by the dance of fire as he uttered, "Time will reveal all."

I followed his gaze to the flames, wondering what he saw there that I did not.

His earlier admission that he worked in the palace surprised me. I would have inquired more about that, but I didn't need him asking me his own set of questions.

"The darkness cannot last," he added. "Light will come again."

I stifled my grunt. In my experience, it was the believers who usually ended up dead.

"I don't hold out much hope for that."

"Hope is all there is. All we have. And love. Or what's the point of any of it?" He was looking toward the bedchamber where Perla and Luna had disappeared.

I inhaled, the breath lifting my chest, thinking how those two things were the most dangerous of all. Even more dangerous than the king's men. Even more deadly than hungry dwellers outside. I had never been my weakest as when I allowed love and hope into my heart.

I would never do so again.

THIRTEEN

Luna

WE TRAVELED FOR almost a week with very little conversation. This wasn't because of any reticence on my behalf. I talked. My whispers filled the space around us. It's all I could do the first few days.

I was nervous and the sound of my chatter helped fill my own head. It also helped block thoughts of Sivo and Perla. I ached with the knowledge that I would never see them again. That I left them alone to face the eventual return of Cullan's soldiers.

Fowler never talked, but I didn't let his silence discourage me. I addressed the back of him, glad for the distraction, needing to forget the ache in my heart.

A nearly impossible task. A lump formed in my throat as I skirted a large outcropping, my palm skimming the rock's jagged surface. Fowler jumped down lightly before me, the sound of his boots hitting the earth signaling the sudden drop in the ground. I followed suit, bending slightly to brace my hand on the ground and landing smoothly where the ground gave way.

It had taken everything in me to say good-bye to them. Sivo had clasped my hands until they ached in his grip. *Swear to me, girl. Promise me you will never come back here.*

So I had promised. Not that Fowler would try to stop me if I decided to break that promise. He would probably be glad to be rid of me. Most of the time, he behaved as though I wasn't even there. Whenever we managed to find a spot to bed down, he would roll out his pallet, and turn his back on me without a word.

So I clung to the diversion of my one-sided conversations.

"How long have you been on your own?"

"How did you meet Madoc and Dagne?"

He never replied. His silence wore on me. I understood he didn't want me tagging along after him, but must he pretend I didn't exist?

My steps grew swifter and I began to answer my own questions as though I were him.

I deepened my whisper into an imitation of his tone, angling my head to the side. "I am from a little town called Foolshaven."

Angling my head in the other direction, I replied as myself, "Never heard of it. Is it anywhere near the village of Idiotsville?"

He made a slight sound, an intake of breath that might have been a laugh or a grunt of disgust.

"It's a bit near there." I adopted a deeper voice again, attempting to sound masculine. "A lovely place. I miss it dearly."

He turned to face me, the air churning with the sudden swirl of movement as he advanced on me.

His presence was too close. I stepped back, unsteady on my feet in my sudden haste to avoid colliding with him.

His low, deep voice rumbled out, making a mockery of my imitation. "A bit of fancy drivel, that. You'd never hear such words from me. There's no place left in the great vastness of this world that can be called lovely. Not since the dwellers came."

"Oh." I tried to sound flippant as his words sank through me like rocks. "Now he speaks."

"Everything is bleakness and death," he added, his voice flat, almost reprimanding. As though I should accept this.

How could his voice be so hard and yet reverberate through me with the quietness of wind? Gooseflesh broke out over my skin and the day was not even its usual cold.

I moistened my lips, my fingertips brushing the insides of my palms. My skin felt grimy and I wondered if I looked as dirty and travel worn as I felt. "When we get to Allu, what do you want to do?"

"What do you mean?"

"Well, once we reach there, you won't be on the road anymore. You'll be putting down roots."

"I don't know. Find a shelter. Build it if necessary. Maybe

farm and store up a respectable food supply."

I huffed out a breath. "Those are the things that you need to do. I asked you what you want to do once you get there. Once you're safe."

"I don't think about what I want. That's a luxury I don't have."

"Well, you might get that luxury there if Allu is all you think it will be."

"I'll worry about that when I get there."

"No." I laughed. "You don't understand. Having free time, doing something you want to do, relaxing . . . that's not supposed to be a worry." I lifted my chin. "Haven't you ever enjoyed yourself before?"

His stare crawled over my face, and I sensed his unwillingness to answer the question. Waves of frustration poured off him and I wasn't certain whether it was a result of me or himself, but I had the distinct feeling that he wouldn't mind giving me a good shake.

I pushed another question at him: "Do you remember life before the dwellers?" He had mentioned that there was no lovely place since the dwellers came. "They've been here for seventeen years," I added unnecessarily.

I knew nothing of life without dwellers. Nothing of the time when my parents lived and ruled a kingdom awash in sunlight, where the forests ran thick with game and the fields yielded a bounty of crops.

I heard the rustling of his clothing. "Enough. Let's move."

My shoulders slumped with the slightest disappointment. I lowered my face, unwilling to let him read my expression if he was even still looking at me.

Sivo and Perla rarely discussed life before the eclipse with me—only as much as they felt I needed to know about life in the capital and Cullan.

He started walking again. I fell into place beside him.

"I was two years old when the eclipse happened," he confessed.

My head snapped in his direction at these words.

"So you don't remember anything then?" Two years old was hardly an age to hold on to many memories.

"I remember sunlight. Once it turned my skin red. I stayed out too long and it burned my face. Lasted a week until it faded. A few days later the skin peeled off in flakes."

I shook my head slightly, trying to imagine that. Trying to imagine the taste of warm sun on my skin so strong it could burn.

He continued softly, "Grass so thick under your feet it was like a lush rug. There was none of this barren landscape. There was color everywhere—" He stopped at this, clearly realizing I didn't see colors—that colors would be something I would miss.

"No withered trees and plants," he added after several moments. "It didn't smell of rot or decay. It smelled like . . . life."

I listened, hanging on to his every word. I wanted to ask more from him, wanted to keep him talking. I wanted to paint a picture in my head with his words. "And?" I prompted.

"And—" He stopped abruptly. "And nothing. I don't remember anything else."

He was lying. I heard it in his voice. He remembered more. He simply didn't want to share it with me.

This shouldn't have hurt. It was nothing Perla hadn't done before. Talk of the past, of the way things had been before, was too much for her.

He increased his pace again, marching off ahead of me, extinguishing our fleeting conversation as effectively as the snuffing of a flame. Thunder rumbled in the distance and I looked up to the skies as though I could see the rain there, waiting to drop down on us in a deluge.

Perfect.

I had smelled the rain on the air for the last several hours, but hoped we would somehow skirt the storm.

Sighing, I followed after Fowler, stepping over a bit of fallen log, rotted and decaying as he had just mentioned.

The first droplet landed on my nose, followed in quick succession by more. A steady patter soon filled my ears as rain pelted down, soaking me to the bone through my garments. The wet added to the chill and I was soon shivering. Fowler did not ease his stride. I struggled after him, the sodden earth sucking at my boots.

After several moments, I began talking again, needing to focus on something other than my misery. I stayed close enough so that I didn't need to project my voice over the rain.

I probably appeared mad, muttering to myself, trudging

across the bleak landscape after Fowler, two little ants amid a vast, pitiless quagmire.

As I hurried to keep up with him, ignoring the burn in my thighs and the way my sopping wet clothes stuck to my skin, the sounds of the forest suddenly stopped.

I fell silent, too.

My steps slowed and I cocked my head, listening over the beat of water. I reached out a hand to touch Fowler's arm. He was right beside me. His forearm tensed instantly, all tightly corded sinew and strength beneath my fingers.

"To the trees," he mouthed against my ear, grabbing hold of my hand.

He ushered me to the closest semblance of shelter. A tree amid a dense thicket of dripping wet brush. He directed me to climb it and followed right behind me.

Of course, hiding in a tree offered its own misery. Stuck on a branch, water rolling down my face and dripping off the end of my nose, I had little to focus on except how cold and wet I was.

My teeth chattered and I contemplated reaching inside my pack for my cloak, but then that seemed pointless. It would only soon be as soaked as the rest of me.

I crossed my arms tightly over my chest and blew out a puff of breath, trying to warm myself—helplessly pressed up against Fowler when he clearly didn't want to be stuck with me. It made me long for home.

It made the ache in my heart that much worse.

I settled back against the hard scratch of bark, Fowler's arm aligned to the right side of my body. Another branch hemmed me in on the left. He'd positioned me to be secure even if it meant we had to sit plastered together side by side.

His breath fell beside me, slow and steady. A dweller cried out, closer now. The sound echoed long and thin through the woods. Moments later an answering call followed, much farther in the distance.

"Good," Fowler declared softly, the word a warm breath on my cheek. I shivered in a way that had nothing to do with the cold and everything to do with him. "Maybe the first one will head after that one."

I nodded, even though I wasn't entirely convinced. Perhaps the second dweller would head closer to us. That could happen, too.

The rain continued to fall, finding its way through the tangle of branches to where we huddled together. I lifted my face to the opening skies, my fingers swiping uselessly at my wet cheeks.

"This is good," he murmured, his lips still close. I felt their movement beside my hair. The rain was on his skin, too. I could smell the combination of water and salt from his flesh. It was a heady thing. A little dizzying, in fact. "They don't like hunting in the rain." His deep voice stroked over me like a feather's brush. "It makes them slower. . . . Sometimes they go to ground altogether."

I knew these creatures were led by sound, perhaps even smell. The wash of rainfall would dull both those senses.

"I imagine it impairs their hearing," I murmured, wrapping

my arms around my knees and drawing them up to my chest, resisting leaning to my right where his warm body pressed into mine.

"Does it impair yours?" It was a simple question, yet it felt intimate squashed together as we were. I wondered what it would feel like if his body relaxed—if he didn't hold himself so rigidly beside me. What would it feel like if he were to turn and fold me into his arms.

My face grew hot. "I suppose it does."

"We'll wait. Make certain they're gone and then push on for as long as the rain lasts."

I nodded. He was always so sensible.

"How long will it take to reach the isle?"

Silence stretched over the pattering rain. I was beginning to think he would not reply, but then he said, "By my calculation, three to four months."

A few months of me talking to his back. Months of us being together but not together.

My chest pinched considering it. I might have been trapped in the tower for the extent of my life, but I'd never been alone. I always had someone.

Now I had no one.

We stayed half an hour longer in the tree before climbing down, and then we tromped through the rain, moving as quickly as we could in the dragging mud, taking advantage of the sudden downpour.

I trailed behind Fowler, listening to his near-silent tread, following in his steps, gauging the shape and direction of Fowler in front of me as the air passed around him.

We walked until I was well past the point of exhaustion, until I could no longer feel my nose on my face. I pressed my lips into a mutinous line, determined not to complain.

"This way," he directed as though I could see him.

I followed him up a steep, rocky incline.

Suddenly I was out of the rain, my boots no longer squishing over sodden earth. I rotated in a small circle, wringing the water from the thick plait of hair that hung over my shoulder. "There is no wind."

"It's a cave. Sit down. Rest."

"Should we not push on through this rain?"

"You're dead on your feet. You need to rest—"

"I'm not wearied. I can continue—"

"Stand down. I'm wearied, too. Does that make any difference to you?"

I sniffed in response, mollified at least that he admitted this.

"We covered a great deal of ground," he continued. "This is an ideal shelter and we should take advantage of it."

I nodded, relenting. I listened as he dropped his pack. Following that, he divested himself of his garments, slapping them on the nearby rock.

My cheeks burned, thinking that he was naked—or nearly so.

"You should spread your clothes out to dry."

"I'm not undressing in front of you."

"You'll catch an ague, and that would do us no favors. Besides," he added, "we will be in close proximity for months. Am I never to see you in an indelicate state? That's not very realistic. If you want, you're welcome to go deeper into the cave."

I turned, facing the chasm. The damp air felt colder in that direction and my flesh broke out in goose bumps. Who knew what lurked in there?

"Come, I'll turn my back."

Still, I hesitated.

"We're going to be together for a long time," he reminded me.

He was right, of course. There had to be trust between us. I shrugged out of my jacket and draped it on the ground. Hopefully it would be dry before I donned it again. My fingers moved to the ties at the neck of my tunic, hesitating. I felt his stare. "Don't look at me," I whispered.

He chuckled and the sound made my skin turn to gooseflesh. But I heard the rush of air as he turned around. More important, I no longer felt the hot crawl of his eyes over me.

With shaking fingers, I undid the ties and pulled the tunic over my head. Next came my trousers. I spread both articles out to dry and stood only in my thin shift, shivering still, but not nearly as cold as before.

I felt a ripple of movement and stilled. "Are you peeking?"

"Tempting as I find drowned little wrens, no. I'm not spying on you."

Face burning, I crouched and dug inside my pack to find my

bedroll, still mostly dry. I stretched out on my cot and pulled the blanket over myself.

Keeping the blanket tight, I pulled my shift over my head. The cool air of the cave dried my damp skin. Naked, I tucked the blanket all around me, exposing no part of me.

"You may turn around."

His tread sounded near me. "Comfortable?"

I nodded.

"Sleep. I'll take the first watch."

"What of you? Will you wake me—"

"Don't concern yourself," he instructed as he settled his back against the cave wall.

It hadn't been precisely the answer I was seeking. It was an assurance, however, and even though I told myself I should be careful not to place my utter and complete trust in him, I dozed off.

I woke with a start, sensing hours had passed. I rubbed at my cheek, feeling disoriented. He had let me sleep. The rain had stopped. There was a freshness to the air, as though the rain had washed the world clean. Impossible, I knew, but I allowed myself to enjoy the scent for a moment.

Clutching the blanket to my chest, I strained my ears for evidence of Fowler. I heard nothing. There was no sign of him. Perhaps he had not left me to sleep. Perhaps he had just left me.

For a moment, the possibility went down my throat in a bitter swallow. I sat up, lifting my head off my pack, which I had used as a pillow, pebbles and bits of rock sticking to my palms as I pushed myself up. Cool air wafted over my bare skin and I recalled that my clothes were spread all around me, drying.

I brushed my hands off on my blanket. A bigger rock slid and rolled somewhere to my left. A booted foot scratched against the cave floor and I turned in that direction.

"Afraid I left you?"

I breathed a little easier, relieved at his return. "I suppose I should wonder at that. You haven't made any effort to hide just how much you resent my company."

"I gave my word."

"That's right. Your word." As though that should mean something to me. It had been enough for Sivo, but then in Sivo's mind there had not been much of an alternative.

"Let's move. You can eat as we walk."

"Could you turn around so that I can dress myself, please?"

He gave a snort, but obliged. I dressed quickly. My clothes were mostly dry and I knew I must have slept a long while.

I put away my bedding and then fished from my pack the last of Perla's flaky biscuits. Setting off after him, I chewed slowly, wanting this last tangible item from Perla to last. I would never have another one. I swiftly pushed away the stab of pain that thought triggered.

I wasn't certain if Fowler had slept at all. His voice sounded rusty with weariness. "Did you stand watch all night?" I asked.

He ignored the question.

"Fowler?" I pressed.

"Don't worry about me."

"Oh. You needn't sleep like the rest of us? Is that it?"

"I can look after myself. I've been doing it for years."

"I see. I'm not to express concern for your well-being, but if you should collapse, I shouldn't worry?" We were in this together and I wanted him to admit it. Perhaps then I wouldn't feel so alone beside him.

He grunted, the only acknowledgment that I might have made a valid point.

"Then I do have a stake in your well-being, after all."

"Very well. I'll abide your opinions."

At that, I laughed softly. "Good to know considering we will be travel companions for the next several months."

"This goes both ways, you know. You must endure my opinions, too."

"Indeed. Have you any opinions?" I struggled to lift my legs high out of the bog-like ground. "You of so few words?"

"I do."

"Feel free to share."

He stopped and faced me, his voice biting. "You fail to realize the dangerous nature of our journey."

"I'm perfectly aware of the dangers."

"And yet you insist on trying to make conversation and interacting with me as though you wish to be my friend."

He uttered "friend" as though it were a dirty word.

I exhaled a breath, heat crawling up my neck because he sensed that need in me and he viewed it as a weakness. "What's wrong with being friends? We will be together for a long time—"

"We are not friends. I had friends once. Family. They are all dead."

I swallowed against the lump in my throat. "And you haven't the desire for any more?"

"I haven't anything in me at all. No room for anyone. Including you."

His words struck like one of his well-aimed arrows. I forced my hands to remain at my sides even though I wanted to rub at my chest where I felt the sting the greatest, directly over my heart.

"I understand." Nodding, I strode ahead of him.

He stayed behind me for a short time before eventually reclaiming the lead.

The chirp of bats drifted overhead, moving as one in a great cloud. I froze and listened. I knew we were too large a target for them. They were hunting smaller prey—rabbits and rodents. I still didn't relish a run-in with the creatures. I shivered at the sound of them, their leathery wings flapping on the wind, their heavy weight as they landed on the brittle, creaking limbs of nearby trees.

Fowler stopped beside me. "Don't worry. They don't attack humans. If we leave them alone, they'll ignore us."

That's what Sivo always said, too, but it didn't cure my apprehension. I waited a moment longer, listening to their flapping wings fade in the distance.

We traveled steadily thereafter, hearing no more bats. Sometimes we heard dwellers in the distance, their eerie cries bouncing through the forest. I'd hold my breath as we quickened our steps, skirting them, but I knew it wouldn't always be like that. We had a long way to go and sometimes we were going to have to fight them.

"How much longer until we leave the Black Woods?"

"Another day or two."

I was almost surprised he answered me. During the last few hours, I had settled into tense silence, thinking over our exchange. We'd never be friends. Clearly, barely tolerated traveling companions were all we would ever be. If Sivo had not extracted a promise from him to take me to Allu, I'm certain he would have abandoned me by now.

"I need to stop," I announced after a while.

"Soon. Keep going for now." He kept walking, not bothering to explain why, not bothering to ask why I wanted to stop.

With a huff of frustration, I turned and headed in another direction.

It didn't take him long to realize I wasn't following. I suppose he was paying some attention to me after all.

"Wait. Where are you going?" His feet sounded after me, quick thuds on the earth, but I didn't stop. My chest burned prickly hot. I wasn't stopping. I wasn't going to turn around and let him see the weak emotion that made me want to drop my pack, curl up into a ball, and bury my face in my arms and weep.

I'd only ever wanted to leave the tower despite the dangers.

I wanted an adventure. But without Sivo and Perla, I felt achingly alone—a fact that didn't improve with him declaring that we couldn't be friends.

His hand clamped on my shoulder, and I spun around, pulling away. "I told you I needed to stop."

"We won't cover any ground if you need to rest every—"

"Oh, how often have I asked to rest?" I demanded, my temper rising. "I need to relieve myself. Do you mind? Can I have a moment's privacy?"

He didn't say anything and I forced myself to face him, hoping he didn't see any hint of the vulnerability I felt in my expression. I felt his stare as potent as Perla's mulled cider, a heady thing crawling over my face, seeing everything, missing nothing.

Deciding the silence had stretched long enough, I stomped off to where the wind felt the thinnest, the air circulating less within the dense thicket. Plenty of cover from his gaze.

Not that he would spy on me. A boy that didn't want to talk to me or be my friend certainly wouldn't be interested in spying on me as I went about my business.

Strangely, that offered little comfort.

FOURTEEN

Fowler

"Do you hear that?" Luna's voice rippled over the chilled stillness, a current swimming in the breathing dark. Her question was the first time she had spoken to me in hours and only a thin thread of sound.

I froze in place and listened, already knowing to trust her ears over my own.

There was nothing at first, simply the rush of blood in my ears and a solitary bat chirping in the far distance. Then I heard it. Them. A low, intermittent rumble of voices, ebbing and increasing and then disappearing altogether.

"They're . . . people." Her voice shook a little and I knew that she would have been less nervous had they been dwellers.

I peered into the dark. There were no torches. No flickering fire through the trees. But we were headed straight for them. Or they were headed in our direction. Either way, everything inside me tensed.

I squinted into the opaque air. We could try to skirt them, give them a wide berth, but there was always the possibility that they had their own scouts ferreting the perimeter of their group. Especially if they were soldiers. That was common protocol.

Normally, I would investigate to verify who—or what—was out there. Constant awareness is what kept me alive this long, but I wasn't functioning under normal circumstances anymore. I had Luna to consider.

"Maybe they're friendly," she offered, breaking into the quiet of my thoughts.

I shook my head, tension knotting my shoulders as I stared ahead into the cold ink of dark. A quick glance upward revealed the thick tangle of branches obscuring the moon's glow. That was being hopeful. She didn't fully understand. Aside from soldiers, she thought the dwellers were the worst thing out here. She thought everyone else was like us, survivors banding together for a like purpose—to further our existence. She would understand in time.

"Stay here," I commanded, unloading my pack and adjusting the quiver at my back.

Her shoulders squared, and that rounded little chin of hers went up. I could tell she wanted to argue. Or simply ignore my instructions and follow me. Just like the boy, Donnan. An ugly feeling swept through me at that reminder of him, and my movements became more jerky.

"I'm going with you—"

"No. I'm not Sivo or Perla for you to twist and manipulate. Out here, I'm in charge." The hard fall of my words made her back away, stopping only when she collided with a tree.

I sighed. "If you stay here, you'll be safe," I said, my voice softer. I stared down at my hands a long moment before looking back up at her. Skepticism was writ all over her features.

"I'll move faster knowing you are here waiting safely." It irritated me that I felt the need to prove myself sincere.

She brought her arms up to hug herself. "Are you coming back?" Doubt tinged her voice. "Tell me the truth."

I told myself distrust was normal. Good even. I blew out a breath and squeezed my eyes shut for a moment before opening them again. The slightest quiver to her bottom lip revealed she wasn't as unaffected as she pretended to be leaning there against the tree.

I gestured to my pack as though she could see it there in the dirt by her feet. "I'm leaving my supplies."

She nodded stiffly, but didn't appear to fully accept my explanation as proof enough that I would be coming back.

I started to leave, walked several feet, but the image of her face—the big dark eyes—burned an imprint onto my mind. I knew that visual would follow me, and I didn't need that. Not when I needed a clear head.

With a muffled curse, I whipped back around. She was scared and not totally convinced I would be returning for her. What if I was gone longer than she expected and she took it into her head to leave?

Several strides put me back in front of her. My heart thumped hard in my chest. Even though she was taller than a good many women, I still looked down at her.

Resolve fueled me. I reached for her, taking her face firmly in both my hands, fixing her unseeing stare on me. She jumped a little at the contact but didn't pull away.

This close, the freckles spattering her nose and cheeks were clearly visible—a collection of brown dots of varying sizes, all several shades lighter than her dark hair.

Trapped in my hands, staring sightlessly up, she seemed so vulnerable. A single budding lily in a world of night. One clap of my hands and she would be crushed, her light snuffed out.

"I will not abandon you, Luna." It was the reassurance she had asked for before, but I had been unable to say the words then. "Ever," I added.

It didn't mean she would never get hurt. It didn't mean either one of us would make it, but if something happened to her it would not be because I had failed her. I would never do that. Not again.

Her lips parted in the slightest gasp. She blinked, looking as startled as I felt at my avowal.

"Do you understand?" I slipped my fingers deeper into her hair, cradling the back of her skull. "You believe me?"

Her shock at my promise was palpable.

And there was my own awareness of her slighter body so close to mine. Her fragrance filled my nose. I felt alive for the first time in a long time. My skin prickled and pulled tight, sensitive even to the slightest gust of air. There was no part of me that didn't feel.

If she touched me, I might come apart. My stomach pitched and turned, hoping she did. Hoping she didn't.

She was a girl who somehow managed to smell good and fresh in a world of stinking rot. It was not a situation I would have chosen for myself, but here I was.

She nodded and those lips of hers—so loose and soft and appealing—grabbed all of my attention. I gave in and dropped my forehead against hers. I breathed in deeply, filling my lungs with her.

My blood pumped thickly through my veins. She sucked in a breath, her only reaction to our sudden closeness.

My lips rested at the corner of her mouth, not quite touching. I only needed to turn slightly, and our mouths would meet. A shudder passed through me.

I flexed my hands, my fingers spearing through her satiny hair. Her forehead felt smooth and warm against my own. Her breath, sweet and minty, crashed against my lips.

My heart heaved painfully as I lifted my head to look down at her again, denying myself what I wanted to do. Kissing her, tasting her lips. The wonder in her expression was an invitation even she wasn't conscious of.

My fingers grazed her cheeks before falling at my sides.

"Why did you do that?" she murmured.

"Do what?"

"Touch me . . . like that."

I shook my head. There had been a girl or two since Bethan. No names. Shadowed faces. Quick encounters to escape the numbness. We clung to each other in the dark and moved on. Luna was not like them.

"I don't know," I replied.

Turning away, I disappeared into the thick press of trees, quickly pushing away the thought of silky hair and soft skin and the kiss we almost had.

I slid back into my normal role, slinking through trees, setting my boots down carefully, choosing each step with calculation.

They were still there, the voices snatches of muted sound. As a group, they didn't move with the most stealth, but they weren't walking around with torches, so they possessed some deliberation.

I pulled an arrow from my quiver and nocked it. They were approaching. I crouched low behind a tree and waited, slowing my breath until my heartbeat filled my ears.

I smelled them before they came into view, the rotting stink of them like a carcass left out to the elements too long. The filthy bunch stepped into view: four men and two females. Blood and dirt covered them. Their hair was matted nests and clothes hung off them in tattered scraps. The bony joints of their skeletal bodies peeked out like gnarled branches.

One of the men was entirely naked, but he strolled along indifferently to the fact. He raked his fingers up and down his already bloodied arms, gouging them raw.

A man walked at the helm holding a battle-ax that looked as if it had never been cleaned. Blood and bits of debris clung to the blade's edge. An older boy trailed behind him, feverishly picking at his gums until crimson coated his teeth.

I knew something was off before I even spotted the dead bats two of them carried, slung over their shoulders as they walked. One girl pulled at her hair, ripping chunks from her scalp. Raw patches, oozing blood, peeked out through the tangled snarls. These people were demented.

My lip curled, and I instantly knew.

Bat fever.

I'd heard of it afflicting those who hunted and ate from the surplus of bats populating the land. The people of Relhok had always been warned against it. In fact, anyone caught hunting bats was instantly banished. It curbed the impulse among the hungriest. No one wanted to leave the safety of the walled city of Relhok. No one but me.

But out here people were desperate and hungry enough. There was no coming back from bat fever. It poisoned the blood and addled the brain. I began to inch back—until the dig of a blade at the back of my neck stopped me.

FIFTEEN

Luna

I WAITED IN the familiar dark, feeling its weight on my pores. The Outside was a pulsing heartbeat. Even when it was quiet, the stillness held its breath, waiting for the inevitable to happen. I expelled a silent breath, emptying my lungs.

Up to this point, my life had been waiting. Waiting to go Outside. Waiting for Perla to grant me whatever small dose of freedom. Waiting for my life to begin.

I believed Fowler when he promised to come back, but what if he couldn't? What if something happened to him? How long should I wait, hoping he would return, before giving up and accepting that I was on my own out here? As much as I believed

I could survive on my own if I had to . . . I didn't want to.

I was done waiting. I was going after him.

Bending, I picked up the bag he left and draped it over my shoulder. In my other hand, I freed my sword, deciding to have it at the ready.

I started in the direction Fowler took, moving cautiously in the strange terrain, following those distant sounds of people, clenching the hilt of my sword as I wove between trees.

The voices grew louder, overlapping. I was close now, so I stopped and listened, wary of getting any closer to the group. I thought I would have come across Fowler by now. Their foul, putrid odor draped heavily over the already thick air. I covered my mouth with one hand to stifle the impulse to retch.

I itched to distance myself. Fowler had to be nearby. Unless he had circled back and I missed him.

I frowned at the thought that I might have missed him. I concentrated on the angry voices, pinpointing their exact direction, marking each one of them as I hovered impatiently. Sivo taught me the importance of assessing my surroundings and never rushing in. Sometimes we would sit on the balcony and he would have me count the dwellers we heard.

"Thief! You should have found your own bats and not tried to take ours," one voice rang out with so much venom that I took an automatic step back.

Bats?

"Now you're going to suffer. Thieves always pay. We will make you pay. Ask the others."

Someone laughed wildly in the group. "Can't ask the others 'cause we made them pay! Nasty, nasty thieves! They had to pay! And now so will you."

"I'm not after your bats." It was Fowler's voice.

I started to step forward, ready to call out to him, but then stopped, setting my foot back down slowly.

"Yes, you are! Yes, you are! A nasty, nasty thief who must—"

"Oh, he's very pretty. Let's keep him for a bit."

Feminine laughter followed this, and then several different treads shuffled over the ground. A sharp slap cracked the air. "Keep your hands off him. He's not your pet; he's a thief. Aren't you a thief?" There was a thud and then Fowler grunted. They were hitting him. I jerked at a second thud, my hand opening and closing into a fist at my side. This time there was no grunt. Fowler was holding silent and taking it.

"Everyone wants to take our bats for themselves. You can't have them!" a shrill female voice accused, heedless of her volume. Another thud, another blow against Fowler. "You hear me?"

I adjusted my weight on my feet uneasily, certain if any dwellers roamed nearby, they could hear her. None of her companions hushed her. Indeed, they all seemed as senseless as she was.

"Why would I want to take yours?" Fowler's voice was calm, but there was a thread of pain from the abuse he'd endured. "There are more than enough to hunt."

"Liar! Kill him! Kill the nasty thief!" My heart pounded faster, harder. She meant it. "They're our kills. We hunted them. We shall have them, not you."

They ate the bats? One was never supposed to eat bat. Even before they became so monstrous in size, one did not eat bat. Even I knew that.

A beat of silence stretched before a man announced, "Kill him before he tries to steal our bats for himself."

One person in the group was scratching incessantly at something. Listening, I determined it was the sound of his nails scoring flesh. I inhaled. The scent of blood and rotting meat turned my stomach. I wasn't certain if the odor emanated from the bat corpses or the mad bat-eaters themselves.

"On your knees!"

There was a sound of struggle before the heavy thud of Fowler hitting dirt.

"Now stay down."

"You don't have to do this," Fowler said, his voice still astonishingly calm.

I was shaking now, my breath coming in quick pants.

One of the others grunted. "Kill him, Cauly. Take the nasty thief's head!"

I shifted anxiously, stopping myself short of lunging forward. I couldn't take on the entire group by myself. There were seven of them at least.

The thought streaked across my mind that a pack of dwellers wouldn't be so bad right now. The distraction could give Fowler a chance to break away. Even this crazed, motley group wouldn't be so concerned with killing Fowler if they were fighting off dwellers.

The solution was that simple, I realized. Fowler had only one chance. And as his fate was tied up in mine, it was the only chance I had, too.

Opening my mouth, I did the one thing I had never done before. The one thing no one would ever dare do.

I filled my lungs to capacity—until they burned—and screamed.

SIXTEEN

Fowler

FEAR SLICKED THROUGH me as I stared at the filth-encrusted blade high above my head and tried to cling to some final thought that would give meaning to my life in these last moments.

Everything slowed to a crawl. The man wielding the battle-ax grinned down at me with a rotten-toothed grin. They'd made short work of confiscating my weapons and shoving me to my knees in the middle of the group. The two women snatched hold of the two bat carcasses and eyed me with wild stares, shielding their kill as though I still posed a threat and might steal them.

I didn't want regrets in my final moments, but they slithered their way in nonetheless. Only it was not for Bethan or my father or the countless other failures littering my life. It was regret for Luna. For abandoning her.

At first I thought the scream splitting my skull was the half-naked giant's battle-ax cleaving open my head and ending it all. But it was an actual scream, full-bodied and shrill. It stretched and kept going and going. Even when the cries of dwellers went up in response, it was still there, an endless echo that I felt in my bones.

Everyone froze for a moment before full-blown panic set in. I took advantage of the chaos and lunged, barreling into the man holding the battle-ax above my head.

He fell with a grunt, the ax flying. I jumped to my feet and grabbed it. That terrible scream ended, but the eerie cries of dwellers had taken its place. They were coming.

I went for the man who'd confiscated my weapons, grabbing my bow from his hand and wrestling the quiver from his shoulder. He started struggling once he realized what I was doing. I struck him in the face with the flat of the ax, cracking his nose open. Bone flashed and he went down, blood spurting.

Everyone else scattered, fleeing in panic—except the two women, who played tug-of-war with their precious bats.

Over the cacophony of dwellers' cries, I crouched and retrieved my sword and knives from the man I felled. Tucking them into their sheaths, I stood and jogged into the undergrowth. I didn't make it a few feet before a slight sound at my back had me whirling, bow ready and nocked. I very nearly released my arrow into Luna.

Cursing, I lowered my arm. "What are you doing here? I told you to stay put." I didn't give her time to answer. Grabbing her hand, I pulled her after me. Leaves rustled. The dragging steps of dwellers were all around us.

"You're welcome," she snapped.

I stopped for half a breath to look at her.

Her dark gaze fixed on me in that uncanny way of hers.

"That was you?" Snorting, I pushed on.

I pulled her through the woods, jerking to a stop occasionally, listening and dodging oncoming dwellers. She followed in her usual wraithlike silence, not even flinching when the first scream from one of the bat mad rang out over the air.

I shouldn't have felt relief, but I did. Every dweller homed in on that cry. Even if we weren't so quiet, that scream was a beacon above everything else.

I relieved Luna of our supply bag when I realized she was carrying it, and we continued, moving swiftly, striding at a hard pace as the cries faded in the distance. I glanced at her several times, processing what she had done. Screaming like that had been bold and stupid and brilliant.

She had saved my life.

"Thank you," I said, still holding her hand as I led her through the woods, unwilling to let go just yet. I adjusted my grip on her slim, cool fingers.

"You're welcome," she replied.

"I suppose you're going to be insufferable now."

"Why? Because I saved your life—twice now—and proved I'm not such a complete burden?"

"I never said you were a burden." Precisely.

"No. You just didn't want to bring me with you."

"That's because I work better alone." At that reminder, I released her hand.

"Except for tonight."

I sighed, closing my eyes in a hard blink, still seeing that ax descending toward me. She was right.

Tonight I needed her.

SEVENTEEN

Luna

FOWLER HANDED ME a piece of bread, his fingers grazing mine. I snatched my hand back, bringing the coarse-crusted bread to my mouth and tearing off a bite, comforted at once. The salty burst of flavor tasted of home, and a pang punched me in the chest.

For so long I had yearned to be free of walls. It wasn't supposed to be this ugly out here. People weren't supposed to be so horrible.

The back of my throat burned, and I gulped, trying to chase away the sensation. Perla had known. I swallowed back a bitter laugh. She had always known. She understood what we had and what I would be giving up.

Frustration bubbled up in me, mingling with the bitter twist of other emotions. "I just wish—" I stopped. He didn't care.

"What?" His voice rang out impatiently, almost like he resented asking me.

"I wish I had appreciated what I had," I snapped.

The gift of all those years with Sivo and Perla, when I had lived relatively safely, when I had been surrounded by love, brought fresh tears to my eyes.

"Life is full of regrets. They'll cripple you if you let them."

I laughed hoarsely. "It's that easy for you? You can simply will all your regrets away?"

As usual, he didn't reply.

"Tell me something, Fowler," I added. "Are you not crippled?" Wasn't being numb, an empty shell, a punishment in itself?

"We aren't talking about me."

"No. We never do that."

Sniffing, I blinked against the sudden sting in my eyes, taking another bite of bread and chewing faster, as if that would somehow stave off the regrets.

So far my adventures had revealed only the ugliness of life.

Except that moment with Fowler.

The brief press of his face to mine when I had thought he might kiss me had been unexpected and wonderful. Even if he didn't know why he had done it, he had. I had that.

"It's the last of Perla's bread," he said, his tone clearly suggesting I slow down stuffing my face.

Cheeks burning, I covered my mouth with my fingers and slowed my chewing, trying to savor this last small bit of Perla.

He shifted, his boot scuffing against the ground. I inhaled, catching a whiff of his spicy scent. I'd never smelled anything like him before and I didn't think it was due to my lack of exposure to others. It was inherently him.

I exhaled through my nose, enjoying the flavor of the dark, hearty bread on my tongue. "I'm going to miss it," I murmured, turning the bread over in my fingers. "I could never make bread quite like her. Even when we reach Allu, I doubt I shall be able to replicate it."

I waited, hoping he would say something. A few words about the better future that waited me in Allu. But nothing. Silence. He offered nothing that revealed he even thought I would reach Allu with him, which only seemed to confirm my suspicion that he thought I wasn't going to make it there.

I tore a small bite with my teeth and chewed slowly, reaching for my flask and washing the mouthful down with some water.

He expelled a breath that wasn't quite a gasp but close.

"What? What is it?" I jerked, immediately thinking that some bat-crazed individual had found us.

"Firebugs."

I straightened, alarmed. "Firebugs? What are those?" I was accustomed to bugs, but that didn't mean I liked them. The world was teeming with them. They owned the night right alongside the dwellers.

He hesitated. "Have you never heard of firebugs before?"

I shook my head, trying not to feel so unworldly even if I was.

"When I was a boy we used to trap them in jars. They're small flying bugs and their bodies light up in the dark."

"They're here now?" I asked, turning my face left and right nervously. "Will dwellers see them and be attracted to the light?"

"They never bother with them. They're not a food source, so they ignore them."

I relaxed somewhat, but still searched for evidence of these creatures that lit up like fire.

Almost in response, I felt the brush of something soft against my cheek.

"Oh," I started, swatting at it, accustomed to swatting away insects.

Either the same firebug or another one skimmed my nose and I swallowed back a startled yelp, nearly toppling over. I sensed them swarming all around me.

"No, it's fine." He scooted closer, his bigger body dragging across the dirt and grass to sit beside me, so close his arm brushed my shoulder, so close I immediately felt his warmth radiating toward me.

His presence beside me felt so solid and larger-than-life. I knew from memory that muscle and sinew roped tightly beneath his skin. There was not an ounce of fat to him anywhere. How could there be? Out here, living like this, there wasn't excess to be had.

He took my hands and lowered them from my face. "Don't," he murmured.

I trembled slightly, hating feeling all the tiny bugs around me.

"They won't hurt you," he added, pushing my hands down into my lap. He kept one hand over mine. That single hand was large enough to wrap around both of mine. His hands weren't as brawny as Sivo's, but his fingers were long and tapering, blunt tipped, the nails shorn to the quick.

Suddenly I wasn't certain what made me more nervous: his touching or a horde of bugs flying around me.

"They're harmless," he assured me. "And beautiful."

He uttered this last word on a breath, so close to my face I could almost imagine he was talking about me and not the firebugs.

Heat crawled up my neck, sweeping over my face and ears. "Easy for you to say. I can't see them."

He said nothing for a long moment and I tried not to shudder when I felt the tiny bodies brush my face again.

"They're like blinking sparks of yellow light all around us . . . around you. It's magical."

My chest tightened, sensing his awe. But he was using words I could never understand. He spoke of colors so naturally and easily. "I wish I could see them," I said. It was the first time I ever wished for sight. The first time I uttered those words.

Frustration welled inside me. I wanted to see what he was seeing. I wanted insight into whatever it was that was making him loosen his tongue and talk to me.

"Wait a moment." He released my hand and moved away. I curled my fingers inside my palm, trying to ignore how bereft I suddenly felt without him touching me.

There was a slight rustling as he fumbled through his pack. He was back moments later, picking my hand up again. He unfurled my fingers and placed something in it. "Here. It's like this."

I cocked my head, feeling the object he placed in my hand. I brought my other hand over it, stroking it. It was smooth in parts but with several tiny prickles that jutted out from the glassy smoothness.

"What is this?"

"It's granul rock." He adjusted my grip, forcing my fingertips to stroke the cold smoothness between all the sharp points. "Feel that? The cold evenness?" At my nod, he continued. "That's the night. The darkness. And this here . . ." He lifted my hand, his touch as sure and deft as his words fanning warmly on my cheek. He brought the soft pads of my fingers down against the tiny protrusions, running the sharp bumps over my skin. "These are the firebugs."

My lips parted on a choked laugh as I stroked the sleekness of night before running my fingertips over the bumpy dots that represented the firebugs. I smiled. "I understand." In a way that I had never understood before. He brought sight to me through touch and sensation.

I lifted my face, my smile widening as a firebug brushed my cheek before flitting away.

I glanced down to where our hands still clung together. I flexed my fingers and turned my palm over, bringing it flush with his. I squeezed lightly, savoring the contact. "Thank you."

"For what?" His fingers tensed around my hand for a moment but he didn't pull away.

"Caring enough. For wanting me to see this."

"I . . ." His voice faded. "You shouldn't have to miss it. There's not much beauty left in the world." He touched my face. Lightly at first, then more boldly. His thumb trailed down my cheek. It was just a graze of sensation, but it reminded me of that almost-kiss. Heat crawled over my face. "It's like they're drawn to you. They're all around you."

"Really?" I breathed, turning my face, letting the little fire-bugs brush my skin without fear now.

"Almost as though they don't want you to hide in darkness."

A breath shuddered out of me. I had never had this before. He made me feel extraordinary and beautiful.

Even if I couldn't see, I understood beauty as a concept. That some people were especially pleasing to the eye. Perla told me my mother had been beautiful. Countless nobles had courted her before my father won her hand. Perla had shared, in her very direct manner, that there was only a slight resemblance between us. I simply assumed I favored my father more, but now I wondered. Perhaps I looked like my mother a little, after all.

I heard his sigh and felt his withdrawal the moment before he slipped his hand out from mine.

I reached for him. Instinct drove me. I took his face in both hands, exploring his features, feeling the aquiline nose, the broad cheekbones, and the slash of his eyebrows over deeply set eyes.

"I've wanted to do this since almost the beginning."

"Do what?" he asked.

"Touch your face. Since I first heard your voice . . . I wanted to trace your features. Etch them into myself." My fingers moved as I spoke. A single fingertip slid over the slope of his nose, across his forehead, and then back down to the corner of his mouth.

"What color are your eyes?"

"They're green."

"Green," I whispered.

"Like the grass," he supplied. "Green is how it smells right after a rain, when everything is lush and thriving."

I smiled. Again, he was able to help me understand color.

"And this . . ." I stroked his mouth, running my fingers over the bottom lip and then the upper, feeling his breath quicken against me as I touched the center of his lip where it dipped down like an arrow's head. Something fluttered inside my stomach, tightened and clenched. "Does it have a color?"

A beat of silence fell. He moved in, closing that small space between us. There was a slight rustling as his body inched in, the breadth of his chest like an encroaching wall. His warm breath fanned my lips.

I jerked as a dweller cried out, its eerie shriek threading through the trees.

He pulled back, tugging my hands down from his face. "That's not important."

He moved away, leaving me with my heart beating like a wild

drum in my chest. I wrapped my arms around myself, needing something to do with them, feeling crushed at his sudden departure. A firebug landed on my cheek.

This time I didn't lift a finger to brush it away.

EIGHTEEN

Fowler

WHEN WE LEFT the Black Woods, it was like stepping out from a dream. There were trees, but fewer and more spread out. There was also the occasional fallow field and forgotten cottage. With less foliage obscuring the sky, it actually seemed brighter. Moonlight dappled the land. I could see farther, but of course that meant we could be seen, too.

Luna seemed to sense the change, too, and not simply in the terrain. She sensed it in me. Her expression became more pensive and her face repeatedly turned in my direction as though she was seeking something from me—something I couldn't give her.

More than once, she had made me feel like who I used to be.

I couldn't be that person anymore. I couldn't get lost in her smiles or her voice or her touch on my skin. I definitely couldn't get lost in her lips. Not if I wanted to keep us both alive.

A bat swell passed, obscuring the sky for a few moments, hiding the glow of the moon.

Luna didn't even glance up to the sky. She simply kept moving.

I frowned. She was different from that girl I first met in the tower. It was bound to happen. Out here, no one went untouched.

She fell in beside me and I spared her a glance. I reached out as though to touch her, but stopped short. There was no need. I didn't want to witness her break. I didn't want her to turn into this twisted, hardened scrap of what she used to be.

I didn't want her to be me.

"We've left the forest," she stated more than asked, biting her lip. It was a nervous habit of hers. She did it often, drawing my stare to her mouth. I dragged my gaze away and scrubbed a hand over my face. That mouth was my hell. I'd almost kissed it. *Her.* Or perhaps she had almost kissed me. Whoever was to blame, it had almost happened. And it couldn't happen again.

Together like this, fighting for our lives, it was a natural urge, but one that would only prove distracting. The last thing I wanted was to give her a false idea of what we were to each other. She was the kind of girl who believed in love even in this bleak life.

"Yes, we have," I answered, my voice curt even to my own ears.

"It smells differently," she whispered.

I hesitated before asking, "How so?"

"Cleaner somehow."

"Less rotting vegetation. And greater winds."

Things weren't going to be as simple anymore. The risks and dangers were greater now. With the Black Woods behind us, there would be more dwellers and more people. The wind howled in the vastness, and the lack of any other sound made my skin prickle. Even the smallest animal knew to make itself scarce out here, or at least the art of making itself invisible and unheard.

Another light rain started, drumming all around us as we moved forward in the gloom. It didn't leave us soaking wet, but the clammy damp of our clothes sticking to skin could hardly be called comfortable.

Her plaits hung over her shoulder in heavy skeins, and her normally pale skin practically glowed like moonstone in the near dark. Her collarbones stood out above the neckline of her bodice and dark shadows smudged the skin under her eyes like bruises. Something inside me twisted at the sight. She really needed to eat more. And rest more.

I faced forward again as we left the dense foliage farther and farther behind, gripping my bow at the ready as we walked into a maw of wasteland that had once been working fields.

I hesitated, scanning the horizon, searching for any woods to pass through that would offer some protection. The skyline loomed ahead, a dark gray plain etched against the moonlit sky. There was no easy way around it. We'd have to cross straight through that open space. Our boots crunched over short, withered-up stalks of sugarcane that even the rain hadn't helped to moisten.

Every crunching step made me cringe. I wanted nothing more than to be off this deadened field and onto softer ground. Quieter ground.

I continued to scan the barren landscape, peering as far as I could into the stretch of nothingness. I flexed my grip around my bow.

In the distance, the outline of a copse of trees materialized against the dark. "This way," I murmured, nodded as though she could see my gesture.

Shaking my head, I led her across the field. As we drew closer, I could see that a small farmer's hut backed against the copse. The crank on the old, dilapidated well turned in the breeze.

"Do you hear that?" Her hand fell on my arm.

I stopped, listening.

"It's a voice." Her head whipped back and forth from me to the cottage. "Someone's in there."

My gaze narrowed on the cottage. It looked abandoned. The windows dark, gaping holes. The door was ajar, hanging off a broken hinge.

"There it is again. Someone is in trouble inside there."

I tensed, aiming my arrow at the hut. I didn't hear anything, but I knew to trust her in this.

She huffed in frustration and lunged ahead, quick as a darting hare.

"Luna!" I dropped my bow and tried to grab her back, but she was too fast.

Swinging my bow over my shoulder, I took off after her, reaching her just as she crossed the threshold.

NINETEEN

Luna

THE MAN WAS in the middle of the room. He reeked of sweat and blood. I could even detect the acrid sting of fear. He was still whispering in that pitiable voice that first alerted me to him. "Help . . . help . . . me," he pleaded between labored pants of breath.

I stepped forward to reach him, but Fowler's hand fell hard on my arm. "What are you doing?"

"He needs help." I waved in his general direction.

"You can't just go charging into every situation, Luna."

"I charged into your situation, did I not? Do you regret that?"

He growled low, and I felt a surge of satisfaction. "Fine. You stay here. I'll check him."

His boots thudded on the wood floor as he advanced cautiously. The floor creaked beneath him as he squatted. I hovered close behind. Clothing rustled and I presumed he was searching the man for weapons. His ministrations must not have been gentle enough. The man groaned and Fowler hushed him softly. "Quiet now. We don't want any unwelcome visitors, do we?"

"I look bad." The man coughed and gurgled blood. "But you should see the other one. It won't be going back underground." He laughed, and the sound sputtered and twisted into violent hacking.

"He's unarmed," Fowler said to me as if there was still some doubt.

This man didn't want to hurt anyone. He was the hurt one. He just wanted the pain to stop.

I hastened forward and dropped down beside Fowler. I stretched out my hand to touch the stranger, but Fowler's hand on my wrist stopped me.

I turned my face in his direction. "Something wrong?"

"He's . . ."

"What?" I asked.

"He's missing some of his face."

"Oh." The word expelled from me in a horrified rush.

"I went out at midlight," the stranger wheezed. "Thought I could get back in time . . . so stupid. I went too far. It was just one dweller, but I didn't see him until he was on me."

Fowler spoke into my ear. "There's toxin all over his wounds."

"What's your name?" I asked.

"Amose."

"Amose?" I moistened lips that felt suddenly dry. "Can I hold your hand? Would that be all right with you?" I had barely finished asking the question before he seized my hand, squeezing it tightly as if staying connected to me somehow helped him bear the agony.

"I had a daughter once. She had small hands like yours." He paused on a pained gasp. "She married. Moved away to Cydon . . . maybe she's still there. . . ."

"It's a big village. I am sure she is there and thriving." I had no idea if the village still stood, but I would say anything to him in that moment that could provide comfort.

Fowler tensed beside me and I could read his thoughts. His judgment. No one thrived.

"I'm so . . . thirsty," Amose rasped.

I reached for my water. Instantly, Fowler closed his fingers around my hand, each finger a biting imprint on my cold skin.

"He's thirsty," I explained as though it were the simplest thing in the world.

"We have a precious amount of supplies."

"Then take this out of my share," I said tightly.

He cursed. "Damn it, Luna. We'll need every bit of that. This man is going to be dead soon. I know it's hard, but surviving means making hard choices."

His words were a splash of cold reality. He was right and I resented him for it. I turned my face toward the man wheezing

165

for air on the ground. He was alone in this world. With half his face missing and his blood soaking into the floor of the hut, his only thoughts were for his child. I couldn't refuse him this relief.

Fowler's hand squeezed mine. "Be strong, Luna."

Anger spiked through me and I jerked my hand free. "Not in this. If turning my back on him makes me strong, then so be it. I'm weak." I slipped a hand under Amose's head, lifting him up so his mouth could find the rim of my flask. He slurped greedily. "Easy," I advised when he broke into a sputtering cough.

"Thank you," he huffed.

I lowered him gingerly back down, plugged my flask shut, and claimed his hand again.

Fowler made a sound of disgust deep in his throat and I squared my shoulders, pretending that I didn't care what he thought of me.

"I suppose we're staying," he grumbled.

I tossed the words over my shoulder in a rushed whisper: "I doubt this will take long."

He said nothing. After a while, he moved away, his boots thudding a hard line to the door to stand watch. Or perhaps he simply didn't want to witness this.

I settled on the cold floor, resting Amose's head in my lap, careful to touch only his hair and not the toxin-soaked wounds of his face. "Tell me about your daughter. What's her name?"

"Nessa."

"That's a pretty name."

"Yes. She was . . . is beautiful. Like her mother. Like you."

He touched me then, pressing one finger directly over my heart. "You have it in here." He coughed violently, his hand dropping away from me. "It's a beauty that nothing can take away. Not this world or its monsters." His voice faded. His breath grew too labored for him to talk anymore, just a heavy cadence of puffs and wheezes.

I stopped asking questions and just talked, about everything and nothing, swatting away the bloated gnats and flies that circled him, hungry for their next meal. Conscious of Fowler standing vigil at the door, I whispered a steady stream of words. Stories. We had a few books in the tower left by my parents. Perla often read aloud to me. One of them was a collection of love poems. It was my favorite. I would hold the rich leather-bound volume in my hands, caressing the pages, stroking where the words rested, imagining my mother holding the book, reading from it. It was my connection to her. I had most of the poems memorized and I recited them now, pausing at the scuff of Fowler's boot on the ground, mortified that he was listening to me share words that were so personal, that spoke of longings etched so deeply in my soul. "And in your arms, I find truth . . . the burn of an unbroken light."

Amose's sawing breaths grew more labored and spaced apart until he took a last shuddering drink of air. He went utterly still.

Silence pressed down, a palpable weight on my shoulders as I bowed over him. There was only the noise of whirring insects circling his lifeless body.

I held his rough hand even as the warmth started to slip away from him.

Fowler approached behind me, his right heel hitting the ground a little harder than his left in his trademark tread. "Come on, Luna."

"This doesn't even affect you. Does it?" My lips felt numb as I spoke. And yet my body didn't feel numb. All of me ached as raw and exposed as an open wound. I felt too much. That's what Fowler was probably thinking. He thought me soft and weak and fragile. He didn't need to say the words for me to know.

"You get accustomed to it."

"I suppose that's true." Out here, how could anything else be? He had seen more death than me. Except I didn't want this to be my normal. I shook my head. "But I don't want that. I don't want to be like you." I turned and lifted my face in his direction, my voice cracking in supplication, as though he could somehow stop this from happening to me.

His fingers closed around my arm, his touch solid and impersonal as he helped me to my feet. "I don't want to be like me either." There was a hard edge to his voice that made something inside me wither away with the realization that this world could bend and twist people into things even they didn't want to become. That perhaps I was destined to change whether I wished it or not.

He led me from the hut. I inhaled the musky air as soon as we cleared the threshold, the coppery-sweet odor of death less strong. There was that at least.

"Thank you for letting me stay with him until the end," I said, deciding some acknowledgment needed to be given. "I know you didn't want to. Perhaps you're not as hard as you think—"

"You better hope that's not true. For both our sakes. I can't afford to be soft. Stop asking it of me." He strode away, his purposeful strides biting into the soft ground.

I sucked in a cold breath and followed after him. "He didn't deserve to die alone."

"We all die alone, Luna."

It was a bleak thought that chased me as we continued on our way.

TWENTY

Fowler

WE WALKED FOR hours, staying close to the edge of the copse until we had to break out across barren landscape again. Wind buffeted us, cutting like knives on our exposed skin. I dug in my pack and gave her a scarf to wrap around her neck and cover her chin.

Finally, in the far distance a grove of trees appeared. Twisted, ghostly shapes, they stood in perfect symmetry. A long-ago orchard, the branches cracked like old bones, stripped of leaves and whatever fruit used to grow there. I led us in that direction, eager to leave behind the overexposed grassland and give us some relief from the bitter wind.

Once we stepped inside the orchard's maze, I could see it was vast with rows and rows of trees.

As we moved down one intersecting path, the trees arching overhead, she asked, "What is this place? The trees grow very precisely every few feet without fail." She inched toward one of the blackened trunks, pressing her palm against the tough skin, testing its texture.

"They were planted that way. It's an orchard." I flicked my gaze over one gnarled-up tree that I passed. "Was an orchard."

She hurried to catch up. "What kind of—"

"It's impossible to identify anymore. They're dead."

She held silent after that. Now that our steps fell quieter, I moved at a faster pace, on direct course for Ortley.

There were places like Ortley that had managed to cling to life. I'd passed through a few of them since I left Relhok City. Those pockets of civilization were like that dead field of sugarcane behind us, rotting, withered echoes of the past, still fighting for their last breath even after all these years. Disease, famine, or dwellers still infiltrated, but the inhabitants managed to hang on, growing smaller and weaker after every invasion.

Not Allu though. Miles off the coastline, the island was free of dwellers and close enough to reach by boat. Its surrounding waters yielded plenty of bounty to eat. I just had to cross a continent to reach it. And I had to do it with her.

I glanced back again to catch her wringing out the edge of her tunic. Water dripped free. When she released the fabric, it unfurled, wrinkled beyond repair.

I scanned the horizon and faced forward again, thinking of our destination. Ortley was one of the only cities east of Relhok still standing. I'd heard of it all my life.

The village was reportedly fortified. Much like Relhok City, there was a population that had managed to survive the dwellers better than most. On occasion, merchants from Relhok traveled there to trade. Of the countless men the king sent over the years, a few returned. A type of kelp grew in the lake outside the once prosperous city. It contained healing properties useful when brewed. It could also be cooked into a soup, which was always convenient when you were on the brink of starvation.

I walked steadily down one of the several paths that crisscrossed the orchard. That kelp, along with other supplies, would be useful to acquire for the rest of our journey.

Food mattered. Weapons. Labor and skills. Those were things to trade. I could offer my services and work for a few days. It wouldn't be the first time. It was a long journey to Allu. A few days' sweating for some supplies would be worthwhile.

I glanced back at Luna, uncertain whether she would agree with my plan. If I worked, I would have to find something to do with her during that time. I was sure suitable work could be found for her, too. She had her uses. Like saving my life. And her hearing was better than my own.

She stopped, her head tilting, chin lifting in that way of hers that signaled she heard something even now.

I moved to her side and stopped.

A nearby bird trilled in the distance, so I didn't think any dwellers were close. They always fell silent when those creatures were wandering in the vicinity.

I touched her elbow. "What?" I released the word into her ear, a mere sigh. A gust of breath that I knew she could hear.

"It's not dwellers," she murmured, precisely what I already knew. Her smooth brow creased as though she was trying to make sense of the sound, a reminder that her experiences were limited.

She lowered her face, her expression scrunching up in frustration. She pressed fingertips to her forehead. "Something else is out there." Her nostrils flared. "Rotten and sour. Like death." The faintest tremor shook her voice as she said this.

I studied her pale face, the slim slope of her nose and rounded cheeks so smooth and unblemished, free from exposure to the elements.

Then I heard it.

Footsteps. I whirled in a swift circle, one hand going to her hip, keeping her behind me as I moved. I slipped my bow down from my shoulder and into position and grabbed an arrow from the quiver at my back, nocking it into place.

My ears strained, picking out one . . . two people. And they were definitely people. Their tread was nothing like the shuffling drag of dwellers. They moved with quick purpose.

My shoulders tensed as I held myself rigid. Luna's breath fell swiftly behind me, but I didn't look at her again. My gaze skipped over our surroundings, aiming my arrow at empty air, waiting for them to show themselves.

Then all at once, the sound stopped. They stopped.

They were out there. I knew it with every fiber of my being. The blood rushed in my ears. I continued to rotate, half expecting them to jump out in front of me.

"They're here," she whispered hoarsely the moment before they emerged, materializing in the distant dark.

They stepped out from behind a row of trees onto the path, limned in moonlight, almost like her voice had summoned them.

Awash in the moon's glow, they looked like a pair of corpses and not men at all. They moved with the eerie grace of animals, walking like they belonged to the night, comfortable in their skin and in the moon-soaked air.

They turned to face us, and we all froze for a moment of awareness, staring at one another across the distance.

As though a spark had been lit, they moved again, advancing in our direction. I held still as they approached, bracing myself for the confrontation. There was no sense in running. Not with Luna in tow. I didn't want them at our backs where I couldn't see them either.

As they came closer, I was able to pick out details and features. They were tall and thin, rangy as wolves with clothes that might have fit them once but now hung loosely. Their ragged shirts hung off the knobs of their shoulders like loose curtains.

I trained my arrow on the one walking lead. His cheeks were sunken, the bones of his face like blades under the skin, and that only made his eyes appear bigger, so dark they looked whiteless.

"Hello, there." His voice was a hoarse scratch. "Just the two of you?" Those soulless eyes flicked over my shoulder to Luna. He craned his neck, lifting up off his heels a bit to get a look at her.

I stepped a little to the side, attempting to block her from view.

He settled back down on his feet and leveled his gaze on me. "Haven't seen another person for days."

"Likewise," I responded, my voice flat, arrow still aimed at him.

"That rainstorm was a bit of good fortune. Not that I enjoy getting soaked to the bone, but at least we didn't have to worry 'bout those dwellers none. They never much prefer hunting in the rain." He cocked his head at my prolonged silence. "Rain's gone. Dwellers should start hunting again soon."

"Say something I don't know."

He frowned. "Are you going to shoot me with that, boy?"

"I don't know you." I lifted one shoulder in half a shrug. "Good enough reason to shoot someone."

The strangers exchanged glances. The leader laughed lightly. "A little standoffish. I understand that. Can't be too careful."

My adrenaline pumped. I'd been in dangerous situations before, but Luna being here changed things. My blood had never rushed through my veins so fiercely when it was just me alone.

He nodded to his friend. "We understand your hesitation." His liquid-dark eyes flicked over my shoulder, trying to get to

Luna. "Especially with a girl traveling with you."

My stomach dipped. He didn't even disguise his interest in her.

His raspy voice continued. "Gunner here knows these parts. Grew up as a boy nearby. Isn't that right?" He flicked his gaze to his companion and back to me.

Gunner nodded and spit a dark string of saliva out the side of his mouth. "Don't know if you're familiar with this part of the country, but there's an old monastery not far from here. It fell years ago. It's abandoned now." He pointed beyond us into the dark. "Just over those hills."

I didn't dare take my eyes off the two of them to follow the direction of his finger. Luna hardly even breathed behind me. If it wasn't for the light pressure of her hand on the small of my back, I would have wondered if she was still even there.

"We were going to push on to the monastery, hole up there to dry out. I'm certain the girl would like to get warm and dry. What do you think? Want to join us? We're better in numbers, I always say."

I never subscribed to that bit of philosophy. Greater numbers drew attention.

He smiled, pulling his narrow, sharp-angled face tighter, revealing a mouthful of rotting, mangled teeth. It was more of a grimace than a smile. I had no doubt that he was insincere. The moment I presented my back he'd stick a blade in it.

Gunner followed suit and grinned, too, rubbing at a dark bit of spit staining his chin. "You should join us. The walls are thick and the ground is stone lined. No dwellers there."

I resisted asking why this place wasn't occupied if it was such a haven. There was no sense in engaging. We wouldn't be joining them.

My attention returned to the leader. We held each other's gaze for a long moment, silently measuring, before I answered. "We're fine just the two of us."

He looked beyond me again, narrowing in on Luna with such intent focus, I knew that we needed to get away from these two quickly. At least I hoped it was only two of them. I scanned the surrounding trees quickly before looking back at them again, already knowing what needed to be done.

"It's only us," the leader offered, clearly reading me and trying to offer reassurance.

Luna's slight hand shifted against the small of my back and that simple touch sent a bolt of determination through me. I would get us out of this.

"Fowler," Luna whispered.

I winced at the faint sound of her voice, angry suddenly that she was here and at such risk. I almost hated Sivo right then for placing her here with me even though I knew she wouldn't have been safe with him either.

I pulled my arrow back tighter, stretching the string, letting them know I wouldn't hesitate to let go. "We're fine on our own. We like it that way."

The leader's dark eyes seemed to glow at my words. "I can see that you're fine." His gaze flitted back to me. "Perhaps we want to be fine, too, eh? Have a little bit of what you have."

Luna's breath caught behind me.

At last, he was revealing his true nature. "I'm not the sharing kind."

Gunner laughed lightly, his hand moving to the satchel that bulged out from his hip. "We men need to stand together out here, friend. We're not your enemy."

"I'm not your friend," I snarled.

Words didn't need to pass for them to convey their intent. The dwellers weren't the only monsters out there. There were two in front of me.

Finally the two men looked from me and exchanged a long glance. "Perhaps you're not aware of what you have there."

"Oh?" My lip curled up over my teeth. "What's that?"

Gunner frowned and looked at his companion, giving him a swift shake of his head. "Anselm," he said in a voice low with warning, his long, bone-thin fingers flexing over that bulging satchel as though it were his most prized possession.

Anselm held up a hand palm out toward his friend in an agitated gesture that was meant to silence him.

I smiled thinly. He thought he could handle me.

"You haven't heard the decree," Anselm added, baiting me. "You're sitting on a gold mine and don't even know it."

I took the bait. "What are you talking about?"

Another meaningful glance passed between the men, and then Anselm sighed, as though relenting. "The king of Relhok has commanded the death of every girl between the ages of fifteen and twenty." He tried to peer over my shoulder again. "I'd say she's in that range." He shrugged. "If there's any doubt of age, it's been advised to take no chances."

I felt Luna shudder behind me.

My mind raced, trying to understand the motive behind a decree for the annihilation of a certain group. Young females, no less. It made no sense. The king was maniacal, but he didn't want to end mankind. Enough of our population had been lost to dwellers, disease, and starvation. An occasional innocent slaughtered as a sacrifice was one thing, but this was something else entirely.

"Why?" The word was more of a thought that materialized than an actual question I was putting to Anselm or Gunner.

It's not as though I expected these assassins in front of me to have any insight into the king of Relhok's inner thoughts, but I was reeling. Understanding slowly sank in, like the teeth of an animal latching onto sinew and muscle. This was why Dagne was cut down. I understood now why they had killed her and left Sivo, Perla, and Madoc alive. They were acting on orders.

"He's a mad king, listening to that crazed Oracle." Anselm shrugged and took a step forward. "Does it really matter why?"

I matched him a step, pushing Luna back, too. "Why do it? What's in it for you?" It was a lot of trouble killing girls.

"Every head gets you a month's rations." Anselm shrugged. "Sorry, friend. Who wouldn't take an offer like that?"

Luna made a choking sound behind me.

Gunner patted the fat satchel at his side then. "And we

intend to eat well for quite some time."

A surge of bile rose up in my throat. From the size of the bulging satchel, I knew there had to be at least two heads in there. That must have been the odor Luna picked up. My nape prickled, panic scraping down my spine. If she could smell them, then the dwellers could, too. My gaze darted around, searching for a glimpse of them in the endless dark. They couldn't be far.

"You're not taking her head," I growled.

Luna whimpered behind me, her fingers pressing deeper into my back.

"Now, boy. Don't get in the way. I'm not a man that relishes killing, but Gunner here won't hesitate to cut you down. We'll do what we have to."

I let my arrow fly just as Gunner went for his dagger, sliding it from his sheath and brandishing it in the air. He didn't have time to launch it before the arrow stabbed him directly between the eyes with a thunk. He dropped like a stone.

Anselm launched himself at me before I was able to shoot again.

I fell with his weight atop me, all sharp angles and bones digging into me as he pulled back his arm and sent his knuckles crashing into my face.

Hot blood spurted from my nose and trickled into my mouth. Luna cried out and scrambled on the ground somewhere above my head.

I jabbed him in the eyes with my thumbs, grinding deep and pushing him off me. He fell back with a cry, groping for his knife at his side. I went for my own blade, pulling it free.

I dodged the swipe of his knife and rolled. He came at me again. I hopped up, knees bent. Great breaths lifted our chests. We scanned each other, our surroundings, realizing almost in the same moment that he stood closer to Luna.

She trembled, hands knotted into fists at her sides as she stared in our direction, her head cocking to the side, listening for our movements.

Anselm's chest lifted, his breath hitching. He flipped his knife over in his grip, readjusting it to plunge overhead.

We dove for her simultaneously, but she sensed us coming and turned, sprinting into the orchard. I tackled him, slamming into his back. I lifted my blade and stabbed through his jacket into flesh and muscle.

He howled and turned, kicking me in the face. I fell back.

The eerie cry of a dweller ripped the air. Several more cries went up. They would be on us soon.

"They're coming," I gasped, facing him again.

Anselm's wild, whiteless eyes fixed on my face. He smiled a crazy, mangled-toothed grin. "I always knew I'd die at the hands of a dweller."

"It's to be today then?"

He hesitated, his gaze turning in the direction Luna fled. He glanced quickly at the sky, and I could see he was calculating how long we had.

"Midlight is still a few hours away," I taunted.

Another cry fractured the air, closer this time. I turned

and spotted the shadowy shape of a creature coming down the moonlit path between trees. I could see the receptors at its face writhing like serpents. The dweller lumbered toward us, its head titling sideways to call out an alert to others. Another dark dweller materialized at the end of an opposite path.

"So what's it to be?" I asked, my voice detached. Urgency pumped through me to go after Luna, but I couldn't move until I knew he wasn't going to pursue her.

He snorted, and rolled one shoulder, wincing from where I had stabbed him in the back. "She's likely already dead out there." He lowered his blade. "They won't leave anything of her to take back. Should have given her to me. It would have been a far kinder death." He stuck the knife in his sheath and squatted at his dead friend, his stare never straying from me as he lifted his satchel of heads and looped the strap around his shoulder. He made quick work of taking his weapons, too. Finished, he flung Gunner's body back down and straightened.

Our gazes held. We didn't look away. It was as though we were indifferent to the advancing dweller, now only twenty yards away.

"Better hope we don't meet again." With that threat, Anselm turned and jogged down an empty path with his bag of heads bumping at his side.

I took off in the direction Luna disappeared, scanning for a glimpse of her between every row of trees.

The cries of dwellers overlapped now, a cacophony of shrill, eerie calls. Blood was in the air and they were hungry for it.

There weren't any human screams amid the din, so I knew the only thing they had found to eat so far was Gunner. Yet they wouldn't stop there. They knew we were close.

I wiped the blood trickling down from my nose and then stopped to rub my hands in the dirt, getting rid of the scent. Rising, I kept moving.

I scanned the ground and the trees, conflicted whether I should call out for her or not. She had impeccable hearing. She would hear me, but so would they.

She could still be running, panicked and terrified. Although the image of her panicked and terrified didn't ring true. She was always coolheaded. She was probably hiding.

I rotated, my gaze sweeping the trees. The orchard was too big. She could be anywhere in here.

"Luna," I called, straining for a sound. I moved swiftly, my bow at the ready.

"Fowler!"

I froze at the hushed call. I looked around, up, and spotted her in a tree, her pale face a smudge amid the dark tangle of branches. The air left me in a rush of relief.

Sliding my bow back on my shoulder, I grabbed hold of the trunk and scaled its width, grabbing one low-hanging branch with both hands. I dangled a moment from the branch, swinging my legs and gaining momentum until I managed to get my boots up and over the sturdy branch where Luna was crouched.

She stretched a hand for me and I took it, scooting up alongside her. Right now, the feel of her slim hand in mine felt right.

It fortified me. A few moments ago, men had wanted her head in a bag. My chest clenched tight, almost hurting. In this moment, touching her did not bother me in the least.

"Fowler." My name shuddered out from her, and I realized she had thought she might not find me again. Perhaps she even thought me dead and herself on her own out here. The idea of her all alone sickened me almost as much as that man taking her head. Either one would be the end of her.

"Thought you lost me, did you?" I said, trying to lighten the mood.

A weak laugh escaped her. She quickly killed the sound as a dweller approached, shuffling below us. The feelers at its mouth wiggled, sensing its prey—us.

I'd seen several dwellers up close before. The receptors at the center of their faces varied in number and length. I'd seen one with as few as five and other dwellers with a whole nest of them a foot long, working in a frenzy like an army of writhing antennae.

I'd theorized that it had something to do with their age. Or perhaps it was related to their strength and stamina as hunters.

This one appeared average. No more than a dozen tentacle-like receptors worked on the air as it paused below our tree.

We fell silent, every muscle locked tight. I held my breath. I'd never known a dweller to climb a tree, but there was a first time for everything. After a moment, I realized I clutched Luna's hand. I was holding her fingers so tightly the blood had probably ceased to flow. I eased my grip, but she seized my hand, not letting me release her.

She shook her head, staring in my direction. A long dark strand of hair had come loose of her plait and dangled in her face. I brushed it back from her cheek, tucking it behind her ear.

We listened to the dweller as it moved, turning down another row of trees. Once it was far enough away that I couldn't see it anymore against the dark, I shifted my weight and settled back against the trunk, sliding my hand up her arm and pulling her close. Luna came willingly, curling herself into my body as eagerly and trusting as a child. My heart squeezed.

"Why?" she whispered. "Why do they want to kill girls?"

I scanned the ground below, assuring myself that no dwellers were in sight. "The king," I corrected. "The king wants to kill girls. And I don't know why."

"At least we know why they killed Dagne now."

I nodded, my thumb moving in slow circles on the back of her hand.

"What am I going to do?" The question made her sound so alone, so lost and without anyone.

"We know now," I said.

She nodded, but I could still tell she was troubled.

I tugged lightly at the end of her plait. "These will have to go."

She lifted her chin, her eyebrows drawing together. "What?"

"You're already garbed as a boy in trousers. Let's make the transformation complete."

"You want to turn me into a boy?" Her expression eased. "Ah. Yes, of course."

"I'm not sure it will work. I'm certain you're not the only girl in this kingdom undergoing a gender change. People will be on the lookout for pretty boys, but from a distance you should pass."

"Then you shall have to make me not pretty."

"Easier said than done." The moment the words escaped, I wished to have them back. Her head lifted, reminding me of an animal catching a new, alien scent.

"You think I'm pretty?" Hope rang in her voice.

"Fair enough," I conceded. "I've seen worse."

"Oh." She exhaled, sounding faintly indignant. Even in the gloom, I could make out the heat creeping over her cheeks, the scarlet flush moving like an incoming storm on her pale cheeks. "I imagine you have a great deal of comparison. Growing up in the capital, there must have been a good many girls, far finer of face than I am." She motioned into the night. "More than you might find roaming out here, I am certain."

"Luna," I broke in, but she didn't stop. Her whispered voice grew feverish and fast.

"No, no, I must have sounded pathetic, fishing for a compliment. The girl stuck in a tower all her life, starved for a bit of male attention."

"Luna, enough."

She stopped, her lips pressing into a stubborn line. An awkward pause rolled between us. Her head suddenly turned down, realizing she still clung to my hand. She let go and tucked her hand between her folded thigh and calf.

I looked out at the orchard and then back to her, sighing. "I wasn't exactly being truthful. You're passing fair."

"You needn't say that to make me feel better. I'm blind. What do my looks matter to me?" She snorted. "Why do anyone's looks matter?"

"I'm not lying. Not now—I simply didn't want to admit—" I stopped and stared out into the sea of trees again, their black shapes etched on a slightly less black horizon. Frustration bubbled up in my chest. This was precisely what I had hoped to avoid.

"Admit what?"

A gust of breath spilled from my lips. She was right. There had been girls, women, back home. Most days it felt almost normal. People in the cobbled streets. A bustling market with tradesmen hawking their wares in the square. The swish of skirts as daughters and mothers passed me on the street on the way to the temple, hoping for a glimpse of, a word from, the Oracle. Sometimes there would be laughter draped over the odor of hope and desperation. Laughter as though all was well. You could almost pretend things were normal—except for the unrelenting night and monsters outside the city's walls.

"I admit," I began, the words strangling me, "that I find you appealing."

She stared at me with that impossibly penetrating gaze. It was probing and unnerving.

"You find me appealing?" Her brow knitted as though she was attempting to translate my words.

"Appealing. Attractive. You're pretty." I released a small, breathless laugh. "And you're not a terrible travel companion either."

Her smile was instantaneous then, blindingly bright, her teeth as white as the moon overhead. You'd think I'd given her the greatest gift, which only made me feel like a wretch because I'd given her so little.

"In the spirit of confession," she said, a smile still playing about her mouth, "I'll admit that I share the sentiment."

I laughed briefly until I managed to catch the sound and stifle it. I was quiet for a moment, basking in the strangeness of sitting in a tree side by side with a girl I had not known very long. She had been thrust upon me against my every wish, but here we were like two friends. Friends. I closed my eyes in one pained blink. There was the reality and there was nothing I could do about it now.

"Indeed? So I'm not a terrible travel companion?" I teased, noting the far-off figure of a dark dweller zigzagging between trees, his body a pale outline against the darker night. I paused, watching the creature fade deeper into the orchard. I looked back down at her. "Or is it that you find me pretty?"

"No, well, y-yes," she stammered. "When you talk, your voice is attractive. Which isn't often, mind you."

"So you like the way I talk?" I nodded, enjoying her discomfort. "What else?"

"Your arms and chest . . . the way you smell." She leaned in suddenly, closer to my face, inhaling me. I stilled as the cold tip of her nose brushed my throat.

Sensation zipped down to settle at the base of my spine in a way I had not felt in years. Not since . . .

It all came back to me in a rush. Flirting with Bethan outside her father's stall on market days until finally, one day when he was distracted haggling with an old woman over the price of bread, I pulled her into a nearby alley between stalls. I caressed her cheek in the stale darkness. And I kissed her.

I'd forgotten how it felt. The way the back of my skull pulled tight all the way down to my toes. That utter awareness of another person on a physical level. The want. The need. Desire.

Apparently, I wasn't totally numb, after all.

Luna lifted a hand and inched it toward my face. Even though I saw it coming, I flinched and backed away, knowing, fearing somehow, that the moment she touched me it would be all over. There would be no more ignoring her.

She hesitated, her palm face out. She couldn't see me, but she felt my withdrawal. "May I?"

"Yes," I replied, my voice coming out strained. Touching me was her way of seeing me, and I wouldn't stop her.

She resumed moving that hand toward me until her palm was flush with my cheek. A ragged breath escaped me, but I still made no move, knowing she had to do this.

An airy, light sound escaped her that resembled laughter.

"Are you laughing?" I rasped, every bit of me coiled and ready to snap into motion.

"A little. You're grinding your teeth."

I unclenched my jaw. Her palm shifted on my face. She slid a fingertip over my bottom lip. The gentle touch on my lips fired me. It made me think of her lips and mine and the things they could do other than talk.

I sucked in a deep breath and shifted uncomfortably on the branch.

Her hand lifted slightly from my face. "Is this fine with you?" she whispered.

I nodded and breathed against her fingers as they landed on my mouth again, tracing the shape, her touch both soft and clinical like a physician examining me, although I'd never felt this way before when I had been poked and prodded as a boy. No, I felt afire, overly warm in the perpetual chill.

"Finished?" I asked in a choking voice when I knew she had fully explored my lips. What more could she do without killing me?

She lifted her fingers. "Quite. Thank you." She sighed and settled back against me.

I waited, feeling her gradually relax. Her body softened into mine and I clenched my jaw, willing myself to relax, too— as impossible as that seemed. My pulse hammered at my neck. Every time I breathed, I caught her scent.

"Fowler, I don't care what you say. You're my friend."

I inhaled. "I know."

A glance down showed her lips curving. Her breathing gradually slowed. Her body melted into mine, so trusting. If she wasn't asleep she was on the verge of it.

Sleep wouldn't come for me. I knew this. Not with Luna curled against me and her words playing over and over in my mind. *I don't care what you say. You're my friend.* Not with the memory of those men and their bag of heads.

I thought of all this for long hours, staring into the trees.

TWENTY-ONE

Luna

AT MIDLIGHT, WE dropped down from the tree. I stretched, hands reaching for the sky, trying to work out the kinks in my body from sleeping the last few hours pressed up against Fowler in a tree.

"Did you sleep at all?" I asked in concern when I heard him yawn.

"Never could sleep in a tree. Always afraid I would fall out."

I had slept well, but something told me that was because Fowler had been holding me.

He'd been kind, talking to me and letting me touch him. I almost believed he didn't hate having me with him, after all.

When I had gone so far as to tell him that he was my friend, he didn't even deny it.

Ducking my head to hide the small smile curving my lips, I started to move down the orchard path. I didn't get very far before he stopped me with a hand on my shoulder.

"Hold a moment." Fowler turned me so that my back was to him.

"What are you doing?"

"We need to take care of something first. They're looking for girls, remember? We're going to fool people into thinking you're something else."

I had almost forgotten. There was a bounty on my head in Relhok. Bile rose up in my throat.

He gathered my hair in his hand. "This has to go."

I shouldn't have felt a stab of regret, but I did. Countless hours of my life had been spent with Perla arranging my hair. Perla, almost exclusively, had arranged my mother's hair, creating elaborate coiffures. Perla said my hair was like my mother's. Dark with buried hints of mahogany. It had mattered to her, so it mattered to me.

I turned around, closing a hand on one of the plaited ropes that hung over my shoulder almost protectively.

"Come now, Luna. Nothing says 'girl' more than long plaits of hair."

I thumbed the curling tip that hung practically to my waist.

He sighed. "Shorn hair trumps losing your head. You're already garbed in trousers. This is one simple thing we can do to give you an advantage."

I nodded, releasing my hair. "Of course." To protest was vain and foolish. Still, as I presented my back to him a lump formed in my throat, thinking how horrified Perla would be. He gathered my hair up in one hand. There was pressure as his knife sawed through one plait and then the next.

The twin hunks of hair hit the ground like dead limbs. My head instantly felt lighter with my hair only reaching the top of my collar.

His strong fingers ran through my hair, loosening it around my head.

Cool air fluttered over the back of my neck. He sawed at a few random strands, working to create a semblance of evenness. "There," he announced. "Not bad. How's it feel?"

I moved my head side to side, testing the unusual lightness. A few strands brushed my ears.

"Do I look like a boy?"

He was quiet for a moment and I could feel his stare on my face. I lifted my chin, waiting.

"Maybe if they're squinting."

I let out a rough laugh. "Tell me we didn't cut my hair for nothing?"

"Well, it's dark, right?" He fumbled in his bag. "I think I have a hat in here. Yes. There we go."

He plopped it down on my head, tucking a few bits of hair back from my ear. "There. Better."

I smiled. Better. The word sank through me until the whole

motive for cutting my hair asserted itself, and then nothing felt better.

"Why would they want to kill girls my age?" I had my suspicions that Cullan knew I was alive . . . that he was hunting me, but I couldn't help hoping I was wrong. Eradicating an entire group of people, especially young girls, future mothers, seemed extreme just to get to me. Was he seeking extinction for mankind? What threat could he perceive in me? I was hoping Fowler could give me another explanation.

Fowler expelled a breath and started walking. I fell in beside him. He finally answered, proving, at least, that he wasn't going to go back to ignoring me.

"When I was a boy still wishing for better things, I would sometimes get caught up in wondering things like why. Not anymore." He took a deep breath. "Over a year ago I heard screaming and I followed it." He laughed once, a hard, broken sound. "Thought maybe I could help. And you know what I found?"

I shook my head.

"I found a father shoving his own son at a group of dwellers so that he could get away. The boy kept calling for him. . . ."

I stumbled, horrified at such a scenario. My chest ached, unable to imagine what he was describing.

He continued, "So I don't ask why anymore. Not after everything I've seen. Things are just the way they are, Luna."

But sometimes there was a reason. Sometimes even evil had a motive. Grim acceptance swept over me like a chill wind. The king was looking for me. He knew I was alive. Somehow he knew.

Perhaps someone had seen Sivo and Perla flee all those years ago and had come forth now. I didn't know how, but he knew. It was the only thing that made sense.

"What is it?" Fowler asked. "You're shaking."

"Nothing." I shook my head and started walking, my pace faster.

He fell in beside me. "Did my story upset you?"

"No," I said quickly. "I mean . . . yes." It did upset me, but it wasn't the reason I suddenly felt scared and hunted. I tugged at my cap, hoping it was a good enough disguise to get me through to Allu.

"I just want you to understand what it's like out here."

I knew more than he realized. "You don't ever wish for better things for yourself?"

"It's pointless. So few of us can hold on to anything really good in this world."

"That's dismal," I grumbled, for some reason thinking about our almost-kiss. That had felt good to me. "I don't want to think like that. I want to believe that things can be better." I had to believe that or what was the point? I might as well turn myself over to Cullan.

"Of course you do. You're the kind of girl who gives our precious water to a person about to die."

"Allu is hope for you, isn't it?"

"I suppose. It should be better than all this. A place without dwellers, but it's still a place without light. Still dark. You can't outrun that."

The corners of my mouth lifted. "The dark isn't so bad. It's just the monsters that hide inside it."

"Sorry," he muttered. "It's easy to forget sometimes that you can't see."

"Don't apologize. My lack of sight is my advantage. I sense more, hear more, taste more. Perhaps I feel more, too. I don't know." I shrugged. "I suppose that's impossible to know. I don't know what you're feeling, after all."

"Maybe you do feel more than me," he allowed. "I'm sure you're more capable in that area than I am."

My steps faltered as he continued on ahead. I opened my mouth, wanting to tell him that I didn't believe that of him. Not anymore.

His actions spoke loud enough for me. Everything he had done for me since we first met proved that he was someone who felt deeply. He wouldn't risk himself again and again, if he felt nothing.

I said none of this. Instead, I held silent and followed in his wake.

TWENTY-TWO

Fowler

THE NEXT FEW days passed uneventfully. The closer we approached Ortley, the denser the forest grew. Thick trees crowded around us, each one so large it looked like it belonged in a land of giants. It would take several men, arms stretched wide, to circle the width of these trees. They were tall, too, stretching up into the night-dark sky, branches tangling together and pushing out what little light crept down from the moon.

Every once in a while, we roamed slightly off course until I caught a glimpse of the moon in the sky and marked its position, steering us back in the right direction.

The terrain deepened the risk. There was no sighting of dwellers across the distance in this massive crush of trees. We strictly relied on hearing. Which meant I relied on Luna a great deal more. If a dweller came too close, I would dispatch it. Fortunately we were never surprised by more than one at a time.

I stole a glance at her. Her expression was peaceful. She moved her head as though looking around her, as though she could appreciate the wonder of these magical woods.

We whispered often, sharing bits of ourselves. I didn't fight it anymore. I answered her questions. It was easier letting myself get distracted with conversation than thinking about Anselm and Gunner and their bag of heads.

And yet thoughts of them intruded. As well as the idea of arriving at Ortley and what could happen to Luna. The possibilities settled like rocks in my stomach. There would be men like Anselm and Gunner there. There were always men like them. If they even caught a whiff that she was a girl they'd kill her. There would be other unsavory types, as well, that called themselves humans. If they realized Luna was blind—whether they knew she was a girl or not—they'd mark her as an easy target.

I was already debating hiding her in the woods and going into the village by myself. There would be too many people there. The risk of her gender being uncovered was too high. If I could bypass Ortley I would, but there wouldn't be another outpost for a long time. We needed to stop. I'd gather new supplies, including the much-lauded kelp.

"I smell water," Luna murmured, pulling me from my

thoughts. She walked at my side. Since the orchard, she stayed close.

I glanced up at the moon through a crack in the labyrinth of branches and the sight served as confirmation.

"That would be the lake outside Ortley. We're close." I halted her with a hand on her arm and released a heavy breath, rubbing at the back of my neck.

She lifted her face up to me. I knew she wasn't going to like what I was about to say. "Perhaps I should go into the village on my own."

She looked stricken for a moment, and then her expression cleared into a neutral mask. "You're leaving me out here?"

"We'll find someplace safe for you to hole up—"

"Are you coming back?"

I stared at her, stunned. "You still think I would leave you?"

"You never wanted me along."

"I'm not abandoning you," I replied quickly.

She wrapped her arms around herself, hugging her body. "I'm sorry. I know that—I just don't want to stay out here alone."

Almost in response, a dweller cried in the far-off distance. The sound was common enough and far enough away that it hardly even made me flinch.

"Luna, there will be soldiers there. To say nothing of mercenaries . . . desperate people who would do anything for a month's ration. If anyone realizes you're—"

"I'm going with you." That stubborn chin of hers went up.

"Luna—"

"It's dangerous everywhere." She held her arms out wide at her sides. "What makes you think nothing will happen to me out here?" She stepped closer and seized my hand, clasping it in both of hers. I stared down at our hands, her pale, small fingers wrapped around my bigger ones. "We need to stay together, Fowler. Don't you see that? After last time . . ." She gave my hands a squeeze. "We're stronger together."

I gazed into her earnest face and felt my resolve crumble. "Come on then."

She started to pull her hands from mine, but I tightened my grip around one of them and held fast. Without looking at her face again, I turned and led the way, weaving back through the woods, straining my eyes for the first glimpse of civilization in the thick press of giant trees.

They spotted us first. A soft swishing whispered on the air. I looked up. A silhouette swung across the night, vaulting from one tree to the next like some sort of tree monkey. I instantly dropped her hand.

"Something is above us," she pointed out.

"Smart," I murmured, watching the body deftly maneuver between trees. "It's a man. He's swinging from tree to tree." Aside from branches, various pegs and boards of wood stuck out from the trees, giving him plenty of places to land—a well-arranged system for spying on anyone or anything on the ground.

"A man?" she echoed.

"A watch, I'm guessing. Come on. Let's follow." If he's tasked to report interlopers, then he'd be heading back to the village now.

I lost sight of the figure as we moved deeper into the woods, and, according to Luna, closer to the smell of water. The watch was gone, but the forest felt like it had its own eyes now. Our progress was being monitored.

"Remember, you're no longer a girl," I whispered, assuming we weren't going to be alone much longer.

We were moving uphill now. Her pace slowed. Our breaths fell a little faster and I had to resist reclaiming her hand. If we were still being watched, holding her hand might not help convince them that she was a boy.

"Fowler," she gasped. "I can smell . . . dwellers."

"We're close," I called back. The gold light bleeding onto the dark horizon told me there was something just beyond the rise.

I could almost imagine the village ahead, a smaller version of Relhok City, the great walls protecting its citizens. The lookouts on the battlements would see us and lift the gate so we could take shelter within. I saw this all in my mind's eye.

Eager, I pressed on, reaching the top of the hill. A large platform appeared in the sky, built into the tops of the trees. "Whoa," I breathed, gazing up in awe. So this was how they survived. "They live in the trees."

Never, since I left the capital, had I seen anything like it. It was a vast village. A true city in the trees. I gazed at the underbellies of buildings and paths constructed around the elaborate network of trunks and branches.

There were a few big houses and buildings, but most were small, no more than shacks similar to the lean-tos that had been erected on the outer edges of Relhok City. A jumble of shanties that didn't look fit to sleep a dog. It was the kind of place Bethan had lived in. Her image rose in my mind, her face an elusive smudge of features. I remembered her eyes had been blue, but knowing and remembering were two different things. I couldn't see them in my head. Not her blue eyes. Not her face.

Brown-black eyes set within a pale face swam in my mind. When I closed my eyes at night, it was Luna's face I was coming to see.

I shook off the distracting thought and continued to assess the mad jumble high above, looking for a way up. All the structures were interconnected with paths of wood planks. Light spilled from the buildings and out the cracks between the planks.

Luna choked my name again as she stopped beside me. "Dwellers," she hissed.

I jerked my gaze back down and spotted them. They were everywhere, like hungry ants swarming beneath the trees on the forest floor, hoping for a crumb to fall.

We just had to wade through the minefield of them. And not die in the process.

"Come, hurry!" I dragged her by the hand, not caring anymore if anyone spotted me. This was life-or-death. Her slight fingers were slippery with sweat and I readjusted my grip, determined not to lose her.

We wove between the colossal trees. I had to break stride when a dweller came too close. Cursing, I released her and let an arrow fly, striking the creature directly in the face. It dropped to its knees. Running forward, I kicked it onto its back. Lifting my gaze, I did a quick scan around us and reclaimed my arrow, pulling it free of the claylike body with a sucking sound. Using the same arrow, I took aim and let it fly again, clearing our path of another dweller.

We were surrounded. Their wet, sawing breaths crashed all around us. I kicked one square in the chest, launching it back, knocking two others down in the process.

We were under the city now, and I stole quick glances up, searching the trees, looking for a way up.

Luna stayed close. I felt her warm body beside mine as I dispatched dwellers, her shoulder aligned beside mine, never getting in the way of me reaching into my quiver for arrows.

Sometimes she would call out and warn me of one advancing at my back or side and I would answer the threat, launching another arrow. I might not hear anything over the dwellers' soggy breaths, but evidently she still did.

She was armed, too, holding her sword at the ready. I didn't want her to have to use it though—one drop of toxin off their receptors, and she would suffer. The fractured thought bounced through me that if I was quick with my arrow, the dwellers wouldn't have to get too close.

Until I didn't feel her beside me anymore.

"Luna," I shouted, yanking arrow after arrow from behind me, shooting advancing dwellers with swift thunks. They were closing in, falling on me in an endless pour.

"Luna!" I roared, for once not caring about remaining quiet.

It seemed like every dweller in the world was converging on us anyway.

Then suddenly it felt like another time. Another place.

I had a flash of myself struggling at the cell door of my prison, gripping the bars and screaming Bethan's name until I went hoarse, until the last dwindling rays of midlight vanished. My last glimpse of anything was my father's smiling face up on the ramparts.

"Fowler!"

I shook off the memories. Luna wielded her sword, thrusting it into the pale, soft body of a dweller.

"Luna! Get behind me!"

An indignant expression crossed her face.

"Luna," I growled. With a curse, I jumped several paces until we fought back to back. I pulled my dagger from a sheath at my waist and started stabbing into dwellers, grateful for my height. I managed to avoid the toxin dripping from the nest of receptors in their faces and stabbed them in the heads.

I was worried that Luna wouldn't be so lucky if one got too close. She was considerably shorter and didn't have the best advantage to inflict damage.

"Luna," I called over my shoulder. "We need to move!"

"How do you suggest we do that? They're everywhere!"

I looped my left arm with hers. "Follow me." With a yank, I pulled her after me, charging through and whacking a path with my sword.

I struck dwellers down, swerving around when I heard Luna

cry out. A dweller had closed both its hands on her arm and was lowering its face to her, toxin dripping from its feelers. She was stabbing it in the belly with her sword, but it didn't seem to care. It kept coming.

With a shout, I swung my sword and sent its head flying. Whirling around, I cut down several more dwellers, clearing a path for us to squeeze through. We were almost to the top of another rise now. The air glowed even brighter.

A giant crested the rise ahead of us. My battle cry withered in my throat. I didn't recognize it as a dweller at first.

It rose up out of the night, limned in the red-gold haze from the village in the sky. This one was unlike the rest. It looked like some freakish entity reaching close to seven feet. Even the toxic receptors on its face were thick as my wrists, like wiggling snakes, stretching for a victim. It approached us, its feet falling heavily on the damp earth.

I clamped a hand on her arm and backed up.

"Fowler?" she gasped, and I realized she must have heard its louder-than-usual tread and sensed its size.

I grabbed an arrow and shot the monster in the face. It paused with a shudder, but its great body kept lumbering toward us.

With a curse, I pulled another arrow out and let it fly. The second arrow pinged off the edge of its shoulder and seemed only to enrage it. It huffed and moved faster now—faster than I'd ever seen a dweller move before. Its pasty gray body was almost running at us.

"Fowler?" Fear laced Luna's voice.

I shoved her back behind me and readied my sword, my grip achingly tight. If this was the end, then I was going down first and I was going down fighting.

An arrow whistled past me to land at my feet. More followed, hissing through the air, raining down from the trees, striking the great body of the dweller. It made a gurgling sound and halted just a few yards away from me. Still, it didn't fall. Over a dozen arrows pierced the chalky flesh of its body and it still remained standing.

It began moving again, staggering toward me, the toxin dripping from receptors as thick as black syrup. A shouted command from above heralded another volley of arrows. This time, it dropped to the ground on one knee. I waited as other arrows continued to rain around us, finding targets in the other dwellers.

But the big one wasn't finished. With a wet rasp, it pushed back up to its feet and continued. I stepped forward and swung my sword, cutting its thick neck only halfway. Pulling back my arm, I swung again, this time slicing it clean and sending the head soaring. The giant finally fell, snapping the ends of dozens of arrows sticking out from its body.

I looked up, my chest heaving with labored breaths. Countless faces stared down at us from planks in the trees.

One man dropped onto a platform positioned at a lower level than the village floor. With a grinding crank, the wood platform started to descend.

"What is it?" The knowledge that we were still surrounded

by an army of dwellers was there, in the thread of anxiety in Luna's voice.

"People are coming to get us," I murmured as the lift lowered. "We're going up?"

"We are. There's a man coming down in a lift."

"A city in the trees," she repeated after me. "It's brilliant."

"Almost as good as a tower?"

"Almost." She nodded in agreement. I heard the smile in her voice.

The lift stopped inches before hitting the ground. "What are you waiting for?" The man motioned around us to the army of dwellers still closing in. "Get in. I'm not here to pick up dwellers, too."

I stepped onto the waiting lift, making room for Luna. The space wasn't very big and the three of us had to stand close.

As we ascended, I looked down, watching as dwellers of all shapes converged on the spot we stood only moments ago. Several tilted their heads up, the sensors on their grotesque faces writhing as we lifted higher and higher, climbing up into the city nestled between thick trees.

One glance up revealed we were almost to the top.

"Let me do the talking," I whispered into her ear. "Stay back behind me."

When the lift stopped, I saw that it opened to a landing. Several dozen people milled about, including the archers who had come to our aid.

They craned their necks to get a glimpse of us. Amid the

mass of people there was a decided lack of young women—proof that news of the king's decree had reached here.

The man who shared the lift with us stepped out and turned, his hand resting on the hilt of his sword. "Welcome." He was almost bald. A shadow of gray hugged his skull, the stubble of new hair growth.

I nodded, my gaze flitting from him to the men flanking him. "Thank you." I understood their caution. I would be cautious of any newcomers, too.

But that didn't mean I trusted them either.

"I'm Glagos, sheriff of Ortley. Is it just you and the boy?" His gaze dipped down to the forest floor as though we had left others below. He fingered a thick-ridged scar that bisected his cheek.

"Yes. This is my brother." I tapped my head. "Don't expect too much from him. He's a little slow."

Glagos's gaze considered Luna for a moment. A quick glance back revealed she was doing her part, looking sideways rather vacantly, her expression vague and absentminded.

"I see. Are you both looking to settle here—"

"We're just moving through. Hoping to refresh and gather more supplies. Dried kelp if you have any to—"

"We don't just pass out our reserves to every stranger. We do nothing out of the kindness of our hearts. I don't need to explain to you just how hard life is."

"No. You don't. I'm willing to work for any supplies."

"Good. That's the only way you'll get any." Glagos grinned, but there was something in that smile that made me uneasy. "We always need able-bodied men." His gaze flicked to Luna and he went back to stroking the puckered skin of his scar. "Don't expect he's much of a worker. You'll have to—"

"I can work enough for both of us. Whatever you need."

"Very good." He nodded, looking pleased. He glanced around, scanning the crowd. "Now let's see. We'll board you with—"

"Me." An old woman stepped forward, her cane thumping on the wood planks. Her back was hunched and bent. It looked painful. I was surprised she could still walk.

She smiled a mostly toothless grin, her rheumy eyes gazing me up and down before fixing on Luna. "I'll take them."

TWENTY-THREE

Luna

"HERE WE ARE," the old woman said. "I've two spare rooms. Bigger than what most people have here. It's just me now. My family's gone. I've some skills so they've allowed me this luxury."

A room to myself would be a step above sleeping in trees or buried deep in shrubs or the occasional cave. And yet not being close to Fowler anymore would be strange. I didn't know if I would feel entirely safe without his steady breath beside me.

"My name is Mirelya," the old woman added.

Fowler made a small sound that I took for agreement. "Thank you, Mirelya. We won't be here long."

I immediately evaluated my surroundings, measuring the

airflow, sensing obstructions, estimating the room's width and length. I processed it all, my measurements clicking through my mind like dominoes dropping into position. I had a fairly good sense of where the walls ended and began. My boots thudded lightly over the plank flooring. The front window was open, its leather draping flapping lightly in a breeze, letting in a gust of wind that smelled pungent, ripe with the scent of dwellers gathered below the village.

Somewhere, a few houses over, a baby cried. It was strange hearing that sound and knowing it for what it was without having ever heard it before. A baby alive amid all this made tears burn at the backs of my eyes. This place could have been my sanctuary. High in the trees, it could have been an echo of the life Perla and Sivo described to me. The kind of life my parents had lived. Free. The king's decree made that impossible, of course. Plus Fowler would never stay here. His dream was Allu.

The gentle aroma of candle wax weaved with the warm, yeasty scent of bread. I inhaled deeply, reveling in it. It smelled like home. I brushed my fingers along the back of a chair, thinking of Sivo and Perla, hoping they were well.

"I am certain you desire to leave with all haste." Mirelya laughed then, a full-bodied laugh that cracked like dry leaves underfoot and ended in a hacking cough.

I winced. "Are you well? Do you need some water?" There was a pitcher on the table, crisp water within it.

"I'm fine. Older than I have any right to be. I've buried two husbands and four children, but somehow I'm still here. If I'm lucky, my time will come soon enough."

I shifted on my feet awkwardly, uncertain how to respond to that. I hoped that if I had such a long life, my years would consist of more than a constant fight to stay alive.

I cleared my throat, thinking I should probably say something. Fowler wasn't the most talkative sort, but some manner of acknowledgment should be given to this woman for stepping forward and offering her home to us. "Well, it's very kind of you to welcome us into your—"

"Kind is right. With girls getting their heads taken these days, I expect not everyone would be as understanding to discover that you're female and not a boy at all."

I froze. Even my chest ceased to lift with breath.

Fowler stiffened beside me. The moment stretched forever. I risked movement, raising my arm as though to touch Fowler, but he stepped forward suddenly, closer to Mirelya. My hand fell back to my side, fingers curling inward, brushing my palm.

"What?" he demanded. "You think he's a . . . girl—"

"No use making a grand show of denying it. I knew the moment she walked off the lift." Her no-nonsense voice rang out. "Just as I expect it's never far from your mind either, eh? Is it?"

I frowned, not sure what she was implying. Of course Fowler was aware that I was a female.

Mirelya laughed. "Oh. Still dancing around the obvious, are we? Young people. You behave as though you have all the time in the world for matters of the heart."

Shaking my head, I grumbled, "You make no sense."

"Look at his face. He understands me well enough," she said smugly, a hum of laughter in her voice.

"Your vision must be impaired, old woman. This is my brother."

"Now you're just being insulting. Shall I step outside and gather other opinions? We can settle this entire matter by asking her to disrobe."

My heart jerked in my chest.

Fowler inhaled. It was subtle, almost imperceptible. I felt its vibration pass through me like my own breath. He was beaten and worried. Maybe even afraid for me. Fowler, who never seemed rattled by anything. This only made me more on edge.

I turned my attention back to Mirelya, the woman who held my fate. One signal, one word from her, and my head would be separated from my body. A shuddery breath passed through my lips. Perhaps it was already inevitable.

"What now?" I asked. "Will you tell?"

"Telling gets me nothing. What's one month's rations? My time here is almost over. I need little food these days."

I nodded, feeling only minor relief. Was my disguise that transparent? Had anyone else guessed the truth and simply held silent, waiting for a moment to catch me unaware? Tonight, sleeping alone in a bed, would a blade come down on my throat?

A feeling of aloneness swept over me. I hugged myself, wrapping my arms around my middle. There wasn't a bounty on Fowler. It was on me. He could go. Perhaps he should. There was nothing but the promise Sivo had coerced from him, and the king's decree made things more complicated and more dangerous in an already dangerous world. It wasn't fair to him.

A finger brushed over the back of my hand. Startled, I lowered my arms. Fowler's touch followed. He hooked a single finger around mine, linking us.

"Luna," he murmured near my ear. "It's going to be fine."

My chest tightened and before I could stop myself I turned my hand around to squeeze his and hold tightly.

His palm turned over, fingers lacing with mine. It didn't matter what Mirelya saw. She knew the truth about me.

"I'm good at keeping secrets," Mirelya added. "I don't share the things I can see if it's going to hurt anyone. There's enough pain in this life already. I won't add to it."

"Thank you," Fowler said.

"I'll also keep the fact that she's blind to myself."

At this added declaration, my legs felt suddenly weak. I released Fowler's hand and inched toward the table, following the faint bite of oak.

I sank down into a chair. "How did you know?"

Somehow this woman had seen straight to the truth. Fowler hadn't even realized I couldn't see until hours after we first met.

"I can see things. I've always been able to see things." The floor creaked softly beneath her weight. The air stirred as she sank down in a chair beside me.

I moistened my lips, turning my face toward her. "How? What do you mean?"

I started a little as she took my hand, closing it in both of

hers. Her hands were large and thick with bone, her palms padded with rough calluses. Her fingers stroked my palms, her
touch feather light, following the lines and dips and contours of
my palm.

I tried to calm my shaking hand, hating the telltale shiver
that coursed through me.

"You're saying you possess the sight?" Fowler asked sharply,
moving directly behind me, his boots thudding a few steps. I felt
his shadow over me like a physical thing, a cloak floating above
me, ready to drop and shield me at the first sign of threat.

I shouldn't have liked the sensation. I shouldn't have needed
it. I pulled my shoulders back, thrusting my hand into hers, wel-
coming her to say whatever it was she saw carved on my skin.

"I did not say that," Mirelya hedged, her voice evasive.

"But you see her fate? There on her hand?" There was a
sharp edge in his voice. His hand landed on my shoulder, squeezing ever so slightly like he wanted to pull me away from her.

"I'm no oracle if that's what you're after, but I have strong
intuition."

"The possibility that you're even a little like the king's Oracle,
who might be even more mad than the king, offers little relief."
Fowler practically snarled the words at her.

She tapped at the center of my palm, indifferent to him. "You
should be grateful. What I see here can help you both."

"No," Fowler growled. "We don't want to hear anything that
you—"

"Help me how?" I asked, cutting him off.

"Knowledge is power," she responded.

"Luna," Fowler warned. "You don't want to hear—"

"Now. I'm no oracle, but I see enough to know you're the one they are after."

My head lifted. "Me?"

"Yes, you. You are the one the king is looking for . . . the reason he's killing half the females left in Relhok."

Her words sank like rocks through silt, chugging through me slowly, difficult to hear aloud even though I had already concluded as much. Now I had to face it. Now Fowler knew.

"How d-do you know that," I stammered.

"Oh, my, yes. It's you," she asserted.

For a moment not a sound could be heard. No one moved. It was as though I had stepped in a sudden vacuum of silence. I felt like I had been dropped into a very deep and endless well occupied by no one save me. It was only me and my beating heart. The blood a dull rush in my ears. The king wanted me dead. Either I let him hunt me or I figured out a plan that did not amount to me running for the rest of my life while countless innocents died because of me.

Fowler finally broke the silence. "What do you mean the king is after her? He doesn't know anything about her. She's just a girl . . ." His voice faded, but I heard what he was saying: I was just some girl he found. Not anyone who mattered. Not anyone who could be important to a king.

I shook off my silent stupor.

"It can't be because of me," I finally said, deciding to play ignorant. The less they knew about me, about the truth, the safer they were. "Why would the king be after me?"

"You're the one," Mirelya was quick to reply. "The one true heir to the throne."

I stood with a gasp, the mad urge to run seizing me. She had seen the truth I was desperate to protect. Even beyond my gender and blindness, she knew this most important detail about me. And she spoke it aloud.

"Luna?" Fowler's voice was whisper soft. At my silence, he turned to Mirelya. "What are you saying?"

"Oh, you don't know who she is?" Mirelya laughed lightly. "What other secrets do you keep from each other?"

I tried for denial again, shaking my head, but this time the lies would not come. "I've admitted nothing."

"You needn't admit anything for me to see the truth, girl. You are the late king of Relhok's daughter. The one they said was never born before the queen died the night of the eclipse, at the hands of dwellers—"

"It wasn't dwellers," I snapped, unable to suffer the lie that had been spread following my parents' deaths. "It was the chancellor. Cullan. He killed them both and blamed their deaths on the rise of the dwellers. Then he declared himself king."

My outburst was met with silence and I knew I had essentially just announced myself to be the one true heir to the throne.

"You're the princess of Relhok?" Fowler's gravelly deep voice was quiet but full of incredulity. His hand slipped from my shoulder. I turned as though I could see him just behind me.

"Well," Mirelya murmured. "Would this not make her the queen?"

"Stop! I'm not a princess or a queen." At least I didn't feel like it. Not sitting here in boys' clothes, travel weary and covered in grime.

"Why did you not tell me?"

"It wasn't important—"

"You didn't think such a detail important?"

"No!"

"Well, apparently you're important enough for the king to wish dead," Fowler accused.

It was sobering to hear this announced aloud. He was right. It was bad enough to know that girls my age were being killed all across the kingdom, but to know it was because of me. . . . I couldn't run from this reality any longer.

My shoulders sagged under the weight of this knowledge. It wasn't something I could carry. "I have to stop him."

"What did you say?" Fowler demanded.

I pulled back my shoulders. "He has to be stopped."

"There's no stopping Cullan. Just get that thought out of your head." Fowler paced an angry line across the room. "We'd need an army to do that."

"Or just a girl," I offered. "Once he has me, there would be no need for him to keep killing girls." I exhaled and released an uncomfortable laugh. "It's that simple."

"You're out of your mind. There's nothing simple about that.

Travel back across the entire kingdom to reach the capital? Even if you could, even if we make our way inside the city, what then? You just surrender yourself? They would kill you. You would die."

The echo of laughter faded from my lips. "I know that. I didn't expect to stop him and live."

I would die, but others—so many others—they would live. Is that not what a proper queen would do for her people?

"Absolutely not."

I propped my hands on my hips. "The choice isn't yours."

He stepped up close to me, his face near my own. I felt his warm breath on my cheek. "You're not doing this."

Tension crackled between us, looking for somewhere to go, an outlet that wasn't going to appear. Neither one of us was backing down.

Mirelya's voice broke in. "Why don't you both sleep on the matter? Whatever happens, Fowler is going to have to work tomorrow. That's the price of staying here and gathering supplies. He will need his rest for the day ahead."

"That sounds like a fine idea," Fowler agreed. "Maybe you'll see logic tomorrow."

I nodded as though I would change my mind, but I would not. I knew what I had to do.

Fowler avoided me for the rest of the night and into the next morning, leaving me alone in the house with Mirelya.

"He's not going to come around to your way of thinking,

girl," Mirelya said as she washed our breakfast dishes. I didn't need to ask her what she was talking about.

"Well, I'm not changing my mind either."

"Perhaps you should. For one so young, you're in an awful hurry to die."

"I don't want to die," I snapped. "It's the only way. Once the king has me, he'll lift the kill order."

"Oh, I understand your motives. They're fine and altruistic, but that boy's only concern is for you. You might want to think about that."

I sighed. "It doesn't matter." I couldn't let it matter, even as much as it made my stomach flutter to know that the aloof boy I first met cared about me.

Fowler didn't return until shortly before midlight. I followed him into his room, dogging his heels. "You promised we would talk."

"I promised once you saw logic, we would talk."

"That's not right!" I stomped my foot. "You're about to go out on the lake and you're only now returning? You're not leaving any time for us to discuss—"

"I can tell by your expression that you have not had a change of heart, so there's nothing to say. I don't want to talk about your crazed, suicidal plans—"

"I thought we were friends," I accused, my voice cracking slightly. "Granted, I have not had a great deal of those, but I didn't think friends ignored you when they don't like what you say or do."

"I am a friend. Such a good friend that I'm making this decision for your own good." He rustled through his things, slipping a jacket over his tunic, continuing on as though there was nothing to say on the matter. He would think that. He would think that I was totally at his mercy to go where he directed. "We'll talk more about this when I get back," he said in a softer voice.

"Oh, will we?" I swallowed against the tightness in my throat and chafed my hands up and down my arms as though suddenly needing the warmth. "I thought the decision was made. For my own good? Is that not what you said?"

He exhaled an audible gust of breath. As though I was a burden. A great weight upon his shoulders that he must endure—and that stung and pricked at all the raw and sensitive parts of me that yearned to be free and strong. Didn't he understand by now that I was as independent as he was and not someone who must be cared for as one cared for a pet or child?

When I left home, I'd told myself Sivo let me go because he thought I was strong enough, smart enough to survive in this world.

I had believed that. I still did.

And yet Fowler didn't. His doubt of me crept in, undermining my own faith. He made me feel vulnerable and scared beyond what was right. A little fear kept you alert. Too much left you crippled.

"Let's not do this, Luna. Not now."

"No," I said, surprising even myself at the firmness of my voice. "I want to do this now."

His sigh sounded tired. "Is it so very wrong of me? To want to keep you safe?"

"It's wrong if it's what I want to—"

"To die?" he demanded. "No. That is wrong. That's selfish and—"

"Only the selfish belong in this world. Isn't that what you said? I'm only doing my part."

I heard his swift intake of breath. For a moment I regretted flinging his own words back at him like that, but then I thought about the multitude of girls being killed across Relhok. Because of me.

"I'm trying to stop him and save lives. How is that selfish?" I pressed, gentling my tone as I stepped closer. The heat from his body radiated toward me. "It's my life. Mine to do with as I see fit."

"I promised Sivo and Perla—"

I scoffed at that, knowing how much he had resented that promise. At least in the beginning. "I appreciate your dedication to keeping your word, but Sivo and Perla will never know. They'll live out their days convinced that I've reached the Isle of Allu. They'll never know any differently."

His hands closed on my arms, each finger splayed wide, a burning imprint that seared me through the sleeves of my shirt. A pulse beat in his broad palms, thrumming directly into me, merging with my own racing heart.

I dragged in a shuddery breath, thinking I would forever feel those hands on me, an indelible mark long after this—whatever this was—had ended. And it would end one way or another. Either he supported my decision to leave or I was leaving without him. Preferably with him, but I'd cope either way.

"But I'll know." He hauled me closer and I went forward with a breathless squeak. "I'll know." He was close, his head dipping, bending toward mine.

I lifted my face up, seeking, unable to stop myself even though I knew this would likely end with fresh torment. He'd almost kissed me before. I was sure this would end the same.

"Luna." My name sounded pained coming from him.

He brought me closer, crushing me against him, our bodies fused until I felt every hard line, every dip and hollow and contour of him. The pressure of his hands on my arms deepened, lifting me slightly until I was on my tiptoes.

"What are you doing?" I demanded in a voice I couldn't even recognize as my own.

"What does it look like?" His lips were on mine then, grazing the sensitive flesh while he rasped, "For every day of my life, I will know. And I will mourn you."

He didn't give me a chance to respond. He deepened the kiss.

I shrugged my arms free of his and looped them around his neck, clinging desperately, following some untapped instinct. I stood on my tiptoes and pulled his head closer. It was like a floodgate had opened. Everything poured out of me, all the longing and hope I'd ever felt. Every dream I ever had I unleashed into this kiss.

The poetry in my mother's books wove through my mind.

This was nothing like the emotions suggested in that stilted language. I thought I understood the secrets behind the words that Sivo and Perla had read to me—how a single kiss could brand a person—but I didn't. Now I knew that the reality was so much better. So much more intense. Now I felt it all: the singe of his mouth slanting on mine, the increasing pressure, the growing need, the friction that spread to my very toes.

I lifted trembling hands, spearing my fingers through his hair, reveling in the silky locks filling my palms. He slanted his mouth one way, then another, as though he couldn't get enough. I cupped his cheek, enjoying the sensation of his hard jaw under my fingertips as we kissed.

"I like that," he growled. "You. Touching me."

I shivered. Did he know how badly I had wanted to touch him? More than just those few times? Every day since we came together I had craved this, yearned to feel him but scared to reach out. I had worried that he would turn from me and I would be left feeling more alone than before.

I knew how soft his lips could be, but I had no idea how they could consume me. I was lost in his mouth on mine, in the sensation of his hand holding my face as his fingers dove into my hair.

He crouched for a fraction of a moment, wrapped his arms around my waist, and lifted me off my feet until we were perfectly aligned, my mouth level with his. He started walking.

I tightened my arms around his shoulders, hanging on. I gave the smallest gasp when he backed us into a wall, but that didn't stop the kiss. No. He didn't slow down. His mouth was thorough, soft and hard and hungry. I felt him everywhere. And this was just a kiss. Leaving him would ruin me.

A thump sounded outside the door. "Come on, boy! They're heading to the lift. It's time to go."

My mouth lifted from his at the sound of Mirelya's rusty voice. Our breaths crashed between us. I held his face, my thumbs tracing small circles on his warm cheeks.

After a long moment with Fowler's arms still wrapped around my waist, he said in a voice that stroked a shiver down my spine, "That's why you can't go. Princess." He brushed back a tendril of hair off my face. "I'm going out on that lake and when I get back we'll continue to Allu." He paused as though he wanted that to sink in for me. I didn't have the heart to fight anymore. I said nothing, but my resolve only deepened.

I would go to the capital with or without him. I had to.

"Fowler!" Mirelya's voice boomed from outside our room, all patience gone.

He lowered me back down to the ground and dropped his hands from me. He strode from the room without another word.

I stood in that same spot for a long moment, stupidly staring into the dark of my mind, still as a stone until I jolted to action. Pulling my cap from my pocket, I tugged it back over my head, as if that helped hide my gender. Feeling suitably disguised, I followed him out.

"I'll look after her," Mirelya was assuring him in her creaking voice, sitting somewhere to the right, presumably at the table.

I snorted, finding a bit of irony in that. This ancient woman, nearly as blind as I was, would look after me? Her bones cracked every time she moved and there was the odor of decay about her.

"Thank you, Mirelya," Fowler said.

"Watch yourself out there, boy. There's more than kelp in those waters."

Cold seeped into my bones. "What do you mean? Is it very risky?"

"It's no simple task," Mirelya allowed.

"Well, no then." I turned in Fowler's direction. "You can't go. You're nothing to them. They care nothing for your life. You're expendable to them. One of many to be lost for their purposes—" I strode across the room, my fingers finding and latching onto him, curling into the worn leather of his jacket. I had been so caught up in my insistence to return to Relhok City that it hadn't occurred to me that they might force him into a dangerous situation.

"Luna." His hand closed over mine. "I've survived this long. This isn't going to be the end of me. It would take more than a lake to kill me."

He lifted my hands off him, his warm touch no less firm for all its gentleness. My hands dropped to my sides, empty.

"I'll be back," he assured me.

"I don't want you to go." There was no wavering in my voice. It rang solidly. I needed for him to be safe and well. I needed him not to go off into whatever danger waited in that lake.

Suddenly I understood his insistence that I not go back

to Relhok City. I understood because I felt the very same way. I wanted him safe, and he wanted the same thing for me, but I wouldn't tolerate it of him.

But his life didn't equal the death of an entire group. Mine did.

I wanted him to forget about going out on that lake. I wanted him to wait until midlight and then continue on his journey to Allu as he'd always planned—as he had always intended from the moment we first met. It was his plan before we met. It was his plan after we met. It would be his plan no matter what happened to me.

I swallowed against the bitter taste in my mouth. Whether I was with him or not, he would eventually see that. As long as he survived. As long as nothing happened to him out on that lake.

"We need the supplies. There's no choice. I have to do this."

There was a rustling as he lifted his pack, and the familiar whisper of his bow and sheath of arrows as he picked them up from where they rested near the hearth. "I'll be back."

Then he was gone.

I felt his absence even though his tread fell silently. It was an ache as keen and sharp as the point of a knife's blade at my skin.

"Come, girl, you can help me with laundry."

"Of course." I fell into step behind her and tried not to think about Fowler and where he was headed.

"You well? You're hardly moving."

"I'm fine." I shook off my sluggish movements. "Why wouldn't I be?"

"Because your man might not return, that's why."

The words struck me like a slap. I swallowed back the lump rising up in my throat. "He's not mine. But he'll be back."

I shoved down the rest of my fear and convinced myself that this was the truth. Fowler had been on his own for a long time. This wouldn't be the end of him.

TWENTY-FOUR

Fowler

THE LAKE STRETCHED like an endless sea. Our creaking wagons stopped at its bank with a groan of grinding wheels. I stared out at the water in the muted midlight. The light spilled brighter through breaks in the clouds as if the sun itself wanted to touch the lake's surface.

My heart lifted for a moment. It was the most sunlight I had seen in years. A fractured memory rippled across my mind. Giggling with my mother outside, my small hand tracing her pretty face while she loomed over me, her chestnut hair gilded in the sunshine as she smiled down at me. Such a rare thing that smile, and nearly as blinding as all that light washing over us.

"Come." Glagos snapped out the command. "Can't gawk all day. Time is waning and we need to be on the water."

I shook off the cobwebs of memory and hopped down from the wagon. The sooner this was done, the sooner I'd get back. Back to Luna.

I didn't like leaving her. Even if Luna was disguised, there was a bounty on her head and that fact gnawed at me. The sooner we put Ortley behind us, the better I'd feel.

I had kissed her. I knew I should regret it, but I didn't. I could only think about getting back to her and doing it again. Maybe if I kissed her enough she would forget about going to Relhok City and turning herself in to the king.

I followed the others, gathering nets and tools from the wagons and walking down the stretch of dock to the moored boats, three in total, rocking gently on calm waters.

"You're with me." Glagos waved me after him.

A near dozen of us clambered aboard boats—three or four to each one. We pushed off. I wasn't stupid enough to take Glagos's insistence that I join him as a compliment. I was the newest arrival to Ortley. He was the leader. He had to keep a close eye on me.

I settled in the middle of the boat and took up an oar. The boy beside me did the same. He was no more than fourteen with reed-thin arms and I wondered how well he functioned when he looked fit to expire from hunger. Apparently the boy didn't eat his fair share of the kelp he fished out of the lake.

We rowed, falling into an easy rhythm, our oars slicing water. Glagos studied me as I worked, rubbing the scar on his face pensively, looking for weakness. I held his stare. With a sound that was part snort and part laugh, he looked away to assess the lake. The other boats fanned out, a lantern in each, bobbing on the current and spilling light into a wide circle on the dark waters.

Midlight gradually slipped away and night returned. I inhaled the familiar darkness, the musky earthiness that signaled the return of the dwellers. I scanned the shoreline. No sign of them yet, but they were out there.

"What? Worried they'll swim for us?" Grinning, Glagos followed my gaze. "They won't."

"I wasn't worried."

"Good then," Glagos murmured. "Let's have it."

I returned my gaze to the lake. The water gleamed like black, shimmering glass. It was not the typical dark. The usual darkness was like staring into a black pit. There was no gloss or shimmer to it. No wink of anything buried in its depths.

We didn't go too far from the shoreline. "The kelp doesn't grow like it did in the old days," Glagos grimly remarked. "Might have to dive a bit deeper for it."

"How far down is this kelp? Last time I checked I still need to breathe."

The boy snickered at my joke. "Take a deep breath before going under. It helps."

"That's it? That's your advice?"

"Good advice as any." We dropped anchor and the boy lifted his sword, taking position at the helm.

I removed my boots and stripped down to my trousers. The

boy grinned at me as I shivered in the chilly air. "Wait until you hit the water. It will wither your insides it's so cold."

Glagos stepped over the seat and grabbed my wrist.

I jerked at the contact. "What are you—"

His fingers squeezed. "Hold still." He looped a strip of leather about my wrist. A set of shearers hung from one end of it. "The blades are strong," he said. "They'll slice through the kelp like ribbons . . . and anything else you might come across."

I winced but uttered no complaint as he tightened the strap around my wrist. His gaze moved from me to the water. I tossed the shears once in my hand, catching them. I clenched the worn leather, flexing my fingers around the grip.

I followed his gaze to the water, his earlier comment not lost on me. "What else might I come across?" I asked.

He stared at me again, his expression mild. "We're not the only ones who like to feed on the kelp."

A bleak smile twisted my lips and a short bark of laughter escaped me. Perhaps I had uttered a lie to Luna after all. Perhaps surviving the lake wouldn't be the simple matter I insisted.

"You find that amusing?" Glagos murmured.

"That I would survive this long only to die swimming in a lake for kelp? Yes. It's amusing."

The young boy tossed me the net. I caught it in one hand. "Don't forget that. You'll need it."

I looped the strap over my head and across my chest, securing the net at my hip, testing the opening where I would stuff the kelp.

I looked at Glagos. "It might help if I had an idea of what I'm up against?"

"Hard to say. Since the dark-out, the lake life has evolved to survive."

"Haven't we all?" I muttered dryly.

The boy nodded. "The eels are particularly nasty. Big as a boat, some of them. But you'll see them coming at least." He laughed. "They make this popping sound followed by bursts of light."

Splashing could be heard in the distance as the other divers hit the water. I exhaled and studied the shore. The horizon bounced before my eyes as the boat bobbed. I'd promised her I'd be back tomorrow.

Almost in reminder, I spotted several dark dwellers trudging along the edge of the lake, their hunger a palpable thing as they looked in our direction, no doubt drawn by the lights of the lanterns. They stood sentinel, their bodies pale smudges against the dark.

As long as they stood there, we weren't getting off this lake until next midlight. Gazing out at the dwellers, I vowed that this wouldn't be a pointless risk. Leaving Luna. Coming out here. I wasn't leaving Ortley without the necessary supplies.

I faced Glagos again. "I'm ready."

"Here." I took the contraption he offered me, turning it over in my hands. It resembled a pair of spectacles except with a leather strap that went around my head. "It's dark down there," he explained. "Darker than it is up here, but occasionally an eel will offer you a flash of light. When that happens these will help you see." I tapped the edge of one lens.

"Tortoiseshell," Glagos added. "Should keep water from leaking in and allow you to see."

I tugged them on, wincing at the tight and uncomfortable fit around my eyes.

"Once you fill your net, we'll be ready at the side of the boat to swap it out for a new one. The more you haul, the more you keep. Good luck."

With a nod, I swung a leg over the side. I plunged into the frigid depths, opening my mouth wide in shock. Water filled my throat and nose. Bad idea. I broke the surface, sputtering and choking on the silty water.

Glagos peered over the edge. "Thought you could swim."

"I can," I gasped, swimming in place, still adjusting to the shocking cold.

"Swimmers usually don't swallow the lake."

The boy shooed his hand at me. "Go on, get to work."

I glared at the little runt and resumed swimming. It didn't take long to feel the silky tendrils of kelp that grew up from the depths of the lake bed brushing my bare feet. Readying my shears, I sucked in a breath and went under, headfirst.

I found a long rope of kelp and wrapped it around my fist, following it down until my lungs ached for air. When I couldn't stay under another minute I cut the taut length of vine and broke through the surface, tossing back my head.

Sweet air filled my lungs as I stuffed the kelp into my bag, legs working under me to keep afloat. Something gossamer soft brushed my arm, and I tensed, slowing my tread. I studied the lake's surface as though I could see within.

A sharp burst of pain flared along my side, and I whirled around in a quick circle in the water, attempting to escape it. "Ow! What was that?"

"Oh, did I mention the carp? They've developed a taste for flesh," Glagos called down at me from the boat, an edge of annoyance to his voice, as though this shouldn't give me pause.

I pressed a hand to my ribs, feeling a chunk of skin missing there.

"C'mon, boy," Glagos barked. "You've got a net to fill."

Releasing my side, I sucked another breath into my lungs and dove back under, intent on getting through this no matter how much was left of me at the end. I only needed to survive and get back to Luna. I blocked out the pain and worked until my arms burned, cutting at the kelp, ignoring the nips and tears at my flesh from creatures I couldn't see coming. I lost track of how many bags of kelp I passed up into the boat. I worked a steady, relentless pace, my mind wandering, remembering Luna. The kiss. The warm taste of her.

A shrill scream carried over the water. I froze and looked toward the other boats. I couldn't see the diver closest to me anymore. The men in his boat leaned to the edge, peering over the side and calling for him.

"Don't stop. Keep working," Glagos commanded.

"What happened—"

"He either made it or he didn't. It has nothing to do with you," he called down impatiently.

Luna's face materialized in my mind. I tightened my grip on the hilt of my shears.

I couldn't leave her.

I continued working, alert, trying to feel for the slightest ripple or change in the current lapping around me. I spent as much time cutting kelp as I did swiping at the foreign bodies brushing me in the black waters.

After a while, I didn't hear any screams or voices searching for the diver. I continued swimming down, pulling up kelp, trying not to think about how cold the water was or what was out here with me. I thought about Luna. The smell of her skin. Holding her. Kissing her.

A movement to my right snagged my attention. Someone else was swimming in that first diver's place. I focused on cutting vines, one after the other, and didn't let myself think about what happened to the other diver.

Until the eels came.

The surface rippled as though a giant wind blew, but it wasn't a current. The eels undulated along the surface, passing through the other swimmers. My stomach dipped at the sound of the divers' screams. The eels turned and shot a direct line for me. I couldn't outswim them. This was their world, not mine.

They rolled through the water toward me like a sea of dark snakes, bigger than any snake I had ever seen on land. I braced myself, my pulse hammering at my throat. I flexed my hand around the grip of my shears, every muscle pulling tight in readiness. The slippery bodies swarmed me a moment before the first popping sting. More stings followed, charges of heat exploding on my skin. I jerked, thrashing in the water. I swiped, cut, and stabbed with the shears, but there were so many of them.

I was on my way up for another breath when some other creature grabbed hold of my leg and yanked me back down. It was big. Strong.

I struggled against whatever it was. It pulled me down, the pressure on my ankle increasing, squeezing.

My lungs burned fire, desperate for air. I lashed out, my shears fighting wildly, swiping around me, desperate to gain freedom. Air. Sweet, lifesaving air.

Water choked me, filling my mouth and nose. I continued to go down, descending amid a tangle of kelp vines. Luna. Luna.

I couldn't pull free. In a final attempt to save myself, I dove, chasing after whatever was holding me, stabbing at it, the tip of my shears making contact. A pair of yellow eyes peered at me from the depths. Its body was indistinct, just a big amorphous form.

My efforts didn't help. Its grip on my leg didn't lessen. One of its tentacles clenched tighter, as if sensing that this was a struggle to the death.

Blackness filled my world. A deeper dark than anything I'd known before. The kind of dark one didn't come back from. A dark that was total and final and consuming.

My muscles weakened, but still I stabbed at the tentacle

wrapped around my ankle, hacking at it as my lungs screamed for air.

Amid all that darkness I saw Luna. Luna's face with the impossible freckles that had never tasted real sunlight. Luna, who I'd given my word to return for.

Luna, who I kissed and wanted to kiss again and again.

Luna, who waited for me.

TWENTY-FIVE

Luna

I SAT AT the table in Mirelya's small kitchen, listening to the busy sounds of the village outside coming to life. A cart rolled past and in the distance children played, their laughter ringing out. The woman next door beat at a rug in steady whacks with her broom.

My hands wrapped tightly around a mug of tea made from the kelp leaves that Fowler was out there risking his life harvesting. It had grown cold in the stretch of morning, but I still sipped at it. If it had nutrients and healing properties as they claimed, then I would take my fill. The journey ahead wasn't going to be easy. Especially since I would be doing it alone.

I squeezed the bridge of my nose between my fingers and released a shuddering breath, trying not to dread the prospect with every fiber of my being. It wasn't making the journey alone to Relhok City that filled me with dread. It wasn't even facing the man who murdered my parents and would now murder me. In some ways, that was long overdue. No. It was never seeing Fowler again.

I picked my mug back up and downed the last of the tea. I'd slept restlessly, if at all, thinking of Fowler somewhere on that lake. I knew he would be gone this long. They did runs back and forth to the lake only during midlight, but that didn't stop the worry. Midlight was close. I could smell it on the air.

Fowler's promise to come back played over in my mind, offering some solace.

Despite the heated words we'd had before he left—and despite that soul-searing kiss—I'd made up my mind to go to Relhok City. Where it all began. Where I would end it. And yet that didn't change that I wanted him safe. Before I left, I needed to know he was well.

A familiar thump sounded on the wooden deck outside Mirelya's cottage. The flap that acted as a door shifted, a hand shoving it back. Somewhere far off a horn blew that reminded me of the one that sounded when we'd stepped off the lift the first day.

Mirelya entered and the door covering fell back in place with a slight whisper on the air. "Hello, there," she greeted, dropping a basket on the table.

"What's all the commotion outside?" I asked as she made her way to the table where I sat.

Despite her frail form, the chair creaked beneath her weight as she lowered down into it. "Another visitor arrived."

"Oh?"

"Aye. Unsavory-looking sort, but they let him up seeing as he's just one. I'm sure they'll send him out on the boats next. They always need volunteers for that."

Like Fowler, he was someone to be sacrificed.

I shuddered and attempted to shake off the thought.

"Don't fret, girl. Your man is stronger than most. One look at him and you can see that."

"He's very strong." I nodded in agreement, recalling the sensation of his body, muscled and honed from years of hard living. "He'll be back."

Sitting there, her words ran over in my mind. One look at him and you can see that. Yes, I could feel him. But I would never have a look at him. I understood the notion of beauty. Some people were more pleasing to the eye than others. Such superficiality didn't matter to me one way or another, but I was curious at how others perceived Fowler . . . and me. Sivo and Perla only ever sang my praises, but here was a woman who had no personal stake in cosseting my feelings.

"Mirelya? Am I like other girls?"

"You mean your appearance?"

Heat crept over my face.

"You're asking for that boy of yours?" She cackled. "You're

wanting to know how he sees you? Whether he finds you comely?"

I shook my head, feeling foolish. "N-no."

"Don't deny it now that you've put the question out there. I don't expect you to know that you're comely enough. Not a great beauty, mind you, but passing fair, as I expect that boy would agree from the way he stares at you. Quite free with his stares he is, knowing you can't see him. Watches you like you're some tasty pudding he would like to sample."

The heat in my face turned to scalding.

"And what of him?" I asked before good sense came over me. "What is he like? I already know he's tall and strong of form—"

"Aye, his face is fine enough to draw the female eye. Not that there are too many your age left to admire him."

At that sobering reminder, I pressed my mouth shut. How could I worry about such trivial things when the world was what it was? When girls were being murdered because of me? When he was out there risking his life for us? When even if he did make it back, I would be leaving him?

Outside, steps approached the front of the cottage door. The leather covering rippled once from the movement. I tensed, relaxing after several moments when it became clear it was just a passerby. Mirelya had been helpful, keeping me out of sight so I didn't rouse curiosity. But it couldn't last forever. I was bound to come face-to-face with others again.

The chair creaked as Mirelya rose to her feet. "You should rest. I could hear you tossing all night. Take a nap. By the time you wake, midlight will have passed and Fowler will be back."

It was tempting—the idea of closing my eyes and opening them again to find Fowler before me—but it would be futile. I wouldn't be able to sleep until I knew he was back.

"Go on with you," she pressed. "Have a rest."

Deciding against arguing, I rose and slipped into the room where I had spent the night alone. Curling up on the bed, I pulled the blanket around my shoulders and waited for midlight, begging silently for it to come and then fearful that it would. That it would and he wouldn't arrive with it.

Moments slid into long minutes. I couldn't be certain how much time passed, but then I heard Mirelya talking to someone. I sat up with a lurch, excited with the possibility that Fowler was back.

I swung my legs over the bed, but then paused. The other voice was unmistakably male, but too reedy to belong to Fowler. Standing, I inched toward the door.

I moved to the door covering, my hand hovering in midair, some deeper sense stopping me from pushing the covering and going through.

"I don't care who told you that. They were confused," Mirelya was saying.

"Perhaps you're confused, old woman."

That voice. Anselm.

My breath locked tight in my lungs. I held myself immobile, my fingers curling into knotted, bloodless fists, my nails scoring into my palms. I recognized the voice. I'd never forget it. Not mere days after he had attacked us. Not years from now.

"I'd know if I let any strangers into my home," Mirelya snapped, her dislike strong in her voice, but there was something else. She was speaking loudly, stalling obviously. Everyone knew she had taken me and Fowler in. Any random passerby could confirm the truth. Or he could search the cottage.

I understood her purpose with sudden clarity. She was warning me. Giving me time to prepare. Hide. Run. Turning, I moved quickly, slipping my jacket over my tunic and snatching up my dagger and sword.

"I was told an older boy went out on the boats, but a younger boy stayed with you." Footsteps sounded and I knew he was moving, circling the room, coming closer to the flap covering. "These two sound like they could be my friends." His voice took on a silky quality that Mirelya didn't mistake.

"If they're your friends, how is it you're not with them?" she challenged.

"We got separated running from dwellers."

I inched away, still straining to listen as I came closer to the window. When I felt it bump my back, I turned, reaching for the edges of the tarp covering. I loosened the ties anxiously, my fingers tripping in their haste as I untied the fabric from the knobs at the window's edge. Securing my cap snugly on my head, I swung a leg over the sill and slipped out of the cottage.

I settled my weight carefully on the wood planks, trying not to make a sound. There was only stillness at this back side of the cottage. I didn't sense a flow of people like in the front. I inhaled and smelled only trees before me, the crispness of leaves fluttering softly in the breeze, the pungent musk of the centuries-old bark.

I pressed myself along the exterior wall of the house, not straying far from the window, still listening for sounds within. My ears separated their voices from the other noises around me. I waited, hoping, my lips moving in silent entreaty for him just to take Mirelya's word and turn and leave.

A crash carried from inside the cottage. He didn't believe her.

Mirelya's voice rang out, "You can't go in there!"

I pushed off the wall, knowing he would see the open window with its dangling cover. He need only to stick his head out and I would be discovered. One look at me—disguised or not—and he'd recognize my face.

Breathing raggedly, I moved, skimming a trembling hand along the side of the house until I rounded it and came to the front. My feet flew, relying on my memory combined with instinct as I followed the path that wove between trees and homes, bypassing villagers.

I had not gone very far when I heard a bellow. I froze for a moment before resuming my pace.

The cry came again and it was distinctly male and closer. Reedy and thin, it wrapped around me like a closing fist.

"Stop!"

My heart lurched. The heavy beat of his footsteps followed his cry. He was coming after me.

I ran. Desperate fire burned through me. My ears strained, listening and feeling with my skin, with my every nerve and pore and muscle. It didn't even matter if I fell. If he caught me I was dead anyway.

No one would stop him.

I bumped a woman's shoulder. She snapped at me in annoyance. I rushed ahead. There were more sounds behind me. He wasn't being careful in his pursuit of me either.

Someone stepped into my path before I could stop my momentum. We collided. I fell over him in a tumble of limbs. I staggered back to my feet, gasping out an apology as I continued ahead.

I reached the bigger thoroughfare that we had walked down when we first arrived. It was bustling with people this time of day. The fresh aroma of bread and dried meat filled my nose and made me ache for home even as I was running for my life. Perhaps because of it. The thought of Perla flitted across my desperate thoughts. My warm bedchamber. Sitting with Sivo before the fire as he sharpened weapons.

Someone grabbed at my arm, but I dodged free. The end of the lane approached. I heard the chains of the lift rattling in the breeze. I stopped before the ground dropped down to the lift platform. I hopped off, tottering on the edge of the platform, arms wide at my sides for balance. One wrong step and I would plummet.

I could hear his panting breaths and curses behind me. My pulse hammered, drumming in my neck.

I arrived at the far side of the landing. My hand groped at a giant tree there, finding and seizing a curling branch. I circled my arms around it and leaped, scooting up until I reached its trunk. From there, I scaled a little bit higher, grabbing another branch, then another. Fortunately, the branches were as big as I was and strong enough to support me. My arms burned as I climbed, no clear direction in mind except away.

I heard Anselm below, climbing up after me, cursing and gasping for breath as his shoes and hands scuffed against bark.

My arms worked, straining, pulling me along. I reached for another branch, this one extending from another tree. It was a little too far. My shoulder screamed as I stretched harder for it. I knew it was there. I could sense its presence, hear its creak on the wind. Please, please . . .

I choked with relief as I grasped hold of it and swung, crossing over into the neighboring tree, finding footing on a lower branch.

My mind raced ahead, trying to strategize beyond the idea of merely getting away from him. I needed a plan.

If I made it down to the ground below, I could lose him in the forest. There was no rescue coming. This was all on me.

Following that logic, I started to reach for lower branches, at times even scaling the tree trunk itself, sliding down against the rough bite of bark that rubbed my skin raw in places. My arms quivered from exertion, whimpers escaping me.

My fingers dug deep, nails cracking and splintering from the abuse. My boot lost its foothold and I dropped several feet before

I hit another branch. The impact stopped me—and shot pain to every fiber in my body.

Panting, I held still for a moment, fighting for breath.

My heart pounded as I took a moment to assess for injuries and to regain my breath. All of me hurt, but I could still move. I had to move. I tested my limbs, turning and stretching to my full height, my spine flat against the tree.

The smell of my own blood reached my nose, and I lifted a shaking hand to my face. I flexed my fingers. Slick blood coated my palms, the coppery scent filling my nose.

I could hear Anselm crashing above me. A fresh dose of panic washed through me.

Move, move, move!

I started down again, ignoring the pain. I tried not to think about the dwellers below. I'd take my chances with them over Anselm.

"Come back here before you fall, girl!"

I whimpered at the sound of his voice. He was directly above me. Close. I moved faster, anxiety pushing me. I had to be close to the ground. I had to be. My legs and arms moved quickly, one over the other, taking me down the tree.

My speed cost me. My hand slipped from a branch. My hand flailed wildly, seizing only air.

Crying out, I plunged, banging my way down. My knee collided with a branch and I shouted, tumbling in a whirl of flailing limbs and spinning leaves.

I hit earth. Flat on my back, I didn't move for a moment.

Didn't breathe. Pain greeted my body in sharp needles, poking and stabbing me everywhere.

I groaned and rolled to my side, gasping into the dirt, leaves crunching under me.

Sounds above jerked me to life. He was still coming. I sucked in air, letting it fill and lift me up. With that breath swirling through my nose, the familiar musky aroma of dwellers assailed me.

I turned, inhaling, marking their scent. They were thicker to my right. The slight snuffling sounds they made were there, their wet breaths huffing on the breeze, growing closer.

It was enough to force me to my feet. I staggered, fighting past the throbbing in my knee and overall aches, weaving through the trees, extending my hands, palms out, brushing shrubs and rough bark, feeling my way as I ran.

He was on the ground now, too. "Stupid girl! Get back here!" his angry shout rang out. I could feel them out there, dwellers hunting me, too.

I pushed my legs harder, dodging where I smelled or heard dwellers, but there were so many—like the first day I arrived with Fowler.

"They're going to get you! Is that what you want, girl?"

Gradually, it grew quieter. I felt their sudden absence. The lack of their loamy musk on the air.

They were gone.

I paused, my chest aching, hard breaths sawing from my lips.

I lifted my face to air that felt thinner, not as dense as the night. It was midlight.

I flew into motion. They might be gone, but he wasn't.

Anselm was still after me, coming faster now, hunting me harder now that it was midlight and the dwellers were gone. It was just the two of us.

TWENTY-SIX

Fowler

I HOPPED DOWN from the wagon and moved ahead of the group, eager to rest my eyes on Luna again and assure myself she was well. I ignored the parts of me that felt chewed up by a meat grinder. A little salve on my wounds, a night's rest, and I'd be fine and ready to go. My ankle was still tender from where that creature had nearly snapped the bone before I managed to saw through the tentacle and free myself.

The sooner we left this place behind the better. I would not be going out on the lake again. I'd take what kelp I had earned, and put this place behind me.

My gaze scanned the mist-shrouded ground. The forest

stirred, everything coming to life while the dwellers were at rest. My gaze drifted up to the city in the trees. I waited impatiently as the lift descended for us, shifting on my feet. Leaving Luna this long ate at me. I would never do it again.

I was the first to hop inside the lift. Glagos stepped on with me, waving away the boy who had stood with us on the boat for the last twenty-four hours, tossing down remarks that were of little help as I hacked at kelp and fought off all manner of creatures hungry for a taste of me.

I had almost died out there. Glagos knew that. His cold stare made that much clear. He just didn't care.

"How many die out there?" I asked mildly.

He shrugged. "You made it and gathered a nice amount of kelp in the process. We could use you here."

"I'm sure you could." My lips curled. He'd happily let me continue risking my neck for them. "I did what you asked. I'm taking my supplies and leaving."

He waved a hand, cutting through the milky air. "You might want to reconsider. Alone out there . . . is it so much better than staying here?"

With Luna it was impossible to stay here. I shook my head.

He shrugged. "Fine. There are others to take your place. Drifters come through here all the time." And I was sure many stayed here, buried at the bottom of that lake, bones picked clean.

The lift stopped at the top with a jar, the chains jangling and clinking. I stepped out onto the landing. My clothes stuck to my wounds, the dried and crusted blood tugging on the torn flesh with every movement. Peeling the clothes from my body was going to be unpleasant.

I spotted Mirelya standing among the small crowd that had assembled to greet all those returning from the boats.

She started toward me, her cane ringing out with each strike on the wood. Her gaze darted down once, almost guiltily, before meeting my eyes. Her color was poor, too. Something was wrong. I knew it with one sweep of my gaze.

I reached her in two strides and leaned down to her hunkered and bent frame, speaking in a low voice. "Mirelya, what is it? Where is—"

"She's gone," she whispered for my ears alone.

"She left the village?" I went cold. Had she left without me? Was she heading to Relhok City?

A memory assailed me. I'd fought so hard to forget it, but suddenly it was upon me.

Two years ago, after leaving Relhok, I'd gone south, knowing that I wouldn't be looked for there. The dwellers had ravaged the south. It was rumored no town or city stood intact. My father wouldn't think to hunt for me there.

I had no purpose then. I had not yet decided to go to Allu. That had been Bethan's dream. It could not be mine.

I found a village. There wasn't much left of Edmon. Just a few cottages that surrounded a stone mill at the edge of a loch. The remaining villagers lived inside its stone walls, sleeping on straw pallets, waiting listlessly in the dark for death to come.

Not living, merely surviving. Foraging during midlight for

scraps. Eating bugs and vermin. There had been a boy. Only nine years old. Donnan always wanted to join me, but I made him stay behind when I left to hunt or forage. One day he followed me.

I turned back when I heard his screams, but I was too late. By the time I caught up to him, there was nothing left that resembled the boy. I failed him like I had Bethan. Like I was failing Luna.

No. Not again.

"A man came . . . carried a reeking bag of heads." Mirelya's fingers dug like claws into my arm. "He was looking for you both. He knew she was there. He knew she wasn't a boy."

My voice shook out of me. "He took her?"

"No. She fled. He chased her through the village." She pointed to the trees that crowded the edge of the lift. "She made her way down. She's out there—"

The words had barely left her mouth before I was back in the lift, catching it before it descended to pick up the rest of the men. I paced the small lift space, scanning the countryside as I traveled back down, craning my neck and peering into the cloudy midlight air.

I was halfway down when I spotted movement in the trees. My hands slammed against the caged wall, staring hard at that one spot. A person was running. It wasn't Luna. This was a man. I recognized his gait from the other day in the orchard. My gaze skipped ahead of him, searching for a glimpse of Luna, but trees blocked my view, and then I was too low, almost to the ground again.

I yanked the door open with a rattle. Others crowded me, ready to hop on.

"Hey, where you going?" the boy from the boat called as I shoved past him and took off.

I ran. Legs pumping, blood roaring in a rush in my ears. I flew, weaving through trees, jumping over fallen logs and debris as if I hadn't spent the last twenty-four hours swimming and fighting in that lake.

My breath crashed with the rhythm of my pounding feet.

I heard a sound and pulled to a hard stop, swallowing my breath so I could listen. I jerked to the right and followed the noise. I spotted Anselm's tall, thin frame through the trees and just beyond him . . . Luna. He was strides from her, a hatchet in his hand. He swung down. Missed.

I roared, arms pumping as savagely as my legs ran. I closed in. Anselm whirled around, shock crossing his gaunt features as I jumped through the air and collided with him. I pinned him down, sending his hatchet flying. I choked him at the throat with one hand, bringing my sword down and pushing it straight through his chest.

He choked, and shuddered under me. Glassy eyes stared straight through me. An expression of shock fixed itself to his harsh features.

I gasped, laboring for breath as I fell back. The sword remained buried in his chest. My back hit the ground as I stared up, my gaze lost in the canopy of thick, swaying branches.

"Fowler!" Luna scrambled to my side. She took my hand, her

warm fingers closing around my blood-slicked fingers.

"Luna." My stare slid over her face, drinking in her every feature. The cuts and bloody scrapes and scratches made me wince. I stroked her pale cheek with my other hand, cringing at the smear of blood I left on her. "Are you hurt? Did he harm you?"

"No, I'm fine." She bowed her head, resting her forehead against mine, her sweet breath fanning my cheek. "You made it back."

I smiled. "I told you I would." Sucking in another breath, I rose, pulling her up after me. "Come. We need to hurry and get back." The dull glow of midlight was fading on the air.

I pulled my sword free of Anselm's body, wiped it clean in the dirt and leaves, and then started back toward the lift. She walked close beside me, and I couldn't stop myself.

I reached for her hand, folding her warm fingers into mine as I pulled her closer.

TWENTY-SEVEN

Luna

THE SCENTS OF Mirelya's cottage surrounded me, at once familiar and comforting. I inhaled the aroma of dried herbs and bread as I stretched my aching muscles. I was going to be sore for a good while. Sore, but alive.

Tears burned in my eyes, and I feverishly blinked them back. The coals crumbled and popped in the small stove in my room, warming the air, but I still couldn't chase away the cold. Cleaned up, with a sticky salve that smelled of mint and nisan root applied to my wounds, I inhaled raggedly. I was safe and out of immediate danger, but that didn't stop me from shivering. I couldn't relax. Tension knotted my shoulders, refusing to loosen.

Perhaps that's what being on the Outside was. It was listening hard to every sound and never breathing easy. Never relaxing. Never feeling warm. Never allowing yourself to believe that for one single moment you could be safe.

Always running.

My teeth clacked and I clenched my jaw until my face muscles ached.

I shivered from the cold. It had to be because I was cold. It couldn't be my near brush with death. I shook my head slightly. I'd had close calls before. My life had become a series of close calls.

Fowler was there. I sensed him like my own heartbeat inside my chest. Somehow he had become a part of me. As intrinsic as the blood in my veins. It tempted me to stay, fixed to his side even though I knew what I had to do. That hadn't changed.

"Here." Fowler's fingers brushed my shoulders as he draped a thick fur around me and I shivered for an entirely different reason. We hadn't come into physical contact since he held my hand on the way back to the lift, and I felt the absence of his touch keenly. A physical ache that I had no right to feel, but it was there nonetheless. "Are you well? Do you need Mirelya to see to your wounds?"

I shook my head. "No, she's done enough."

He turned to move, leaving me alone in my room, but I reached out, grabbing his wrist before I could consider the wisdom of touching him.

"You came for me," I whispered, my chest twisting with

emotion as I considered what would have happened if he had been even a few moments later.

The bed sank with his weight beside me.

I felt a flutter of movement near my cheek and I lifted my face, but the touch never came. Instead it was his voice, as hard and final as a hammer falling, that reached me. "We need to move. It's too dangerous to stay here now, Luna. Too many saw him chasing you. It won't be long before they come nosing around."

"You're ready to go right now?" I shook my head, my stomach churning. This would take some planning. It would be harder to slip away from him when it was just the two of us on the Outside. He would track me down before I got very far. "Midlight is the safest time to leave, don't you think? Tomorrow is soon enough."

"Luna—"

I stopped him by pressing my fingers to his mouth.

"Tomorrow," I insisted, my pulse fluttering at my neck. My stomach clenched.

This day would be the last I'd have of him. Perhaps it was selfish, even foolish, but I wanted it. One more day and night together for me to cling to during the days and nights I was on my own.

He'd brought me this far. He hadn't wanted me with him in the beginning, but he cared about me now—at least whether I lived or died. Something told me I was one on a short list of people he cared about. Maybe I was the only one. My heart swelled, feeling privileged to have that.

"Luna." My name sounded pained, strangled and choked

against my fingers. "The things you do to me . . ."

"Show me," I challenged.

"We can't—"

"You mean you won't?" I dropped my hand from his face. He didn't realize this was all the time we would have. He was tossing it aside when I needed it to be everything—a final, sweet memory to carry with me.

I turned away, but then he spun me back around. His hands held me by the shoulders, then my face. Warm palms rasped against my cheeks, pulling me in. Those hands anchored me, holding me as his mouth came down on mine.

His mouth was all I felt. This single searing contact became my entire world. His lips on my lips, moving, caressing, sliding and slanting, giving and taking.

I clung to his shoulders, my fingers curling deep into the hardness of his body.

He lowered me back on the furs. I went willingly. He balanced his elbows on either side of me, careful not to crush me, but I wanted that. I needed the weight of him, all his warmth to envelope me.

He kissed me until my lips felt tingly and swollen and I couldn't breathe. I didn't need to breathe though. I just needed his mouth. *Him.* My bones melted alongside my muscles. All of me felt like warm pudding, sinking beneath him.

My hands roamed, free finally to touch, free to feel and memorize all of him. My fingers tangled in the strands of hair that brushed his warm neck. I stroked silky tips, tugging gently.

He growled into my mouth and I swallowed the sound, taking it into me. My chest swelled and tightened. A sense of empowerment flowed through me, heady with the rush that I affected him. That I made him feel.

I shoved his jacket off his shoulders. He pulled back slightly without severing our kiss, allowing me to slide it the rest of the way down his arms.

I touched his bare throat, fingers gliding to the top of his chest, as far as his shirt would allow.

"Fowler," I sighed against his lips.

He pulled back and I felt his gaze on me, his hands holding my face. His thumbs grazed the edges of my mouth. "I've fought this, Luna."

"What? What is it you're fighting?"

"You. Me. I wasn't supposed to feel this way for anyone. Everyone that ever matters, I lose."

The tightness in my chest turned into a throbbing ache. "So you're saying that I matter to you?"

A shudder rolled through him that I felt to my very depths. "You matter to me. You're the only thing that matters anymore."

I smiled, trying to hide the curve of my lips with my hand, feeling like one of the lovesick swains in that book of poetry that belonged to my mother.

He tugged my hand down. "You don't need to hide from me. Especially not your lips. How will I kiss them?"

I smiled openly then, exposed. "You make me happy," I admitted, "but I know you didn't want this between us. You didn't want to care about me. I feel as though I owe you an apology. You were set on one course and then I came along—"

"And changed everything. Thank you for that." His mouth brushed mine once, then again, lingering before lifting up. "Don't apologize. I'm not sorry and you shouldn't be either. I'm done fighting this . . . you . . . us."

We kissed again. Feverish, breathless kisses. To think we could have been doing this sooner? I almost wanted to weep at the lost time. Why fight it indeed?

"Exactly," he muttered against my mouth and I realized I had spoken aloud.

Then all words stopped. The pressure of his mouth grew deeper, more urgent. We had almost missed this.

And tomorrow I would. Tomorrow I'd be gone from here and there would be no more of this ever again.

A deep pang punched me in the chest. I wanted this and not just for now. I wanted it to be like this always. But more important than this happiness I had found with him was saving the lives of countless others.

I pushed him onto his back, taking charge, desperate for him, to make the memory of this so indelible that I never forgot it.

"Luna," he muttered, my name slipping free from our melded mouths. His hand trailed through my hair, reverent and caressing.

Mirelya's cane banged on the floor outside the room. "Everything all right in there?"

We tore apart with mutual gasps, my pulse jumping against my throat at the intruding voice.

"Her timing could be improved," Fowler panted.

I nodded shakily, pushing tendrils of hair back from my face as I sat up.

His hand cupped my cheek, thumb grazing my skin in small circles. I covered his hand with my own, clinging to him, turning my face to kiss his palm. I needed him. I needed to make this night everything because it was all I would ever have. Even if I survived what the future held, I wouldn't have Fowler again. He'd be at Allu.

That thought fired through me as I took Fowler's face in both hands, savoring the texture of his skin, the cut of his jaw, the flexing of his cheek muscles beneath my exploring fingers.

When I was a little girl I used to dream my parents were alive. There was no black eclipse. No evil royal chancellor who killed my parents and seized power. The sun still lived. It didn't hide behind the moon. It arrived every day. Crops grew. People were happy. Safe. No one was hungry. No one suffered in the dark. And I could see. When I dreamed of what I thought perfection could be, it was this.

But that wasn't perfection. Not even close. Because it wasn't real.

This was.

"We're fine, Mirelya," I called out. "Good night."

She grunted a response and the thunk of her cane faded across the outside room.

I lowered my head and kissed Fowler again, each kiss slower, longer, imprinting onto the darkness of my mind. His hands roamed over me, slipping under my tunic to trail over my back, his callused palms skimming the line of my spine.

"You're trembling," he murmured when I paused, lifting my head. "Are you still frightened?"

Today had been perhaps the closest I'd come to death. But that wasn't what he meant. He meant this. Us.

I ran my hand through his hair, marveling that it could feel like silk after all the abuse of this world. "The last thing I feel right now is fear." In this moment, in his arms, there was only joy. An end to the loneliness I had felt for so many years.

"I feel it, too," he admitted softly, his lips moving on mine as he spoke, so gentle that it broke something loose inside of me. "I'm afraid."

"Why are you afraid?" In my mind, nothing ever scared him.

"Because you make me feel, Luna." His hoarse voice was almost unrecognizable. "I haven't felt anything in a long time. That's the way I wanted it. I convinced myself it was enough. But you make me want more again. What happened today . . . what could still happen, it terrifies me." I felt his tremble pass through him and bleed into me.

"Shhh." I kissed him. "Not now. I don't want to speak of anything bad right now. Tomorrow is soon enough."

"I just want to get you out of here."

"Fowler, you aren't responsible for my life." I needed him to know that. "People live and die. People you care about. You can't bear that burden." I let that hang between us, hoping it sank in and he remembered it later when I was gone. I knew he'd loved and lost before. I didn't want him to hurt again like that. Not because of me. "We can't stop loving and caring about others just because it hurts when we lose them."

"I'm not losing you." His hands held my face, his grip all at once tender and fierce.

His words tore through my chest. The boy who had started this journey with me wasn't the same one before me now. Somehow along the way he had changed from a hardened warrior who treated me only to terse words. He cared about me. He wanted to be with me now and not because Sivo had forced me on him.

"Close your eyes and kiss me," I whispered, realizing that he wasn't the only one who had changed. I was different now, too. I lifted a hand to his face, stroked the hard line of his jaw, reveling in the light rasp of his unshaven cheek and the brush of his mouth on mine. "Pretend we're already there."

TWENTY-EIGHT

Luna

I LEFT ORTLEY at midlight, putting as much distance as I could between myself and the village and the herd of dwellers that lurked beneath ground, waiting for the coming dark.

I ran the full hour, my heart pounding in rhythm with the steady beat of my boots. I stopped when the woods quieted and the air thickened with the impending end of midlight, climbing a tree to crouch on a sturdy branch. There, I sat, awaiting the darkness.

It was impossible to keep my thoughts from straying to him. I thought about how I left Fowler nestled deep in a fur blanket, snoring softly, his warm body smelling of peat smoke and leather and Mirelya's herb tea. I hoped he found others. People he could trust to join him on his journey to Allu. I didn't want him to be alone, to feel the way I did right now.

I'd kissed his slightly parted lips a final time, tracing them lightly and memorizing their texture before departing the room, knowing he wouldn't stop me. He'd have to wake up to do that and there was no chance of that happening. Not with the sleeping draft Mirelya had given me to slip him.

I knew I should be thinking about what loomed ahead for me. My mission to Relhok . . . how I was going to get inside the capital to speak with Cullan and make certain he knew he had me so that he could stop the mass killing

Except Fowler filled my mind and heart. When he woke, would he understand or hate me for leaving like that? Hating me would be easier. Kinder, I supposed. He would be able to forget and move on if his feelings could be reduced to hatred. A lump rose up in my throat.

I lifted my chin against the weight of night. It was different alone on the Outside. Scarier, if I allowed myself the luxury of fear. Purpose fueled me though, blocking out fear-inducing paralysis.

Without so much of my attention on Fowler, every scent flooded my nose. Sounds rang sharper in my ears. It felt as though I were submerged underwater, every noise thundering against a backdrop of swooshing silence.

I shifted until my body was balanced, then leaned back against the trunk and waited, listening for dwellers as they emerged, making certain none were too close. Leaves rustled in the distance, ground breaking with plops as the soil broke and turned over.

A dweller groaned several yards away, and I held my breath, waiting as it pulled free and rose to its feet. It passed beneath me, its heavy tread dragging through topsoil and rotting leaves. I counted the moments until I could no longer hear the whisper of its sloughing breath.

I climbed down and continued, no longer running, but walking hastily, listening and altering my direction based on the cries of dwellers.

A new sound emerged. A faint scrabbling, like the scratching of nails against wood coupled with a low, mewling whimper. It was no dweller. They never cried liked this. The whimpers grew more pronounced. Whatever it was, it was in trouble. My boots turned in its direction, curious enough to investigate. I palmed my dagger, although the plaintive whimpers told me that the creature wasn't in a position to attack.

I knew the minute it spotted me. The whimpers turned to low growls. I paused, recognizing the growls of a tree wolf. The instinct to run surged inside me, but then I realized it couldn't hurt me. If the vicious beast were able, it would have sliced me to ribbons with its razor-sharp claws or buried its fangs deep in my flesh.

The wolf's body thrashed, trapped somehow. I inched closer and the growls intensified, broken with an occasional warning yip for me to keep my distance. From the pitch of those yips I could tell it was not yet full grown.

"What's the matter?" I whispered, holding out my hand,

wincing when my palms came into contact with a thick hedge of thorns. I stretched my arms above my head and then far at my sides, assessing how tall and wide the hedge extended.

The tree wolf snarled and jerked inside its prison of thorns, but that only made it cry out more sharply. A dweller's eerie shriek stretched out across the distance and wrapped around me. I took a step to flee, but stopped at the tree wolf's whimper.

He was a waiting meal. Easy pickings for dwellers. I didn't know why, but I decided the wolf was a he. A dweller would make short work of him. That fact struck me as an injustice. Tree wolves had survived this long because of their ability to climb, their strength and hunting prowess.

I took another step, my fingers tightening around the strap of my pack, and it almost seemed like the tree wolf whimpered even louder, pleading for me to help him.

"Very well," I grumbled. "I'll just cut some of the thorns away." I squatted before the trapped creature, careful not to get too close. Using my dagger, I started snapping thorny branches. "I'll just give you enough room to move." I sawed at a particularly thick vine. "Just don't kill me. If you could extend that courtesy, I would appreciate it."

He had enough room now to move his paws. He started scratching at the ground furiously, clearly attempting to aid in his own escape and dig free. I cut loose another vine and pressed my blade to another, pausing with a long exhale before snapping it free. "Just promise not to maul me. Would you do that for me, Digger, hmm?"

I jerked at the unnerving shriek behind me. The dweller was closer than I anticipated. My fingers fumbled on a branch as another cry floated on the wind. My dagger dropped. With a curse, I patted the ground, searching for it, my movements growing frantic as the dweller's solid tread shuffled closer.

Digger growled, the sound deep and menacing. It was coming. The wolf could see it, and I could smell its earthy musk.

I whirled around, forgetting about my dagger and withdrawing my sword. Only one advanced. I should be able to dispatch it quickly. Being with Fowler hadn't made me that reliant. I wasn't weak. Sivo's lessons weren't forgotten.

I braced my legs, and adjusted my hand on the leather-bound grip, ready to swing high when a great furred body launched over my shoulder in a rush of wind. The tip of the tree wolf's long tail trailed behind it, swiping at my cheek as he passed.

The wolf was free. The dweller screamed as the wolf's razor claws buried in its chest and brought it to the ground. My sword lowered as the beast mauled the dweller. Blood sprayed everywhere, the scent thick, the taste of metal in my mouth.

I backed away slowly, trying not to call too much attention to myself. The snarls faded to low rumbles, and there was a heavy thud as the wolf released the dweller, dropping it to the ground.

"Easy, good boy," I whispered, feeling the animal's stare on me. Its paws padded toward me on the soft soil. "We're friends, remember?"

I held myself utterly still, not daring to breathe, trying to project absolute calm. "I helped you." My voice cracked a little and I swallowed. "You helped me. Let's just go our separate ways."

The tree wolf stopped directly in front of me, panting heavily. His head almost reached my waist, confirming he was still young. A full-grown tree wolf could weigh a few hundred pounds, but this one was perhaps half that size.

The fog of his blood-soaked breath filled the space between us, reminding me that for all his youth, he was still dangerous. The dweller's nearby corpse served as a reminder, too.

His entire body radiated heat. Beneath the coppery-sweet scent of blood, the pungent aroma of his fur made my nostrils twitch.

I exhaled as time slowed to a crawl. My nerves stretched taut as this beast panted in front of me. His tail swished against the ground lightly. Sivo had described their unusual tails to me before. They were strong and wiry, but also long, curling into a loop. The tails unfurled when needed, gripping branches and helping them maneuver through trees.

I shifted on my feet and Digger huffed, not missing the movement. "What do you want?" I tried to sound like I wasn't worried he was about to devour me.

He continued to pant, his tongue darting out to lick his lips wetly. Angling my head, I considered why he wasn't attacking me. It couldn't matter to a wild animal that I had helped him. Could it?

Deciding to find out, I lifted my hand toward him, pausing at his soft growl of warning. Dropping my hand back to my side, I sighed. "So we're not friends? Then what are you still doing here?"

A pair of dwellers shrieked, calling to each other, the volley of shrill screams bouncing off the forest.

Digger shifted, a low rumble swelling up from deep in him.

"See," I said. "They're coming. Time to go."

I stepped to the side and my boot struck something hard, sent it sliding over the ground. Bending slowly, I recovered my dagger. I stuck it back in my belt and started to edge away. Tension knotted my shoulders, and I half expected the wolf to pounce on me, but I had to risk it. I couldn't stay here.

He must have reached the same conclusion. As though he had no interest in me anymore, he turned with a soft whine and loped away, leaving me unharmed. Air shuddered past my lips, but I didn't linger.

Turning, I moved out. Alone again.

I nestled deeper into the fur, my fingers delving into the toasty-warm blanket. Insects hummed around me. A bug whizzed past my head, large enough to create a breeze. I didn't even flinch, simply burrowed deeper. The languor of sleep clung to me, clouding my head and tempting me back under.

I sighed, a smile curving my lips. With one hand, I searched for Fowler, chilled fingers seeking the firmness of his skin, the hard curve and dip of muscle and sinew, all that life and vitality that was supremely him. But there was only a pelt of fur, which moved, lifting with rhythmic breaths under my seeking touch.

My heart lurched in my chest as the reality of where I

was—where I wasn't—crashed over me. Not in Mirelya's warm cottage. Not beside Fowler.

I was Outside. Up a tree. And when I last closed my eyes I had been alone.

I jolted upright. A low growl rumbled loose from the great ball of fur beside me, strangely almost like a whine. Clearly, the beast did not approve of my movements.

I jerked back, quickly losing my balance. The belt yanked hard at my waist, the only thing that stopped me from plummeting to solid ground. I dangled in the air for a moment, arms flailing, my stomach screaming in protest from the belt digging into my middle.

The wolf shifted his weight, branches and leaves rustling as he settled in to observe my antics. I waited for a moment, debating whether to cut my belt and risk the drop, or climb back up and share the branch with a vicious animal.

The branch shook for a moment as he scratched himself.

"You're not going to kill me, are you?" I murmured.

His paw dropped back on the branch with a soft thud. His panting breath filled the silence between us, his only response.

My hands gripped the strap of leather as though it was a lifeline. Arms straining, I used the belt, pulling myself up hand over hand. With clawing fingers, I hauled my weight onto the branch, pushing all the way up until I was sitting astride it.

Gasping for breath, I untied my belt and squared my body in front of him, resting my back against the thick tree trunk. I pulled my legs up to my chest and wrapped my arms around my knees, marveling that this wild animal would come this close and not want to eat me.

With the barest whimper, he scooted forward until he rested his muzzle on the top of my boots. His tail swished with a scratching sound against the rough tree bark.

"Digger," I breathed, reaching out slowly, touching the downy soft hairs on top of his nose. "Good boy."

Stretching out my arm, I delved farther and stroked his thick coat, marveling that he permitted me to do this. "We're friends now, boy." An invisible band constricted around my chest. "I could use a friend." My throat thickened and I blinked back the sudden burn in my eyes.

Suddenly, I didn't feel quite so alone.

TWENTY-NINE

Fowler

IT WAS MIDLIGHT when I woke.

I sat up with a lurch. To wake to any light at all was a wholly unknown experience. Sleeping so deeply and peacefully through the long stretch of dark that I missed the coming of midlight had never occurred before. That only happened to dead men.

Usually I was awaiting it, ready to seize the opportunity to be up and moving without the threat of dwellers. I had planned on being far from this place with Luna by now.

I dragged a hand through my hair, trying to shake off the vestiges of sleep. A quick glance around the room revealed it empty of Luna. I frowned, missing her, wanting to see her and kiss her again. Hold her. I sat up and swung my legs over the side. I doubted that would ever get old.

I moved to the small window, lifting the cover, attempting to estimate how much of midlight had passed. I rubbed at my eyes with the heel of my palm, staring out at the busy town. People moved on foot and carts passed, carrying kindling and other goods.

With a curse, I turned from the window. The day was lost. I couldn't leave with Luna now. I pressed a palm to my aching forehead. The fog of sleep stuck to me like clinging cobwebs. I wasn't right. Perhaps an additional day was for the best.

Luna's indentation could still be seen within the bedding. I smoothed a hand over it. Any warmth from her body had long faded. She knew we were supposed to leave today. Why didn't she wake me?

Faint sounds drifted from the front room. I pulled my tunic over my head and stepped out.

"Oh, finally decided to join the world, have you?"

I shook my head. Everything seemed blurrier, the edges of my vision shadowy. I pressed a hand against my temple. "Yes," I replied. "I suppose I needed the rest." I'd been operating on a paltry amount of sleep over the years. Perhaps my body had finally decided to claim what it needed.

Mirelya smirked, her milky eyes considering me. "Or it might have something to do with the sleeping draft the girl slipped into you."

My head snapped up, a sick feeling starting in my gut as I

narrowed my gaze on her. "What?"

"You recall the drinks she fetched you both in the middle of the night?"

I did. She'd complained of thirst. When I offered to fetch them, she had insisted she could get them, and I let her go. I didn't want to treat her like an invalid. After everything we had been through together that would have been insulting.

"Yes . . . why?" I pressed fingers to my aching forehead.

Mirelya shrugged. "She asked for my help."

I lowered my hand. "So . . . you did something to my drink?"

"She has a right to make her own choices."

"You did something to my drink," I bit out.

"You weren't allowing her to make her own choices."

I stared at the old woman, my hands clenching into fists at my sides. "Where is she?"

"She left last midlight. You were dead to the world. I put a sleeping draft in it."

I glanced toward the feeble light trickling around the edges of the window coverings. My stomach churned sickly. She had been gone for some time now. She had a good head start on me. A full day.

I strode back into my room, making quick work of dressing and gathering up my things, checking all my weapons and making certain they were in working order.

There was no question in my mind. I was going after her. I was going to find her long before she ever reached the king. I would tell her everything. I would make her understand that turning herself over to him would make no difference. It wouldn't help. He would not even lift the kill order once he had Luna in his clutches because that's what kind of twisted man he was. He'd keep the kill order in place just to be certain that the late king's heir was in fact dead. On the off chance Luna wasn't who she claimed.

Whatever it took, whatever words I had to say, I would make her understand that she didn't have to do this. That we could be together in Allu. We would.

"Let her go," Mirelya murmured as though she could read my thoughts. Maybe the old woman could.

I shook my head. "Never."

"She's trying to do the right thing. Let her go."

Swinging my pack over my shoulder, I passed her and headed for the door, calling back, "She can try all she likes to do the right thing. But so will I."

THIRTY

Luna

I moved with all the stealth Sivo had taught me, retracing the route I had taken with Fowler, my ears straining, my nostrils flaring, filtering smells. Digger traveled several paces behind me, his paws padding lightly on the ground with a cheerful rhythm in direct opposition to the sinister sounds of the infinite night. Every once in a while he would run ahead of me and then backtrack, dashing past my side almost as though he was playing with me.

Our friendship existed on his terms. He approached me only when I stopped. He chose when I could touch him. He chose when to sniff me, when to graze me with that looping tail of his.

If I climbed a tree, sometimes he joined me. Other times he ran off, not returning for several hours. I didn't mind. I was glad for his company on any terms.

I decided to head south and follow the Kangese River before turning west to Relhok City. I would briefly cross into Lagonia's lands. Sivo's lessons played over in my mind. He had taught me all about the kingdom—my kingdom, as he had frequently reminded me. He had schooled me in its geography. Beyond that, he told me about the other kingdoms that surrounded Relhok: Neliam, Carondale, and Lagonia. He had even imparted everything he knew about the far distant lands on the other side of our seas. Not that any of that mattered greatly now. I only needed to worry about reaching the capital, giving wide berth to the villages and cities that may or may not even exist anymore along the way.

Sivo had provided me with a mental picture of the world, including how it used to be and what it was like now—at least as much as he knew from residing in seclusion.

The world as it truly was, what it was actually like to live in . . . Fowler taught me that lesson.

The world was a merciless place. Hard and cruel. Except when you found someone to trust and love. Life, however fleeting, possessed meaning then. Knowing Fowler and loving him had given my life that meaning. I could always cling to that. I always would. Until the end.

I was being followed.

At first it was just a vague sense—a possibility that I dismissed as a result of my constant state of vigilance.

I listened but could hear nothing over the wind and drum of my own heart. Digger had left on one of his private excursions a while ago, and I tried not to long for him too hard. He was a wild animal that roamed where he wished. He wasn't a pet. Shaking my head, I told myself I was just being overly anxious. Out here, alone, my nerves were a stretched string ready to snap.

It was midlight again. I could tell by the crispness draped over the pungent marshland I presently trekked across. The air felt less cold on my skin, too. I was covering good ground at least, despite the nasty stretch of bog sucking and pulling at my boots.

It wasn't an outright swampland. Each step plunged me down with a squish, mud splattering all the way up to my knees. I pushed on faster, my strides gobbling up ground, determined to put more distance between Ortley and me. Fowler and me.

I doubted Fowler would give pursuit. He had dropped his walls to trust me, and I had left him. I doubted he would understand and overcome that betrayal easily. No, he would push on for Allu.

And that was for the best—no matter how it swiped a claw at my heart.

Even the bitter sting of my thoughts didn't block out the prickle at the back of my neck. The sensation at my nape swept up, pulling my skull tight. I slowed my strides and stopped, immediately sinking deeper.

Standing still, I listened. It was there. A steady whooshing that fell evenly, like the sound a towel makes when it's whipped in the air. It was more than that sound though. It was a sense, too. Something was coming in fast and hard at my back. Given that it was midlight, this wasn't a dweller. I turned my head left and right, assessing for a place to hide from whatever it was that was coming. I was out in the open, a stretch of barren landscape with only a few shrubs and far-off trees. My flesh puckered to gooseflesh. I was exposed and vulnerable.

Swallowing back a wet breath, I ran hard for the nearest tree, splashing through the bog. In my haste, I tripped once and ate a mouthful of foul water. Spewing the sludge from my face, I pushed back up to my feet and kept going.

The wind shook the tree's branches. They sounded brittle, but I only hoped they were sturdy enough and had enough leaves to provide some cover from whoever was out there. Slogging through the mud, I told myself it would have to do. Midlight was already fading. I didn't want to spend the day stuck up in a tree if I didn't have to. Hopefully dwellers avoided this swamp like they did lakes.

Reaching the tree, I climbed it easily, scaling up its length, muttering one of Fowler's curses. It creaked under my weight, bits of bark flying off and crumbling under my clawing fingers. One of my nails cracked. I pushed on, whimpering as a sliver of wood imbedded itself in my palm.

The trunk was nowhere near as large as those of the trees that had surrounded Ortley. It swayed in the wind as I reached as high as I could go. It was with some effort that I balanced myself in the nest of fragile branches. Finding as solid a perch as I could,

I waited, listening again to all the obvious and not so obvious sounds around me.

The whooshing grew louder. I turned in its direction, hanging on tightly from my position. It was a person. I marked the even two-footed tread, the loping gait. That one foot . . . the right foot that always hit the ground just a fraction harder.

Fowler.

Relief coursed through me. My head dropped and I sagged, tension slipping from my shoulders. Outrage followed, eclipsing all else. I adjusted my weight, stiffening at the sudden protesting crack of a branch. My nails dug deeper into rough bark. Leaving him was the hardest thing I had ever done. Even harder than leaving Sivo and Perla. I didn't know if I had the strength in me to do it again.

I waited, hoping against all hope that he might pass the tree and keep going. It was possible. Any tracks would be hard to read in this bog. Any steps I'd taken had to be swallowed back up the instant I made them. If I could just hold silent and use the branches for cover and not make a sound—

"Are you going to come down from there or am I going to have to come up and get you?"

My heart jumped in my chest at the deep stroke of his familiar voice. "What are you doing here?"

"I thought that would be obvious."

I clutched the branches and leaned down to call to him. "You should have let me go, Fowler. I didn't want you to follow me."

"I gathered that, seeing how you tricked me into drinking a sleeping draft."

I batted back the niggle of guilt over that. "I wouldn't have had to do that if you'd just let me go."

"Luna, come down here so—"

"No!"

With a curse, he grabbed onto the tree and started to climb up.

"What are you doing?" I cried.

"You won't come down to talk to me, so I'm coming up." The tree shook with his weight and movement.

"You can't make me go back with you, Fowler," I said as he came to a stop on the branch across from me.

I braced myself, prepared for his argument. Instead, he circled the back of my neck, leaned forward, and covered my lips with his. The familiar scent of him overwhelmed me, heady and male with that undercurrent of wind and woods.

My heart lurched to my throat. He kissed me long and hard. There was punishment in it, but also something desperate and needy. I felt its echo run through me.

When we finally broke apart, I breathed in the changing air. I felt dizzy and more confused than ever. Air crashed from my lips like I had run a great distance.

Turning my head sideways, I softly uttered, "Midlight is gone."

"I know," he replied.

I dipped my head, hoping it somehow lessened his impact on me. He couldn't stare directly at my face, and his mouth wouldn't be so close, the memory of his taste beckoning me in that hairbreadth of space between us.

"Fowler," I began. "Think about all these girls dying. Because of me."

"Not because of you," he returned. "Because of a madman."

"But if he had me, the killing would stop."

"You can't be sure of that. He kills all the time. Indiscriminately. That's what he does."

I angled my head, mulling over his words. There was an edge to his voice I had never heard before.

"I can't go with you. I can't leave Relhok while this is happening." I winced at the volume of my voice. I lowered it to say, "I won't be able to live with myself."

"And what about me? Us?" He hated to ask the question. I could hear that in his voice. He hated that need. He hated exposing that vulnerability in himself.

A lump rose in my throat. "You'll go on without me. To Allu." I stopped to swallow again, fighting back that lump. "You'll find other people. Good people and you will—"

"No," he bit out, almost as though he sensed I was intimating that someday he would find someone else to love. "You can't go. You don't know. You don't understand—"

"What? What don't I understand, Fowler?"

"You don't understand what kind of man my father is!"

I jerked as though slapped. Everything inside of me repelled away from him. My spine arched. Another fingernail split from the pressure of my grip.

His father. *Father.* The word reverberated through me and

my stomach twisted. I pressed a hand to my belly and swallowed back the bile. "Your father?"

I felt him nod. His clothing rustled and a branch groaned as he shifted closer to me, his voice a feverish rush. "Don't look like that, Luna. It's not—"

"The high chancellor . . . Cullan . . . he is your father? The king?"

"Yes. But I left. Two years ago—"

"Your father killed my parents." The truth washed over me awfully and settled like poison in my stomach, curdling there. I pressed a hand to my mouth, certain I was going to be sick.

I peeled back my fingers to choke, "When you found out who I was back in Ortley . . . why didn't you tell me then?" My voice sounded alarmingly calm to my ears despite all that I was feeling. It felt like the person closest to me in the world had just perished with all the unfairness of a vicious and sudden death. I was left grieving, sick to my stomach, and bewildered.

"I couldn't. I didn't want you to do what you're doing now."

"Which is what, Fowler?"

"Looking the way you do. Like you think I'm a part of him," he snapped, his voice fierce and raw. A curse followed and I heard the flutter of his hair as he dragged a hand through it.

"You are," I whispered, working my lips, trying to suddenly rid the taste of him from me. My eyes stung and I blinked them rapidly, shaking my head. "You're his son."

A new sound rose, penetrating over the murmuring wind. We stopped. Not a word. Not a move. I couldn't even hear

Fowler breathing beside me anymore.

The swamp stirred, the wet ground shifting, bubbling like soup in a pot.

Fowler whispered my name in warning. Squelching sounds gurgled under us.

I nodded and bit my lip to cut off all sound. I didn't need to see to know what was happening. Dwellers were waking, rousing in the swampy ground.

The ground right below our tree frothed and rustled. Clawed fingers slapped mud and silt. A dweller pulled itself free near the base of the trunk with a great sucking sound.

More of them came. They were pulling free everywhere, the mud sucking and sluicing down their stout bodies as though the swamp wanted to keep them buried forever. I assessed the landscape, counting over twenty. Maybe the ground was easier to penetrate here. There were so many, groaning as they came to life, their heavy bodies roiling, squelching the sodden earth.

Fowler's hand closed over mine. I squeezed back. We held ourselves as still as stone. I didn't dare make a sound. I held my breath, my fingers flexing against his warm flesh.

A cracking sound split the air and suddenly the tree gave out. It tilted to the side, jostling us in the branches. I lost my balance and fell forward. My legs swung free, but I locked my arms around a branch. A sharp cry escaped before I could smother it.

Fowler's arm wrapped around my waist and hauled me back up, plastering me against him. I panted into his neck, clinging to him.

"I got you. I got you."

I nodded fiercely, a hot tear spilling down my cheek. I buried my face in his chest, listening as the dwellers rumbled and surged against the tree, aware of us now. The tree shuddered against the force of their actions.

They started battering the base with their bodies. I clung tightly to Fowler. He held on to the tree for both of us.

"It can't support us," Fowler whispered.

I nodded, pressing my lips against his skin directly above his collar. This was it.

The pack of dwellers was frothing under us, clawing and tearing at the trunk, those horrible wet breaths sawing from their lips. The tree made another crunching sound and jerked a foot down. My stomach bottomed out. I whimpered and bit my lip until I tasted the coppery flow of blood against my teeth.

"Luna, Luna." Fowler's steady voice drew my attention to him. "They're not going to go away."

I bobbed my head, latching on to the sound of his voice, so calm and mesmerizing. I inhaled, searching for composure. If I wanted to live, if either one of us was going to have a chance, then I couldn't be a hysterical mess.

"We can't both stay up here." I nodded again, even though his words did not fully penetrate. Was he saying we were going to have to make a dash for it? Through all those dwellers? I bit back a cry as the tree jerked again with a splinter of wood. Even if we fought our way free, how could we clear them without getting a fatal dose of toxin from so many receptors?

Fowler released a deep breath and cupped one hand against my face, his thumb stroking my cheek tenderly. "Luna, I don't regret it. Any of it. Not since the first moment I met you in that forest." He paused with a deep inhale. "Understand me?"

I shook my head, bewildered. "No, no, I—"

"Say you understand," he cut in, his voice hard, allowing for nothing else but my agreement.

"Yes. Yes."

"Hold yourself silent and still. No matter what happens. Be quiet. Stay in the tree. Let them think there's nothing more up here for them."

"Fowler?" I angled my head. "What do you mean—"

He kissed me so hard that our teeth clanged, but I didn't care. I only felt the hot press of his mouth and his strong fingers diving into my hair, holding me for him. He lifted up his head at the same time he released my face. "I love you, Luna."

My chest clenched as his arms loosened around me. He sucked in a sharp breath. My mouth worked, searching for a response as his words reverberated through me.

His palms rasped the rough bark as he shoved off the branch. It sprang higher with the sudden loss of his weight and I tightened my grip to stop myself from falling even as I stretched my other hand out for him, groping air wildly.

Thud.

Dwellers went wild under me, snarling, clawing each other for a piece of him. I opened my mouth on a silent scream, but Fowler's words held me in check. I would do what he asked of me.

His sacrifice couldn't be of no value.

I listened hard for him. I heard several of his grunts over the dwellers' din, but he didn't scream. I had to hope he wasn't being torn apart. Who could hold silent during that?

Hot tears streamed down my face, but I held quiet, choking on sobs, drowning in the sound of the savage thrashing below. I grasped my branch with aching, bloodless fingers, desperate for the sound of him. A cry. A single word. I needed to hear him. I needed something to tell me that he was fighting them off, getting away, escaping like he had always managed to do before.

Only nothing ever came.

Gradually, the noise stopped. My ears strained, but I could not even detect the dwellers' telltale breathing. I sniffed, searching for the coppery-sweet scent of freshly spilled blood. Nothing. Silence hummed, floating in the loam-laden air, and I knew they were gone. They had gone underground and taken Fowler with them. I held still for several moments longer, my heart racing, my thoughts churning. It couldn't end like this. Fowler could not end like this.

Calm swept over me. Suddenly I knew what to do.

Unsheathing my dagger and pressing a palm flat to the tree's trunk, I gathered my nerve, inhaled several quick breaths, and dropped down from the tree. I struck the sodden ground on my knees. Mud splattered me in the face, sticking thick in my eyelashes. I wiped at my eyes with the back of one hand.

An eerie quiet surrounded me. I moved quickly, frantically, covering a wide area, distaste coating my mouth as I patted the surrounding ground for remains of Fowler. As I suspected, they took him. They had all gone back below with their quarry. He could still be alive—for a little while anyway.

I continued crawling, hurrying until I found where the ground was the softest. Not even ground anymore, but more like a pool of mud. This was where so many of the dwellers had emerged.

I flexed my hand around the hilt of my dagger, sucked in the deepest breath my lungs could hold, and dove headfirst.

Into the abyss.

ACKNOWLEDGMENTS

Beginning a new book—a new series—is always nerve-racking. It's like a first date. You're excited and nervous and have no idea at all if it's going to live up to all the hype in your mind. Such is the angst of writing. From that first kernel of an idea to typing "The End," it's a roller coaster of emotions. Thank you to my family and friends for hanging on (as always) as I take that ride.

The world of *Reign of Shadows* would never have happened without a long-ago conversation with my agent in which I shared a crazy-pants premise that would become this book. Thanks, Maura, for being so succinct and ardent in your instructions to "just do it . . . go write that book." Also, thank you to Jennifer Klonsky and HarperTeen, who so quickly jumped onboard; and to my editor, Emilia Rhodes, for pushing me to go deeper and encouraged grossness (yes, I'm looking at you, bat fever)! Your enthusiasm and attention to detail helped me bring this book the final stretch home. Gina Rizzo, you do wonders for my ego and your support goes above and beyond. Thank you to all my writer friends who supported and plotted with me throughout *Reign of Shadows* (hoping I don't leave anyone out!!): Sarah MacLean, Carrie Ryan, Tera Lynn Childs, Shana Galen, Jennifer Armentrout, and Victoria Scott (Tori, where would I be without the scary-as-hell pictures of the star-nosed mole you sent me?).

And to my dear readers, I hope you enjoyed Luna and Fowler. I can't wait for you to see what happens next!

Read on for an excerpt of

ONE

Luna

THIS WAS DARKNESS.

Of course, I was sightless, so darkness was all I had ever known. It lived in me, *on* me, like scars written on my skin. But this darkness went deeper. Thicker. Denser. It suffocated me. Thick as tar, I was drowning inside it, flailing, searching for air to fill my starved lungs.

Diving underground after Fowler, I knew precisely what I was doing. Even if an earthen tomb would likely become my crypt, it was what I had to do. Fowler was gone. Dwellers had taken him. He was lost somewhere in this tar. Dead, maybe. Probably. I expelled my pain-laden breath. No. *Find him. Find Fowler.*

I dropped, falling into a thick pool of sludge. I swam through the mire and sucked in a sharp breath that felt like razors scraping the inside of my throat. My palms slapped the surface of emulsified earth, keeping me from sinking. I was already underground. Who knew what lay farther down? The very bowels of the earth, perhaps.

I lifted my fingers, letting them unfurl from their grip on ground that only seemed to break and crumble under my grasp.

For a moment, I wobbled on my knees, my balance thrown. Lifting my chest, I took another gulp of air and inched forward, patting wet earth. The ground started to dip, so I flipped to my bottom and slid down the slope.

Damp earth rushed past, sticking to every inch of me. Sludge clung to my hair and clumped in my lashes. I blinked, trying to clear it away. Rich, pungent loam filled my nostrils. I sucked in a breath and swallowed earth. Coughing, I spat out debris and sealed my lips shut, determined to not breathe too deeply down here.

I came to a stop, landing on actual ground. *Their* ground. I'd followed Fowler into their domain. For the first time *I* was the invader.

I sat still for a long moment, listening and taking slow sips of air as I attempted to still my racing heart in the dripping silence. I was certain dwellers could hear me. *Terrified* they could hear the wild beating in my chest, that organ that I'd thought dead. Fowler had killed it, crushed it with the awful truth, but the stupid thing knew how to keep beating, fighting no matter if it was dead. Fowler was Cullan's son. Cullan, the man who killed my parents and hunted me. The man who killed every girl in the land for the crime of *maybe* being me. That monster was Fowler's father. Fowler's past, his legacy, was wrapped up in that evil.

I shuddered and pushed out the thought for later. For now I couldn't think of that. I wouldn't. I could think only of saving Fowler and getting both of us out of here alive. Nothing else mattered right now.

I flexed my fingers and remembered that I still clutched my knife. I was comforted to feel it in my hand. Water fell overhead, echoing in tinny pings all around me. I shivered in the bone-numbing cold that permeated my wet clothes. I shifted uncomfortably, plucking at my tunic and vest. It was pointless. There was no relief, no way to feel warm or dry or safe.

I didn't feel at home like I usually did in the dark. There was nothing comforting. Nothing familiar. I wanted to crawl back out and escape through the quagmire. Except Fowler was here somewhere.

My breath came faster. My heart felt as though it might explode from my too-tight chest. *Fowler*, trapped in this world under our world. It didn't seem possible that strong, capable, unbreakable Fowler could be here—that this was his fate, that he had embraced it, sacrificing himself to dwellers to save me.

I shook my head against the terrifying possibility that I was too late. He was still alive. I would know if he wasn't. Something like that . . . I would know.

I deliberately shoved away the memory of the words he had said to me, that confession, that horrible truth that had always been between us like a serpent in the grass waiting to strike, waiting to inflict its poison with immense fangs.

I kept going. My legs felt wobbly. Bracing my hands along the moist wall of earth to my left, I continued to edge forward, half expecting to come face-to-face with a dark dweller. But no, I was always good at sensing them, at knowing where they were before they knew where I was.

Most dwellers were aboveground hunting, with the exception of the ones who had taken Fowler. Hopefully, they'd just dumped him and returned aboveground to hunt. There seemed no end to their hunger, after all.

I hastened forward, skimming my hand along the earthen wall, the odor of bracken and rot stifling. I shuffled one foot after the other, feeling my way rather than plunging headlong down another incline. With luck, the ground would stay level. I needed to keep my bearings.

A distant dweller's cry echoed faintly through the underground labyrinth of tunnels. I froze, angling my head and listening, holding my breath. No other cries came. Water dripped over the blanket of calm.

I started forward again, turning left when my hand met the open air of a tunnel. I focused intently, using my heightened senses and marking the distance my feet traveled, noting every turn I took so that I could find my way back to the spot through which I entered.

Another cry sounded, and this time it wasn't a dweller. It was wholly human. I followed the direction of the shout, my steps quickening as hope pulsed inside me. *Let it be Fowler.*

TWO

Fowler

I'VE ALWAYS LIVED in darkness. With dark dwellers and death, death and dark dwellers. The two were interchangeable but the same, and by some miracle I still lived.

I'd lost consciousness at some point, but I wasn't gone. Not yet. I remembered that rush of adrenaline as I flung myself from the tree into the arms of the waiting dwellers. I did it for Luna. I could accept that. I had no regret. As long as she lived, I was fine.

In this absolute absence of light, I waded through air like ink, lost.

My ears pricked, listening. Not far away someone wept. Panic bit me in the chest. Was it Luna? Had they taken her, too? She couldn't be down here as well. Fate wasn't that cruel. I tried to move my body, but my arms were wedged tight.

Maybe it was punishment for all my wrongs. I'd withheld who I was—what I was—from Luna long past the point when I should have told her. Fear held me back and now this was the price. Faulty logic, maybe, but it was all I could manage.

My head and shoulders were free, and I looked about wildly, tossing the hair back from my eyes and squinting into the darkness, peering in the direction of the person crying.

"Hello?" I called into the murk. The tears stopped abruptly as my greeting echoed over the chilled air. "Who's there? Luna?"

"Who are you?" a voice demanded. Not Luna.

Relief eased over me. "Fowler," I replied, and then almost laughed. What did my name matter? I was stuck in here with this hapless other soul and we were both about to die.

For a moment her ragged breaths were her only response. "I'm Mina. They took me . . . and my group. A few days ago, I think. I don't know. There were seven of us. I'm all that's left." Her voice cracked into wet sobs. "There are others in here, too. But I don't know them."

A few days? They'd kept her alive this long? And there were others. Maybe that meant I had more time. Time to give survival another chance.

Determined not to give up, I tried to move my arms again, hopeful that I could break loose. My breath puffed out as I exerted pressure. If I could get free, perhaps I could find a way out of here. There was a way in, so there had to be a way out.

There had to be.

THREE

Luna

I CHASED THAT echo of a cry long after it faded. Even when
the air around me softened to mere drips of water, I didn't stop.
I prowled down tunnels and passageways for so long that I worried it was only a matter of time before I came face-to-face with
a dweller. I lost all sense of time in a world where every moment
counted.

The space around me was empty. I moved, straining for any
sound. My nostrils flared, the odor of dwellers rich around me:
loam and copper. Metal in my mouth.

Even with the scent of them so strong everywhere, they
weren't nearby. This was their territory. The stink of them

embedded in the bones of this underground tomb.

The silence was finally broken again by another shout. Human.

I followed the sound, my lips moving in a silent mantra. *Let it be Fowler. Let it be Fowler.*

I couldn't be certain how long I was down here, but I sensed time was fading fast until midlight—that brief duration when the ink dark faded and a haze of feeble light surfaced and chased the dwellers back underground. In an odd twist, midlight was something I didn't want to occur. The idea of dwellers returning and prowling the same space I occupied made my steps quicken despite any reassurances.

Suddenly the ceiling above me started to shake and froth, mud dropping down and raining on my head. Was it a cave-in? I ran, trying to escape the earth falling on me, keeping my hand on the wall to my left. I ducked down the tunnel, chest heaving.

Pressed into the wall, I turned my face up and held out my hand. Nothing was falling anymore. The ceiling of earth was stable. Holding myself as still as possible, I listened.

A dweller's wet, sloughing breath filled my ears. Its dragging steps felt like a scrape of a blade across my flesh. The heavy weight of its body thudded and settled into the damp ground with each move. My heart beat so hard my chest ached. I heard the whisper of the sensors at the center of its face slither on the air, and smelled the drip of toxin.

The monster wasn't alone. A human struggled against the dweller's razor talons, sobbing and choking out garbled pleas.

Hopeless words. There was no reasoning with these creatures. Not pity to rouse. No help. No rescue.

They drew near the smaller tunnel where I hid, and I debated my next move. Hold still or run? Lungs locked, I held my breath, waiting for them to pass. *Hoping* they passed. If they turned down this tunnel it was all over. I was lost.

The dweller passed me, dragging the hapless human behind, and I swallowed against the dryness of my mouth. Fortunately, the dweller was so focused on its victim it didn't detect my scent. Or perhaps being coated head to foot in mud aided in disguising my smell.

I waited several long minutes before continuing. Part of me wanted to take cover and hide, but the longer I hid the closer we drew to midlight. And once midlight hit . . . I shivered. Dwellers would be coming home. I had to move. Fowler and I needed to be out of here before that happened.

I took several more bracing breaths, in and out, to calm my heart as I moved down the narrow corridor. I didn't hear that dweller or its poor victim anymore. Faint, very human moans trickled over the vaporous air. It was colder down here than above. My teeth clacked slightly as I continued, growing closer to the sounds of humans, my hand skimming the uneven wall beside me. The tunnel opened up into a great space where the air flowed swifter, the current similar to when I stood in an open field with the wind blowing, lifting the hair off my shoulders.

I hovered, standing at the threshold, shivering at the cusp of something . . . a great maw of space that contained several humans. They were trapped. Their moans met my ears, soft anguished cries lined with defeat. Their hands slapped and clawed at the ground, trying to pull themselves free. Some were injured. I smelled the cloying sweetness of their blood. I lifted my face, smelling, listening, assessing.

It was a nest, a vast stretch of earth with holes that imprisoned humans.

"Fowler?" I whisper-shouted over the pitiable sobs and pleas for help. Swallowing, I took on more volume. "Fowler! Are you in here?"

His response was almost immediate, alongside the cries of others, answering me, begging for their release. "Luna! What are you doing here?"

Elation burst inside me, sweeping over me and making me almost limp. "Fowler!" I started to step forward, but his sharp warning stopped me.

"Careful, Luna. You'll fall in. Drop to your knees and crawl."

Lowering to my knees, I started forward, patting the ground ahead of me. It didn't take me long to figure out why I should crawl. The ground broke off into a pattern of holes. I crawled between them. Sticky residue was everywhere. I practically had to peel my palms off the narrow stretches of ground between holes.

Other people pleaded with me, calling for my help, but I kept an even line to where Fowler was lodged. His voice was a steady wind of encouragement that I followed until I reached him. My hand landed on his shoulder.

"Fowler . . . are you hurt?" I skimmed the curve of his shoulder, quickly understanding that he was wedged deep in the hole, his arms trapped. This must be why none of them were moving.

"Luna, you have to go." Panic sharpened his voice. "You don't have long. Get out of here before they come back—"

"I'm not leaving you. I'm here. Now help me get you out." My hands roamed, trying to find some leverage to pull him out.

"I'm stuck tight and this sticky mess everywhere isn't helping. It's like one giant spider's web."

"Then I'll cut you out," I declared.

"What do you—" His words died abruptly as I used my knife and started hacking at the edge of the hole trapping him. I worked hard, panting as I cut and clawed the crumbling ground away from him with my fingers.

"Luna, there's no time."

I shook my head, pelting mud-soaked strands against my cheeks. I'd come this far. I wasn't leaving without him.

He released a grunt of frustration and then started struggling, apparently grasping the fact that I wasn't giving up and he might as well try to break loose.

My arms burned as I hacked at the ground. He jerked inside the hole, wiggling his upper body as I widened the opening a fraction at a time.

"It's not . . ." Whatever he was about to say was lost as one of his arms suddenly broke free. He flung his body to the side and squeezed the other one out. I grabbed his shirt and helped haul him out, although now that both his arms were free he managed most of it on his own.

The others came alert and called out, their voices ringing around us, begging for help.

Fowler grabbed my hand and tugged me to crawl after him, ignoring them.

"Fowler," I began, listening to the sound of a woman near him, crying and begging for us to save her. "We need to help—"

"There's no time, Luna." His fingers tightened on my hand as if he feared I would slip free.

I turned my head, facing the direction of her sobbing pleas.

"Please, please help me, too. Don't leave me here. Don't leave me here to die!"

I pulled against Fowler's hand.

"Luna!" he growled, turning his body to snatch me by the shoulders. "We have to go! They're lost. Most of them are covered in toxin, and it's nearly midlight!"

For once in my life, midlight signaled the end of safety. Not the dawn of it. The irony wasn't lost on me.

I shook my head, but then everything started shaking. The very ground we crawled over vibrated. The underworld cavern trembled and shuddered, great clumps of earth falling from the ceiling.

"Dwellers," he growled over the buzz of their return, as though I didn't know. As though the rot of them wasn't choking. "They're coming."

This time I didn't resist as he pulled me after him.

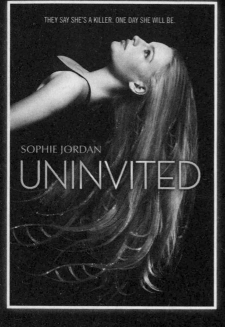
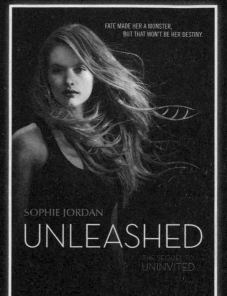

FORBIDDEN LOVE.
HIGH-STAKES ACTION.
HEARTBREAKING CHOICES.

Don't miss any of the books in the sizzling Firelight series!

HARPER
An Imprint of HarperCollins*Publishers*

www.epicreads.com